THE SANDS OF AKHIRAH

ALSO BY MARTIN KEARNS

Beneath the Veil: The Valor of Valhalla Book One

THE SANDS OF AKHIRAH

BOOK TWO: THE VALOR OF VALHALLA

MARTIN KEARNS

NEW YORK, USA

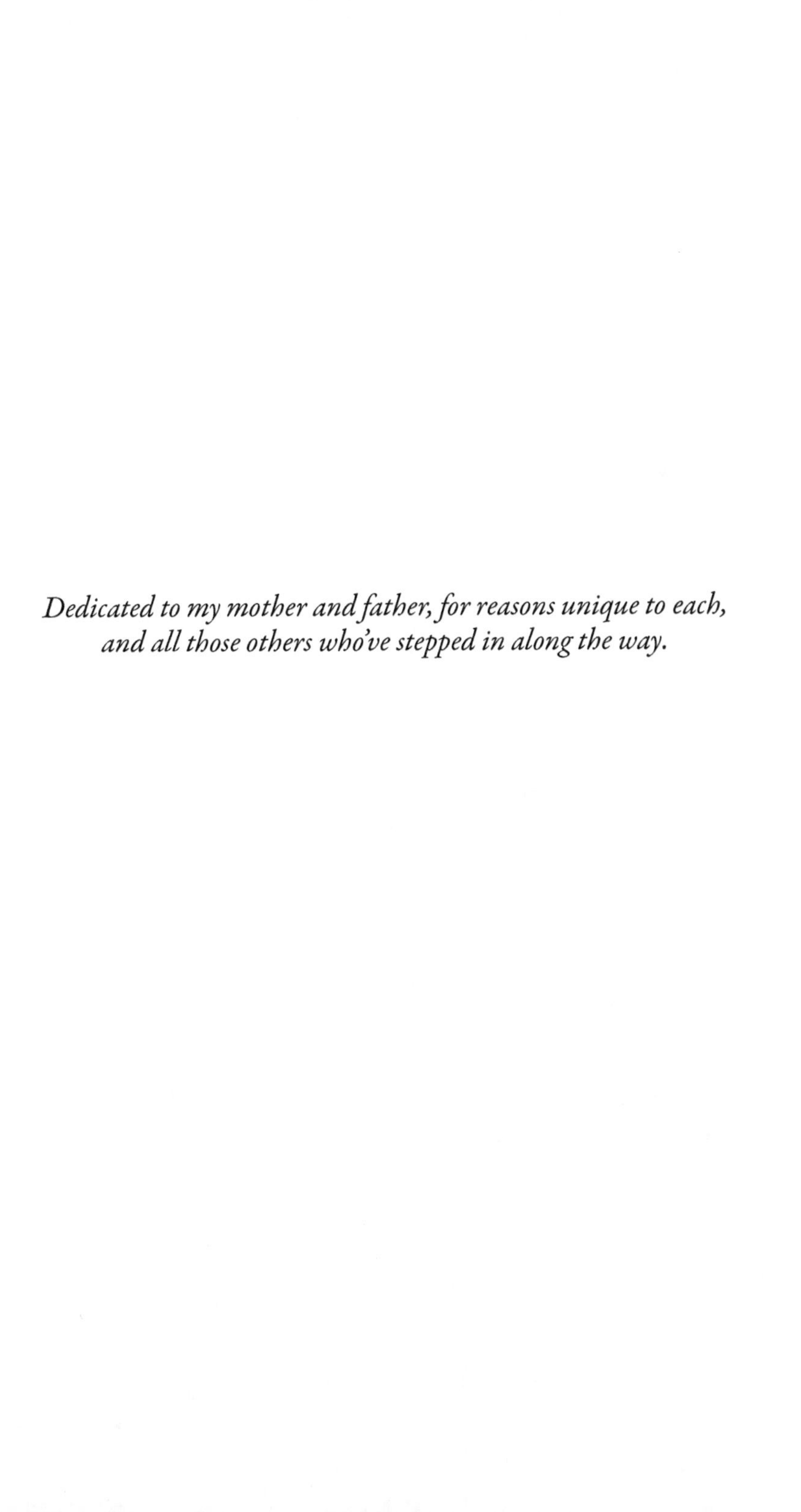

*Dedicated to my mother and father, for reasons unique to each,
and all those others who've stepped in along the way.*

Which way I fly is hell; myself am hell;
And in the lowest deep a lower deep,
Still threat'ning to devour me, opens wide,
To which the hell I suffer seems a heaven.

— PARADISE LOST, BOOK IV

THE SANDS OF AKHIRAH

PROLOGUE

Sixty miles southeast of As Sukhnah, in the sandblasted wastes of Syria, Rami Maalouf sheltered within a shoddily erected domicile as the sky tore itself apart.

No dark wall of coarse mayhem signified a coming storm when the sun fell behind the horizon, yet a fierce wind assaulted the walls of his shelter, and the structure threatened to collapse inward upon him. The only cause Rami was able to consider was that the war was spilling over around him, though his location atop the cavern-pocked hills was too remote for a serious skirmish. Soldiers lacked the strategic need to squabble over wasteland. Would they have been in hiding in these hills, he may have considered this possibility more earnestly, but fighting was taking place far to the north and east. This knowledge was why he'd sheltered himself and his flock in this meager outpost in the first place.

Pulling up stakes had metamorphosed from a plan rooted in denial to a decision grasped under duress when the war raged closer and closer to the Maalouf family. Rami sent his elder father, mother, and three sisters on ahead to seek refuge in the farmlands of Lebanon, where they were welcoming refugees. He had chosen to take their flock and, with the help of Aviate, the family's Bedouin Shepherd dog, he had set out on an eddied path to meet his family. The very reason he'd chosen to weather the coming night in these hills was due to their safety; thick armor would always vie for second place behind the fortresses of nature.

Blasts from the sky indicated there had been an error in judgment along his way, and all he could do was hunker down and pray he was spared from the explosive contest occurring beyond the walls. The boy dared not risk Aviate to keep the flock from disbanding among the hills around them while the sky cracked. Rami would have to set out at first light to round them up, should opportunity be on his side, and he not be forced to abandon the sheep and goats altogether. These animals were to be used to have the Lebanese welcome their family with open arms. Pay for farming increased for those who had their own means. Otherwise, the terms were tantamount to indentured servitude. Slavery.

Time passed, and the blasting became less constant, the flashes which had forced light through the cracks in the boarded windows fewer and farther between. Rami's anxiety lessened, and the toil of his travels eventually took him to his rest, where he dreamed of Adam laying prostrate before the great Iblees standing over him. Bile and blood spewed from the demon's mouth as it cursed the first man in a tongue unknown to Rami or any Maalouf before him. Wakefulness came abreast dust dancing in beams of sunlight.

The shepherd boy hurried to pack his sack with belongings and move to secure his flock. The door swung inward, and Aviate broke into the day, issuing his purposeful barks, but the good pup needn't have rushed to his work with such vigor. The flock stood unbroken in its entirety just where Rami had settled them for the night. He made his count to be sure none had strayed and found his assessment to be true. Perhaps the instinct for flight was overcome with the need to stay close to their owner, though this was an uncommon reaction from dumbed beasts.

Rami set himself to the rear of the flock and pushed them toward his future. Aviate harassed the edges of the bugling mass to keep order, and they made good time descending from their high vantage. It was midway down that Rami noticed the multitudes of rock and sand below, which had been heaved about during what turmoil robbed him of his early sleep. The normal signs of battle were not in evidence, however.

Devoid of blast marks, the rocks appeared to have been lifted by sheer force rather than by concussive explosions. Sand walled into steep dunes from short bursts of wind, and there were no shattered casings of rockets nor ammunition shells strewn about them. He was still above the blasted field, but from what he could see, there'd been no conflict between men to have caused the apocalyptic commotion the night prior.

His travel took him to the base of new hills, which strained against the earth's crust to rise to mountains, and Rami progressed quickly over the flatlands, heading west toward succor. Much of the oddities lay behind him and his flock, but as they walked through a deeper and more pure sand, Rami was forced to shield his vision. His eyes had grown accustomed to the cruel sun and were normally protected by his keffiyeh, but now the sun raked across his vision from reflections on the ground ahead. The sheep and goats bottled together to avoid stepping on the reflectors as they passed by the glinting pocks of ground, and Aviate ceased his harassment of the animals to join the boy's side—an odd occurrence for a working dog.

Rami's travel-worn sandals continued forward until he was astride the source of this phenomenon, and he made a small detour to inspect it. The base of an oiled walking staff jutted out toward a glossy substance on the ground and slid smoothly along the top. Rami crouched and choked down on the shepherd tool to place it under the edge of what he saw to be glass. He tried to lift at the edge, but the glass had been kilned to more than two inches thick, and it spread out far ahead of him to the north. He looked up from his crouch and spotted many islands of the glass in the field to the north. The sun danced about the ridges and pits formed within them.

His great grandfather had long ago brought home a platter-sized piece of sand glass formed from the intense heat of a lightning strike thrown down from the sky to the desert. Such occurrences were few, and the family treated the glass as an heirloom, one of the few possessions they had chosen to travel with as they fled on ahead of him across the wasteland. Rami now looked upon amounts many orders more voluminous than his family treasure. Whatever had occurred out here last night as he'd slept had brought heat down from the heavens upon the earth in a torrent far more powerful than anything this land had seen in many generations, if at all in the time of man.

Rami raked his nails behind Aviate's ear as he contemplated this before he stood. He turned to face his future to the west and followed his herd away, leaving the bad omens pervading Syria behind him.

PART ONE

THE PRINCESS OF NOTHINGNESS

CHAPTER ONE
LOST CHILDREN

Pericarp wandered the unstructured nothingness, but for how long, it didn't know. Nothingness held no time, and it knew no seeds of hopes to come nor valorous preparation for strife or struggle. Existence simply was and carried with it none of the weights to tip the scales between pain and joy. So it was that Pericarp ambled through the nothing as three parts of one.

The first of the three, an automaton donning a mask of no expression or care, simply glided to and fro through the murk as though a task needed tending, before jerking to a stop once it realized there was no wrong to be righted.

The second behaved in a manner to tend to the first—relentlessly peppering it in its baseless tasks with grasps and tugs at its arms and waist. This endeavor proved equally meritless due to the first part of Pericarp feeling no compulsion to change its course whatsoever.

The third and final pillar of psyche stood out from its counterparts in that it clearly assumed some form of cognitive etiquette. It would fly to the side of the other two and direct the second should it be too harsh in its handling of the first. Pantomimes of petting and handholding were expressed often as the third rushed to train the second in a more wholesome methodology and, at times, it broke from the other two to peer off into the nothingness before returning to observe. There were flashes of inspiration within the third in those moments of staring, as though its gaze might conjure an image or shape to break the monotonous melancholy of the murky nothingness.

Pericarp carried on in this way in its existence without thought, and Pericarp was not alone. Many others had been cleaved into three and engaged in similar spectacles across the nothingness, but all were as lost to one another as each was lost to itself. The nothingness served as a nursery of sorts, its function to scrub the conscious and unconscious of filthy and parasitic interlopers before visitors were ushered on to the next phase of their existence. None would remember their ride with Kharon while immersed in this murk, not at first, but memories would emerge as they themselves were reborn from this place of changing.

Samael entered the nothing uninvited, rarely choosing to survey the souls he delivered to the banks of the Styx who were still tethered to the world of the living. Odd instances of delivery did occur, that was sure, but the angel of death was often uneasy watching millions of souls as they were processed through a machine of readying, only to be categorized and downloaded to respective destinations. He found the process eerily clean in its purpose, and the machination to be perverse, even in the world beneath the veil.

He had found helping Uriel in his efforts to save David from this fate to be far more enticing. The two angels working in tandem to catch both David's earthly body and his ethereal presence and separate them for the next phase of the wise angel's plan had titillated Samael in a way he hadn't felt in time immemorial. He found himself reliving the experience to feel it again and again. Though he'd left the part of David in his charge on the shores of the Styx as he did all others, he'd left him a future outside of this machine, and that action filled him with renewed purpose.

The current moment served as an unusual undertaking not dissimilar to his fond memory, and Samael separated the mottled nothingness before him as he ventured through to find a faint light in the void. Care had been taken to hide his actions. Meddling in the affairs of Anubis would likely carry with it notice, questions, and, possibly, retribution. Though retribution did not worry the angel whose wings devoured all light, the prospect of adding more pieces to the board of play on which they endeavored did not appeal to Samael—there were quite enough already.

Shapeless clouds of murk separated and swirled, revealing countless souls before Samael spied the Pericarp. He walked to the first of the three and scooped it into his arms as though lifting an errant child. The fraction of a once singular mind did not protest nor struggle, but it looked after its invisible objective with longing. Samael turned and strode back the way he'd come, and the second and third followed the first, as they always had and always would.

Ω

Wind stirred sand against the stone walls of a cold-looking structure that towered over the tops of all other nearby homes.

Brahman listened to it as he took his tea after his morning meditation rituals. Dank air within his domicile had grown thick with heat as the hours brought midday closer, and the aging mystic took his shirt down to allow the parched breeze a chance to lap the moisture from his skin. A stone-covered well across the earthen floor held his attention when a knock at his chamber door pulled his thoughts from it.

"Master Brahman, may I enter?" Acrit asked.

"Come," Brahman said.

A boy, whose stubble-budded face had not yet been scored by more than fifteen years, crept inside of the small chamber, his shoulders hunched as though he feared bumping his head despite the high ceiling.

"I brought your provisions from the market," Acrit said.

"You're early. Was there a problem with your payment?" Brahman asked.

"No, I've received my pay, and the money from the provisions budget was sufficient. More than sufficient, sir. That is not why I am intruding," Acrit said. He looked to the door as though it had been a bad idea to come. "I've heard word of a stranger."

Brahman nodded as he sipped from a mug marked with the bold initials AC.

"I heard tell when I was in the market from your man, Mikhail. The stranger is looking for you."

"Lots of people have sought me out," Brahman said. "Seems like there are more every year, son. Not something for you to worry about."

"I believe this *is* worrisome. Mikhail indicated the stranger was, well... He was not menacing, but he carried with him a strong aura. A heat, yes, that is what Mikhail told me. The stranger may mean you harm, sir."

"I appreciate your concern." Brahman stood and patted the boy's head. "And I am not upset by you breaking the rule and interrupting me during session." Brahman gripped a handful of thick black hair and hunched to peer into his face. "You are a good boy, Acrit, but don't bother with this stranger. Let me know if you hear anything else, will you?" Brahman released Acrit's hair and turned to set down his cup. "I'll see you in another day and a half, after my solace is over."

Brahman offered the boy a smile, and Acrit left in a hurry, his narrow shoulders never losing the tension wound within them.

The mystic wondered what horrors had been inflicted upon the young man. He was stern, but he had never raised a hand to Acrit. He'd never even raised his voice. It was possible that the constant state of conflict in Palestine was to blame for how the young scurried about as though rodents seeking safety. Brahman tended to think of them as he thought of most people—in measures of how useful they were to him, and little more. Palestine, as a whole, had been quite helpful in his endeavors. He needed only pay off Hamas to have total control over his stay here. Intel was piddly, not much to do about that, but the help was capable, and his only true need was for solitude to prepare for the communion.

The man who called himself a mystic turned from his finished tea before engaging in the vigorous physical torment that would carry him through midday and on to evening. The regiment, designed and made more rigorous over the past five years, drew Brahman to find himself precariously tethered to the ethereal plane. That link grew in sinew and strength with each cycle of solace.

Fever built along with exhaustion, and the heat it generated melded with the swelter of this land. Brahman fancied himself a kinsman to natives in the Americas who sat in extreme temperatures to gain higher insight. His body and his mind were to be divided, this was the plan and he felt it working.

Brahman found himself forced to temper his excitement at the pain surging through his muscles, to calm his mind as he hefted boulders from the ground to his chest and then cast them across the sand-covered floor. Crossing, hefting, and heaving. Crossing, hefting, and heaving.

Echoes of his frenzied breathing reverberated off the heavy walls, and a ringing returned to his ears, beginning the trance he pursued. Hours would pass before he would allow himself to drink from the carafe of water situated on the table next to where he'd lay his body when the time for rest would come.

Ω

Glints shone from Lilith's eyes as she watched the water cast light back toward the heavens. Her fingers ran atop pebbles at the bottom of the streambed as the sounds of wings filled the sky. The tengu landed and stood between his mother and the sun to shield her from its light.

"Tchakyen, lower your wings," she said. "I want to feel the heat on my skin."

"Yes, Mother," Tchakyen said and tucked his wings behind his shoulders. The resemblance to how one of the Host would fold its wings when not concealing them was not lost on her, and she found herself resenting this child for his likeness to her tormentors. Feathered wings were the only similarity a tengu such as Tchakyen might share with an angel—they held a sense of honor which juxtaposed them from most all of her other children—yet many of his kin bore no wings at all, and all of his race shared a common cleverness.

Tchakyen served without question to please Lilith, and he rightly deserved Asmodeus's vacant place at her side. Perhaps this had been so even before the demon of lust's destruction. Still, the chasm between the abilities of Asmodeus and her other children was wide, and she missed him terribly for this, if nothing else. The pain she felt at his loss was not of an aggrieved mother, but more akin to the general grief at having lost a vital piece of the war machine. Lilith tried to keep Asmodeus from her thoughts, as they were pavers to the realization of her own weakness, but when she was unable to keep him from her mind, she did as most anyone might expect of the mother of demons. She raged.

"We have moved my brothers and sisters to the locations across the ocean, as you instructed. There are no further actions to complete your order," Tchakyen said.

"Good. I assume this means they have set their foothold in the deserts to the east?" Lilith asked.

Tchakyen hesitated. "Yes, but there is much difficulty in keeping it. The shaitan do not appreciate our presence in their domain. They attack us on sight. We have lost many, and this has made it difficult to settle matters with the boy as he traverses the sands."

"No matter." Lilith waved her hand and cast droplets of water into the air. "We are numerous. The denizens of Azazel won't be our match while he lays locked in his prison."

Tchakyen bent down and gathered soil rich with sediment into his palms and ground it between his fingers. "We are strong here, Mother. We have our roots in the soil of the forests. Out there"—Tchakyen flicked his eyes eastward—"we are without footing. I do not find joy in bearing sour news to you, but to lie is an affront to my charge. Your children have found little more than slaughter at the hands of David Dolan, the jinn, and the shaitan of the east."

"So be it. If Lucifer claims to command legions, then we will prove ourselves twice as numerous. The demons of the deserts cannot match our numbers. This you should know," Lilith said.

"As you command," Tchakyen said, betraying no emotion.

"Kill the boy, or we will be destroyed by him," Lilith said.

She rose to show her round belly as it morphed with the movement of her pulsing spawn before walking off into the trees.

Ω

David floated through a canopy above a bed of lotus flowers and marveled at their colors. The air felt soft on his skin and tugged him gently along to a small clearing.

Upon landing, a young woman with jewels adorning her caramel skin brought him a plate filled with sweet morsels and sat beside him to run her hands through his hair. Another appeared from the leaves with fresh pillows, propped them behind David's back, and rubbed his shoulders. Another woman appeared, and then another, and another, all while David sat waiting on the bed of lotus, and he knew this would be paradise for most and could have been the very thing that Odysseus chose to dally with for years while Penelope fended off suitors in his honor.

One of the women was whispering in his ear, and David reached around her waist to pull her close. His fingertips glanced upon her neck, and she laid her head back to moan at the sensation before he grasped the neck tightly and pushed the woman to arm's length. The other women gasped, and David swept his arm through the air to dispel them for the mirages they were.

"Did you think I wouldn't notice I was being led into a dream, Mære? I don't dream anymore," David said. He let the demon wriggle from his grasp. It barked at him and tried to flee beneath the lotus flower bed, but the leaves and pedals disintegrated around him— along with the cotton candy colored sky above.

"Ah-ah," David said as they floated together in the darkness. "My mind, my rules."

Mære appeared incensed at losing control in a realm where it had only known superiority and chose to dispel its own disguise to reveal itself. David's first thought was of a hobgoblin as he looked the creature over from its toes to the tips of its pointed ears. It was a stark contrast from the sultry images of a scantily clad incubus he'd grown so accustomed to in pop culture.

It wriggled to find purchase in his mind, to find some means of escape before David grew tired of the game. He knew it was stalling, having sacrificed itself to leave him vulnerable within his room as he waited for daybreak.

"This is goodbye. You won't be causing anymore nightmares," he said before crushing the demon to the size of a penny with little more than his imagination.

David blinked in the dank silence of his small room. He'd sought this spot out for its proximity to the edge of a residential area, and because he'd learned the owners did not ask questions. Having entered the state of Palestine without papers, questions would bring problems for him. Problems cost time, and he was not so patient these days.

He wondered at the frenzied efforts of Lilith's children to bring him down and considered his adversaries carefully at first, but the repetition of tactics and lack of true threat continued to lull him into a feeling of safety, if not superiority. This was not the first time a demon had attempted to enter his mind and force it to a dream state, for example. Preying on someone like David, someone on a more-than-even playing field, as opposed to on children and the forlorn, was apparently not something which Lilith had made them accustomed to.

David stood and opened the door, noticing the unusually warm day had broken to a cooler evening. He ventured out to dispatch those lying in wait before once again retreating to his room to think about the treasure he had lost and tasks to be done.

CHAPTER TWO
HOBBLED

Chelsea Dolan filled her trusty water can from a rusted tap affixed to the foundation of her home and watched hummingbirds feed from their reservoirs of sugar water. Liquid filled the vessel, and she was cued by the absence of echoes from the hollow to instinctively shut the water before turning to see to her bushes and early spring flowers.

The roots were young and exposed to the harsh whims of confused seasons. She had put extra care into them to keep invasive thoughts from finding her, but Rose tumbled through her thoughts as she cast insulating mulch to ward off late frost.

Time had done little to dull the pain of losing the girl, but Chelsea had found within herself the fortitude to press on. There were serious matters afoot. Ones she couldn't ignore while in a hole of depression.

For one, she had to see to Dodd's recovery. Asmodeus had broken his leg in four places. Two of the fractures had been compound and protruded from the skin of his leg. His journey of recovery was one of agony and wouldn't be short, though physical therapy was working, and he was able to walk with the help of a cane, if just for brief jaunts.

Still, Dodd had been adamant about attending Rose's memorial service and standing while her casket was lowered into the ground, his face a mask of grief as he watched. Chelsea, too, was shattered by the loss of the girl she considered her own. She sought vengeance often, even if only in her thoughts. Her efforts to locate Lilith were tempered after David left without word or warning to seek out answers from where he believed they were buried in Syria.

"Tell me about my father," David had asked her on the night of Rose's burial.

Chelsea sighed. "There isn't much more than you already know. It was a one-night stand while I was at the dig in Syria. We were a hodgepodge group of archaeologists from a few different countries, and your father was little more than a stranger. Sorry to say, but love didn't factor in that night. I was young and lonely."

"His name?" David had asked, his eyes staring through her at some long-distant thought he was chasing.

"Silbi. Arthur Silbi," Chelsea said. "If you plan to find him, you're going to run into some roadblocks. He's off the grid, as far as I can tell."

David left less than a week later for parts unknown to Chelsea, until he'd contacted Dodd to run a name for him.

"Brahman was who he was asking after," Dodd had told her. "I had nothing on the database about his whereabouts overseas, but he is a big baddie stateside. Something of a corporate fixer, he bounced around to regions ripe with resources and facilitated the destabilization of those in control. Companies, governments, didn't matter. He'd eviscerate them. Then he and his buddies swooped in and took over in Venezuela, India, half the continent of Africa... the list goes on. A lot more digging and a few calls turned up that Brahman's posing as a pseudo-medicine man living somewhere in the Mideast." Dodd had easily read the dismay on her face. "Don't over worry. The kid sounded fine, Chelsea, just driven."

Chelsea knew David was driven. He had explained all that transpired the night he left to save Rose. The appearance of other angels and their involvement in his life was spoken as little more than an afterthought, though his description of how Uriel had been taken after breaking some sacred law was riddled with nearly as much anguish as he held for his lost love. She knew plenty about the names David mentioned, and she had been doing her own research on how to seek an audience with these divine interlopers. One way or another, she intended to get answers as to why David was being kept in their plans.

Chelsea's phone alarm rang, and she looked down to see it was nearly time to get Dodd from his physical therapy. She lifted the can and emptied its contents on the bushes lining a small stone inscribed with a single phrase on each side. *Rose* was visible to the sky and for all passersby to see. David had used his nails to grind out another word opposite to the one Chelsea had etched into the stone.

Lost.

Ω

"I'm not asking for much, Dodd, just a workup on a few characters that Mom was cagey about when we were speaking," David said. "Silbi isn't a common name, even overseas. There's got to be something on the guy."

Dodd breathed heavily into the receiver as he walked out of the hospital to be picked up by Chelsea. "I'm not CIA, kid. Shit, I wasn't even FBI. I'm a retired detective with some good friends left over who will stick their necks out for me. I can't snap and receive a write-up on every nefarious figure you come across. This will take some time."

"I know, and I'm not asking for you to make a miracle happen, but any leads you can send my way will save time," David said. The connection was spotty, and Dodd sounded as though he was small through the phone. David bet the large detective *felt* that way after having been hobbled by his run-in with a demigod, demon, or whatever the current title might be.

"I'm working for ya, kid. Rest easy and be safe out there. If you get yourself hurt traipsing around war-torn countries, your mother will give me a lot more to worry about besides a broken leg and few ribs," Dodd said.

"I know," David said. He was working his way through a crowd and didn't want to be seen whispering into his burner phone. "Thank you, Dodd. Tell Mom I love her."

"I will, kid. Be careful."

The connection cleared, and David walked through the throng of Palestinians crowding the street. His complexion was not cause for alarm or worry here—many westerners came to the strip to report on the eruptions of violence between Hamas and Israel, but it did draw attention, which David could do without. He needed to find this mystic, whom he'd heard knew of the yam burial places of fallen angels.

A young boy walked past but held his stare on David overlong—his eyes belied knowledge beyond the distrustful stares other people issued toward the American. David sidestepped into the boy's path. "Cup of tea?" He asked in Arabic.

The boy's face blanched. "No, sir, I must be getting home to prepare dinner for my family."

David nodded. "That sounds like a noble cause for leaving. Allow me to walk with you." His palm opened to reveal a mass of folded bills.

The boy swallowed his first words before they could leap from his tongue and asked, "Who are you?"

"David Dolan. Please, continue on. I don't want to make you late."

"Very well. You may call me Acrit, sir." The pair walked in silence for a time before Acrit broke the spell. "I am surprised at your Arabic, Mr. Dolan. It is quite good."

David smiled. "I'm adept in most languages, I've found. Yours holds a particular beauty." He observed Acrit's smile. "Please call me David. After all, I'm not much older than you, and I hate formal titles when they're put on me."

David had stopped using pseudonyms after arriving in Israel. Being attacked by the children of Lilith on his second night proved they were useless. He saw no value in wasting time attempting to hide from them, since they had some means of tracking unknown to him, and if they wanted to be slaughtered, he'd let them.

"Why are you here, David?" Acrit asked.

"I need information before I move on," David said. "Information few people have."

Acrit pulled the loose collar of his linen shirt up around his neck and the bottom of his face. "People have been discussing your inquiries. You have found that questions tend to lead to suspicions here, I trust?"

David nodded. "Difficult to gain the trust of people who've been upended so often in their history, particularly in the last half century, Acrit."

"Yes. Most everyone whom we haven't aged with is a person of suspicion. Given how Hamas has chosen to operate—and Israel— we've no choice but to whisper softly," Acrit said. "Do be careful what you say regarding Hamas here. They have a way of reaching into barred doors and taking those who have criticisms."

"Oh, I'm not planning on making trouble for anyone here, even them. That is, unless my path leads me there," David said.

Acrit led David around a corner and to a row of doors lining the side of an overlong building made of tan brick. "This is our home, David. Our journey together has been short, but pleasant."

"A fine walk on a cool night. Thank you for your time, but I would be a fool not to ask you for another meeting," David said as he extended the money toward Acrit.

Acrit gently folded David's fingers over the bills and pushed his hand away. "I will meet with you again. Please come here tomorrow at this time, and we will sup together. It is a kindness to offer a traveler food and drink. One tradition people should never forget. We may discuss your questions then."

David watched as Acrit entered his home. The boy seemed to hold wisdom well beyond his years.

He turned and walked the road the way he'd come, feeling eyes dance over him from all sides.

Ω

Samael traveled with Pericarp's three selves for a vast distance after leaving the waiting place behind. They hadn't needed to cross the

31

river nor trouble the ferryman on their journey, as they were already beyond the veiled banks and deep within the murk. Samael correctly assumed Pericarp had crossed the river Lethe, a cascading torrent of forgetfulness, as was deemed appropriate by the vast mechanism sorting souls after death. It was often the chosen passage for those who had died as victims.

The quartet made their way smoothly, despite the unpredictable nature of Pericarp, and soon they reached a crossroads nestled neatly in the countryside—or so it appeared from Pericarp's perspective. Samael had learned to hoist the baser form of the three along and worry not about the other two following. They had little choice.

At the branching of three paths, Samael led them to the center fork without hesitation. Less fanfare was called for at this passing than Uriel had deemed necessary for David. Pericarp wasn't on a journey of self-discovery, after all, but one of reclamation and uncertainty. The fractured psyche needn't be subjected to judgment. The simple reason being that it was unfit in its current state.

Low growls arose from the nearby brush to signal the guardians' attention was on them, and the angel calmed them with the utterance of a single word before striding through the area in a manner devoid of worry.

The second Pericarp behind him cooed at the animals who'd threatened them as they passed, and Samael paused to appraise it. This was the first time it had given attention to anything but attending to the safety of the first. Now he looked at the path ahead that insisted on bounding around through the landscape in a comically exaggerated layout. This wouldn't do for his needs, and his needs were budgeted in time.

He lowered his charge until its feet touched the ground and allowed the first Pericarp to wander about while he concentrated on the scene. The essence of Pericarp was chaos, albeit benign, but chaos as pure as the wanton abandon of order could conjure. He had to align Pericarp to a degree in order to create uniformity in the path ahead and shorten their passage.

Pericarp's first and second parts cajoled with one another while the third pinched pebbles it found on the ground, pausing now and again to mew in the direction they'd come. Samael walked to it and gently took it by the hand. The third was not as easily led as its more primal lower selves, but it came with little more trouble than being patted on the arm to keep its attention on the task at hand.

"Stand here and do not move," Samael said before leaving to carry the first to where he'd left the third. The second followed as it was compelled to. He placed the second behind the third and likewise the first behind them both and put their hands on the shoulders of those in the front until they appeared as a misfit conga line. He walked to the front and raised the lead Pericarp's chin. It gazed at the landscape with eyes losing their unquestioning ways.

Satisfied, Samael walked to the back and placed his own hand in the center of the back of the first Pericarp. He pulsed his will through the three and observed their alert posture, but he felt no feedback to show a shared consciousness or purpose. He gave a light but swift kick to the pants of the second Pericarp and felt a jolt run through them. Small, like the sound of many voices at low volume, but it was there.

"Good. Now think *straight*," Samael said.

The three parts of one remained scattered, and Samael concentrated harder to pull their wills taut with one another. As he did, the pathway ahead rolled trees and dislodged boulders as it pulled itself from a meandering mess and into a fine vector.

Once the path completed its alignment, Samael moved to release the three parts of Pericarp, but before his fingers left the link, he felt a sharp pain. The three parts of Pericarp had united, and memories were beginning to coalesce from their shared past. Samael sensed confusion and anguish from each being, uniquely expressed at experiencing these memories, and he quickly released them from their union. The pain and terror fled from his mind, but the experience told him putting this mind back together would take some talent.

"All right, Huey, Dewey, and Louie, let's get a move on. Tut tut," Samael said.

The three parts of Pericarp ambled one after the other along the path, and Samael considered his plans to unite them. A labor never before completed, nor attempted, he had his reservations about his odds.

Most of our hopes hinge on Ma'at, the goddess of the sands, who divines order from endless chaos.

CHAPTER THREE
SHAITAN

Brahman's endeavors carried his mind through the setting of the sun and into another night of toil. He warded off thoughts of thirst as his arms, large with the memory of similar acts, pulled a troweled rake through the thick sands of his chamber floor. The distance might fool an observer into believing the task to be simple, but the sand Brahman toiled against was comprised of zircon—the heaviest on earth. Though laced with salt, thus less dense than had it been pure zircon, the sand proved more than adequate for hours of painful exertion. He raked the sand and smoothed the thoughts pervading his mind.

The trance was tantamount to the rower's high he'd experienced when competing as an oarsman in college. Days long passed, but whose memory never faded fully from the man's mind, just becoming more muddied and less descript with age. His senses had been at a heightened level as he pushed his oars through the air and pulled the water into submission with the muscles in his back, and so too were they now when he became aware of an uninvited presence in his chamber.

"I'm not pissed if you have serious business with me, Flueric, but if you're here to interrupt my process out of boredom, that's not the way into my good graces," Brahman said.

Flueric entered the chamber and strolled to the small table where Brahman's meager provisions had been placed by Acrit. The man paid no mind to the carefully measured allotments arranged along the coarse wood grains, and he popped a fig into his mouth.

"The world doesn't stop turning while you chase the dragon, Brahman," Flueric said. "I might grow old and weary waiting for you to have time to meet with me."

"You're older than this sand. I think you could manage a few more hours," Brahman said.

"Older and far grittier, but it gets boring watching the sand fall through an endless hourglass," Flueric said. Brahman stared flatly as Flueric poured water from his carafe and drank greedily. "So, I decided to look in on you. I hate to be the bearer of bad news, but you appear to be failing."

"I'm striving for insight, not sainthood, you dick," Brahman said.

Flueric laughed. "There you are. Steeped in sweat and grime, but you still can't shake that pesky persona you developed over that sordid life of yours. Tsk tsk, mystical Brahman. Maybe you will need to resort to prayer after all."

Brahman dropped the trowel and walked to the table to pour his own water. Continuing his work would be a fool's errand at this point.

"Why are you here?"

"Still have the gimp in that hole there?" Flueric asked.

Brahman nodded before swallowing the warm water.

"You're sure it's a shaitan, and not some other jinn?"

"I lured and trapped it myself," Brahman said. "It's one of Azazel's own."

Flueric smiled. "Good. I think I'll stay and observe your little interrogation."

"You aim to help?" Brahman asked.

"Oh, that's a hard no. Those little shits don't listen to me. Never liked me much, truth be told," Flueric said.

"Ah, I suppose it was too much to hope you'd be helpful," Brahman said.

"Oh, I can help, just not with the shaitan," Flueric said. "How about a little intel for you?"

Brahman's eyebrows raised.

"There's another player about, a special one, and I am just dying to meet him." Flueric bared his ivory teeth in a smile so perfect that it felt insidious.

Brahman nodded. "Yes, Acrit mentioned him. He's looking for me. We heard tell he's been traipsing around the market."

"Indeed. You two are hunting the same wabbit, it would seem," Flueric said.

Brahman's eyes widened at this. Before he'd traveled to the Mideast to find the fallen angel, he had been at the pinnacle of his career. One not often spoken of around the supper table, and one that had made him fabulously wealthy. The first number to be called by oligarchs and governments alike, Erik Brahman liked his status as a fixer on a national scale. The power he felt bringing ruin to whole societies and leaving them ripe for the plunder was almost biblical. Had he been around, the Israelites mightn't have needed the Ark of the Covenant to bring down Jericho.

Flueric smiled. "Oh, now don't get all worried. I doubt your reasons are lined up, but who knows, maybe he can help. Everyone has a price, after all."

"I very much doubt that," Brahman said. "I've been aligning myself for communion with this demon of the sands for almost three years. Not something a traveler with a pipedream of seeing a fallen angel will likely have done."

"No, that's true. But I think you playing at being a monk in cloister is fogging your brain." Flueric leaned forward and tapped his cup against Brahman's forehead, smiling as the droplet of water left there ran down to the tip of his nose. It dangled as though refusing to fall and be torn to shreds by the hungry sands. "He's got some clout, this one."

Brahman flicked the water from his nose. "Stop dancing around the point and just tell me what you know and want to do."

"Well, there's not much really," Flueric said. "A kid from the States barely old enough to vote. He's a bit bright eyed and bushy tailed, for sure. I can't say he's exceptionally violent, either. He didn't threaten your servant, Acrit, when he chanced upon him, so there's that. But he sure runs hot, Brahman. Too hot to ignore, even for me."

"An angel?" Brahman said. "That doesn't make sense. They don't meddle with us, and even if they did, they don't pussyfoot around the slums looking for clues."

"Agreed. Oh, except about the not meddling part. Read a book, oh wise mystic. They've been told to stomp out more than a few score of your kind. Don't think that card won't be played again someday." Flueric pressed his palm down on a fig, and its ripe contents spread into the wood.

Brahman considered this and decided to drink the remaining carafe and devour the provisions on his table. Flueric watched and smiled.

"I'll push my timeline up. Dudael must be entered soon," Brahman said, wiping his mouth.

"A prudent thought," Flueric said. "Mind if I stay here until your buddy shows up? The Airbnb scene in Palestine is just so sparse these days. You know, with the blood of innocents running through the streets and all that."

"Do what you like. I need to get rest if I'm to perform the inquisition tomorrow," Brahman said and left the room.

Flueric arranged his chair by the pit housing the shaitan Brahman had managed to trap. He pushed the stone cover to the side, looked down into the darkness, and saw two glowing embers aimed up at him. They narrowed in recognition.

The shaitan was forced to endure Flueric's maddening smile as piss rained into the pit.

Ω

Samael sidestepped the gatekeepers of the world beneath the veil and continued his journey with the first Pericarp draped over his shoulder. Trusting it to follow the path had not gone well.

She cooed and whooped without relenting at the second and the third, who walked along beside Samael diligently without fussing overtly.

"Soon?" said the third.

"Speaking again? That's good. Yes, we will be there soon," Samael said. The third would be the one to regain any powers of speech, and this was an encouraging development, but Samael did not relent in his worrying. The Pericarp would have to come far to regain any semblance of her whole self, and quickly at that. "You must listen to my commands when we arrive, or else you'll likely wish you were cast back into the endless fog of sorting from where I plucked you."

The third continued to stare at her feet and walked on, but Samael believed she understood in the same way a toddler understands the direction of a parent.

They arrived at the entrance to a great amphitheater, comprised of ornate stones and golden designs. The exterior was as well groomed as any Roman construct in its prime and exuded sheer beauty, but upon entering, the interior showed to be timeworn by what would have been hundreds of years of weathering in the living world. The sorting place of Ma'at and Thoth, this was where he'd find out if Pericarp could be restored, or if she would be deemed unrighteous and be devoured.

"Ho, what have we here?" Thoth leaped down from his balcony seat. "Why, we haven't seen you in *some* time, Samael."

"It's tough to schedule social calls these days, old friend. I hope you aren't offended," Samael said.

"You've already forgotten me entirely if you'd think I might be offended by that, ho, yes." The deity of order and wisdom peered closely at the first Pericarp on Samael's shoulders. "A fragmented one, I see. I did wonder what methods you'd use to further Uriel's plans. He played his cards close to the chest, that one, did he not?"

Samael merely nodded at the mention of Uriel in the past tense.

"Ma'at, come look at the odd human Samael has brought to us," Thoth called.

Ma'at emerged from a door in the amphitheater with far less fanfare than her counterpart, though she had no need to rely on such for attention. Her every movement alluded to grace, and most any found it difficult to keep their eyes from her. She sat at the seat of the once bright scales of judgment and rested her arms at her side, partially concealing a beatific assortment of feathers adorning them from wrist to shoulder. Samael lowered his eyes so as to not linger on her sharp facial features and to show her his respect.

"What a pleasant surprise. It is not often we have such a learned traveler call upon us, is it, my love?" Ma'at asked Thoth.

"Not nearly as often as we'd like," he said.

"Even two of the wisest and most unique among us become bored of each other over eons, then? What hope will we have after another billion years passes?" Samael asked.

"Well, I'd better become more interesting before that time comes," Thoth said.

"You're interesting enough, Thoth—or would Hermes better serve as your name?" Samael asked. "I feel like that was your name when I was here last."

"Hermes or Thoth, depending on where you are and who you ask, I suppose," Thoth said. "Though we've become aged relics of the past by now. Not nearly as well-known these days as you, the reaper of souls."

"Such a crude imagining of a beautiful angel, don't you think?" Ma'at asked.

"I've never minded," Samael said.

"No. You wouldn't, would you? Not an ounce of pride left in you, I suspect. So unlike your father. You'll have to teach Thoth how to overcome his own ego. He's absolutely the worst when it comes to talk of speediness of any sort, and any mention of it comes back to his own." Ma'at mocked Thoth's tone of voice as perfectly as any spouse that ever has when she added, "*I could beat light itself in a footrace!*"

Samael laughed and then moved to corral the second Pericarp, who'd wandered off. "Speaking of talents, I have a request of you two. One that shouldn't cause you much trouble."

"Is this the business which brings you here, Samael of the black wings? A fragile mortal who's been fragmented for processing before being sent on..." Ma'at asked. She stepped around the third Pericarp, who observed the beauty of the deity with wonder in her eyes.

"She is of the utmost importance to us at this time. It was Uriel himself who deemed her so," Samael said.

Thoth and Ma'at both looked upon him at the name. "Oh, what a tragedy that was," Ma'at said.

"And for what?" Thoth said. "To snuff out a fledgling demigod? An absolute shame. None used their light such as he."

"If you'll forgive my impudence," Samael said, "there are those who may, and she could count herself amongst them, should you place her heart upon the scale and find her worthy."

"You can speak freely to us. Please never worry about such things, Samael," Thoth said. "We live outside of the cone of narcissism and need no idle flattery to churn ourselves to action."

"Thank you," Samael said. "Your compliment is well understood, however. Uriel was our wisest, and his absence has sent the Host into a crippling cycle of uncertainty. They watch and they wait, as Uriel predicted they would."

The two ancient gods nodded and exchanged glances.

"Well, shall we begin?" Ma'at asked.

Thoth gently lifted the first Pericarp from Samael's shoulders and walked with her toward the scales as Samael chaperoned the second to follow after. Ma'at gently grasped the hand of the third in her own and smiled. The third returned the smile to the delight of the goddess. "Well, aren't you a lovely little thing."

"We have never judged one who is in three parts, Samael. This may not work as you hope," Thoth said.

"Will she be devoured if it goes wrong?" Samael asked.

"Absolutely," Ma'at said. "There is no other path for those who are found to be impure other than to be devoured by Ammit. She will find herself torn apart a second time and likely fragmented beyond reclamation, I'm afraid. A fate worse than any I can conceive." Thoth nodded in grim agreement.

"I trust in Uriel's judgment. We shall continue," Samael said.

"Very well. Thoth, line them up and then step away, please," Ma'at said.

Thoth did as he was bidden. After, he walked to his space at the left scale, and his face took the form of an ibis enshrouded in onyx fur.

Ma'at approached the first Pericarp with care and drew her in. The girl collapsed into the goddess as though a child being consoled after a painful folly. Ma'at consoled her and gently reached a taloned hand into her chest to remove a beating heart and then placed it upon the scale next to Thoth. She repeated the process for the second, and when she approached the third, she smiled. "It is good that you are unafraid, my dear. I sense great light within you," she said. Ma'at reached into the third Pericarp and removed half a heart.

Thoth gasped. "Why is it not whole?"

"This is unusual," Ma'at said.

"Well, did you leave the other half in there?" Thoth asked.

"I did not!" Ma'at said.

"Check for it, ho! We can't go about these things half-hearted—"

Ma'at used her free hand and hit him squarely in the chest to stop his wheezing laughter. "I will not be rooting around in this tender thing for something I know isn't there. She's merely got half a heart."

Samael looked on and considered the possibilities for such an outcome. The hearts were largely a representation of moral value and ethics here, and not representative of true biology. The weight of a person's intentions and past deeds was what was weighed against the righteousness of Ma'at. "This changes nothing. Let's continue the test despite the anomaly," he said.

Ma'at walked to the scale and placed the third incomplete heart of Pericarp next to the others and settled at her place to the right of the scales. She pulled a feather from her left wing and gently laid it upon the second golden plate and then unlocked the mechanism.

The scale pulled heavily down on the left side and the hearts dipped below the height of the feather before the they reverted in a pendulous swing in the other direction. "Do they often swing so wildly?" Samael asked.

Thoth answered, "No."

As if in response to his query, Ammit strode into the amphitheater. Samael was struck by the creature's beauty, despite its composition being that of a crocodile, lion, and hippopotamus. He watched with earnest as the beast walked to Thoth's side and observed the scales.

Thoth reached down and scratched the neck of the creature while they waited, but Samael could see Ammit's eyes greedily measuring the speed of the scale's movement. It would be close, they both knew.

"Soon now," Ma'at said to the relief of none among them. The Pericarps stood motionless in observance, save the third, who watched Ammit with keen interest. Samael wondered if they knew fear of consequence, and if not, how blessed they truly were to have that ignorance.

The scales slowed and reached a stalemate before the left dropped below the equal threshold by the barest of margins. The hearts had weighed heavy.

"Impossible," Samael said.

Ammit moved from Thoth, whose eyes showed sorrow. The beast loomed above the scale, looking upon the hearts.

The first Pericarp sprang into motion and avoided Samael's attention as it walked to the beast, who turned its head to observe her approach. "Don't!" Samael called, but he was too late to stop her and was forced to restrain the second along with the third. Ma'at looked on without protest.

Pericarp's first and most primal self stood motionless as Ammit's large crocodilian head lowered before her, but she did not cow. She reached forward with both arms and hugged the snout of the creature with pure joy on her face. Ammit, could do nothing besides endure the embrace. Not a creature of malice, after all—the servant of Anubis even appeared to enjoy the gesture.

"Look to the scale, Samael," Thoth said.

Samael did, and he saw it swing by the barest of margins in the other direction to make Ma'at's feather measure slightly heavier.

"I'll be damned," Samael said.

"It is lucky for her that you aren't, old friend," Ma'at said. "You wish for her to become whole once more, then?"

"Yes, though I haven't worked out exactly how I will accomplish that," he said. "Other than moving beyond purgatory to the pool of consciousness, as those do before the next step, I am not sure it is possible to be rejoined."

Thoth came forward and whispered into Ammit's ear and then looked to Samael with both hands down at his sides and open for all to see. "Please, trust in us and do not be alarmed. We do not wish for conflict."

"I don't understa—"

Samael was interrupted when Ammit turned and devoured the hearts upon the scale despite their righteousness having been proven. The crocodile then laid its head on the ground and opened its mouth as far and wide as it could, creating a cavern of pink flesh and stalagmite teeth. Thoth grabbed Pericarp at the same moment Ma'at embraced Samael at his waist. "Do not worry," she whispered to him before Thoth threw the first Pericarp into Ammit's gullet. The second and third quickly ran to join her.

Ω

David arrived at Acrit's door as the evening sun flirted with the horizon. The boy whose almond-colored eyes David was meant to trust opened it before David could announce himself with a knock.

"Good evening, David Dolan of America," Acrit said.

"You've done some research already," David said. "Does this mean we are no longer supping together?"

"It does, but not for reasons rooted in malice. We're to go see my master, Brahman," Acrit said.

David stepped aside to allow Acrit to join him outside. The evening air had cooled quickly from the unseasonable blaze the day had been, but its effect was little comfort to those seeking relief from the dry desert heat as it emanated from where it had dug into the stones of the walls around them.

"Warmer than usual?" David asked as he motioned for Acrit to lead them.

"Actually, yes. March tends to be cooler here, yet the sun rages down as though it was months later," Acrit said. "People speak of it as a bad omen."

"Oh, weather spikes and records are set all the time. Don't forget that four generations ago, saw a year without summer," David said.

"I'd forgotten that. Krakatoa, was it?" Acrit asked.

"Yes, that was the volcano in Indonesia that belched enough ash into the sky to black out the sun for a year. Hard to believe it was so recent," David said.

"Feels like yesterday, sometimes," Acrit said. He glanced at David and smiled broadly.

"It would appear you may have more secrets of interest to me than just the location of your master," David said.

"Oh, yes, of course," Acrit said. "But would you begrudge a new friend for not showing his hand of cards? It's not as though we can trust one another just yet, is it?"

"You speak a lot of truths in the form of questions, Acrit. Reminds me of Bob Ross," David said.

Acrit remained quiet as he chewed this over, and David hid his amusement. In truth, David often wondered how Kharon the ferryman would react to the news that he had been correct in his assumption that David was far more than he himself knew. David felt the urge to visit his fast friend, and he might have acted upon it if he had any inkling how he might journey back to the docks the ferryman used to usher the souls of the dead to their proper places in the veiled world.

"Brahman's place is just ahead there. You're sure you wish to continue?" Acrit asked, but he gave no indication as to why David might stop his journey here.

"Yes, I am sure," David said.

He followed the boy to a building much larger than most in the near vicinity. Its domed roof and expansive footprint would have led the mind to consider it to be a temple, though the dearth of ornamentation gave it more the look of a cloister or monastery. Acrit produced a ring of keys and led them inside to a receiving room. David moved to take off his shoes, but Acrit stopped him.

"Brahman will not require you to remove your footwear as there is earth enough inside already," Acrit said.

"Interesting," David replied.

He straightened and followed the boy through archways held

together by bent olive wood. The interior of the dwelling was not so spartan as to seem empty, but the efforts to maintain a sparse amount of furnishing seemed clear. Tables were small and held plants, surrounded by walls which were largely empty, save a few paintings of the desert here and there.

"Why would a man have earth inside of his dwelling?" David asked.

Acrit smiled. "What can better serve a man to reach the pinnacle of his humanity than to be surrounded by the very substance from which he was made?"

David nodded his understanding. "I do believe Mr. Brahman will be worth the time and effort it took to arrive at his doorstep, Acrit, but tell me, who is the other one waiting beyond that door with him?" David stopped walking and leveled a stare at the boy.

"I didn't know of another guest before coming here," Acrit said. "Brahman sent a messenger to me at my home to inform me of my charge to bring you here, and that is all. He lives and trains his mind and body alone, save the coordinate he keeps in the earth within his inner chamber. I do not believe it is this dismal creature you speak of, though."

"No, not the demon. It's a tiny ember next to the other one. *He* burns brightly," David said.

"You are interesting, David. Shall we enter and find out together?" Acrit asked.

David didn't feel that Acrit was lying to him, so he kept silent. Acrit took the fact that David had not turned to leave as his answer and rapped on the door in a pattern that told David he'd been trained to announce himself in this way.

"Come," came Brahman's voice from within.

David and Acrit walked through the smaller door into the center of the domed building. The room was expansive, with a high ceiling allowing for a feeling of freedom compared to the restrictive halls and rooms leading to it. David saw the floor to be composed of soil at the edges and sand in the middle, not unlike the sands of Valhalla's arena. At its center, there jutted crudely stacked stones with a large slab serving as a cover. David would have wondered if it was a well had he not been aware of the demon smoldering within.

"The prodigal son returns," Flueric said from his seat at the periphery of the room. David turned to observe him. He didn't remove his stare when Brahman spoke from near the small stone pit.

"Now, now," Brahman said, "let's not startle our guest. We have it on good authority he has traveled far to join us here tonight."

Flueric said, "He doesn't look jumpy to me. Just awfully serious."

David watched on as Flueric hardened his own expression to mock David's own.

"Acrit, you may leave us," Brahman said.

"I'd prefer if he was allowed to stay," David said, breaking his stare at Flueric and turning to face Brahman. "If it isn't too much trouble, Mr. Brahman."

"Ooooh, and so polite. Mightn't we have a future statesman here?" Flueric mused.

"Very well. Acrit, you may take a seat next to Flueric there. There is water and figs for you, should you be in need," Brahman said. "So, David, what is it that you believe I can do for you?"

"Azazel," David said. The utterance of the name devoured the pleasantries whole like a gluttonous serpent.

Brahman said, "What of him?"

"I need to find him," David said, "and my journey has wound its way to you as the best option for knowing where his prison, Dudael, might be."

"Well, this is quite the surprise," Brahman said. "I'd thought my endeavors to locate the general of the fallen Grigori were quite secret."

"I have means most don't," David said. He turned to walk in the direction of Flueric and Acrit, keeping his eyes on the pile of figs on their table. Flueric's delight at his approach was so palpable that David expected him to burst from his chair at any moment, but he stayed seated. David hadn't gained a mastery of his powers yet, and he wondered at times if he was unaware of some of them entirely, but he'd made good on becoming powerful enough to set on edge the most powerful warrior of heaven. This he knew.

Yet, Flueric, who undoubtedly knew David held great power, appeared giddy with excitement rather than fearful. What was worse, David could sense the great power of Flueric, but his senses had not been honed beyond the ability to delve further. He did not know what Flueric was capable of.

David reached forward and plucked a fig from the table and then turned to face Brahman. "Have you gotten answers from that thing down there?" David asked, popping the fig into his mouth to satisfy his curiosity as to the taste of the thing rather than to sate a need for nourishment his body no longer required.

"The shaitan? No, we have not been able to connect to its consciousness yet, and it does not speak," Brahman said as he patted the stone cover.

"I have a proposal," David said. Brahman glanced at Flueric and then back to David. "Allow me to try to communicate with it. Should I succeed, I will take us all to Dudael."

Brahman's face drew taught. "Even if you could, which I highly doubt, why would you risk allowing us to know? We could merely kill you and go to receive the spoils of Dudael ourselves."

"You're welcome to try, but I believe you'll find that it is far more likely that I would be venturing on alone, and you would be so much ash left to mix with the sand and soil of this place," David said. His tone remained even, contrasting the mood of the meeting with the severity of his statement.

"Oh, I like him, Brahman," Flueric said. "Let's give it a go and see how it pans out."

"You'll kill him if he steps out of line?" Brahman asked.

"Absolutely not. I haven't been this entertained in quite some time, dear Brahman," Flueric said.

Acrit was forced to stifle a chuckle and avert his eyes when Brahman's scowling face pointed toward him.

"Fine, see if you can get answers from the shaitan then, but do not cross me, David. I've means beyond Flueric at my disposal, and I will rain down hell on you should you lie to me," Brahman said.

Flueric laughed openly and clapped his hands together. He stood from his chair and adjusted his suit by buttoning the jacket over his vest and carefully pulling his watch chain so it hung in an elegant arch from his top button to the vest pocket. David didn't find his actions to be threatening in the slightest and believed he had no intentions to harm him, at least for the moment.

"Very well, let's begin," David said. He strode to the well, causing Brahman to retreat some distance out of caution. David reached out to grip the stone and hefted it into the air to peer inside. Brahman gaped at the display of strength, and Flueric maintained his idiot's grin. Acrit watched quietly and ate figs.

"Well, aren't you cute," David said into the pit before casting the stone aside and leaping down.

"Wait, he's by no means tame!" Brahman called across the sand floor.

Before he could make to move more than a few steps toward the pit, David had leaped out with the shaitan under his arm, forcing the mystic to reverse his course and back pedal away.

"Are you crazy?" Brahman exclaimed.

"Maybe," David said as he released the shaitan on the sand floor. The demon hesitated, unsure what to do with its newfound freedom. First, it glanced at Brahman with anger in its eyes and considered heading toward him, but upon spotting Flueric at the periphery of the sand floor, its choice became apparent very quickly. It flung itself toward the smartly dressed man, whose smile never faltered in the face of such ferocity. When the shaitan reached Flueric with hands hooked back to slash forward at his throat, the man removed his hand from his pocket and struck the demon before returning it to the silk lined pocket. David noted the ferocity of the blow and hoped the demon wasn't dumbed by it.

"Now, that wasn't very wise, was it?" David said as he walked to where the shaitan lay and helped it up to a seated position on the ledge of its prison. "I trust you've gotten that all out of your system, then?"

The shaitan looked upon David with the same centuries-old red eyes that burned with hatred for Flueric moments earlier, but for

David, they had softened, as though the demon recognized him in some way.

David took the opportunity to reach out with his mind and found the shaitan had not left the door to its own thoughts open to him. That was to be expected, though, as the creature had been imprisoned here for lord knew how long and had been assailed more recently in the form of a cosmic backhand. David persisted urging his request to communicate across the barrier of space between their minds until the shaitan relented and allowed for a trickle of understanding.

At first, David only received a hazy projection of what he assumed to be Azazel standing within a cavern filled with black flames. David projected his own image of himself as Azazel's son, and the shaitan nodded its understanding. More images were sent through the space of their minds, until David depicted his ability to use the demon's language, but only if the demon used it first.

The shaitan considered this for a moment before attempting to speak using its inner monologue, which David then used to form an inner dialogue.

"They are whore's sons, the lot of them," the shaitan said of his captors. "I will kill that man." It pointed to Brahman, who blanched at its menacing stare.

"There's no need for that right now. I will free you once you tell me where Azazel is imprisoned," David communicated.

"You'll try to kill him?" the shaitan asked.

"I won't lie. There is a distinct possibility things may play out that way."

The shaitan put its hand atop David's shoulder and stood. "I will tell you where he is. He wants you to come."

David's mind filled with images of rocky outcrops and sandblasted terrain he had no way to understand until the shaitan graced him with the image of a crude map from the shaitan's perspective to guide his course. He'd been shown the way.

"Thank you," David said aloud, and he steadied the creature on his feet.

He was about to explain that the creature should be allowed to go free from this place, but the demon's quick movements interrupted his attempts. The shaitan loosed a feral growl at the domed ceiling of the chamber and once again tore its way through the room at Flueric, who stood smiling at the spectacle.

This time, the demon stopped short of its goal, kicking up a dusty cloud of sand at Flueric's pants, forcing a displeased frown from the man at being made dirty. The shaitan smiled at Flueric before using its claws to rip open its own throat, spewing gore and blood on Flueric's clothes.

Flueric, for the first time since David had met him, looked less than amused.

CHAPTER FOUR
SUTURE

Dodd leaned on the banister of Chelsea's staircase as he descended and wondered which would give out first: his femur or the delicate wooden spindles marking his progress down.

"How are you making out?" Chelsea called from the kitchen.

"Not so bad as a week ago, not so well as two months ago," he said.

Dodd's beleaguered rate of recovery wasn't exactly as dire as Asmodeus had predicted. For one, he hadn't decided to eat a bullet in lieu of continuing his existence on Earth, and for another, he was already walking with a cane. Though, the demon had been correct when he predicted Dodd's size would hinder him. His bones, once a riot of splinters and maligned cylinders, now felt like stones rubbing together with each step he took. He'd lost weight, about thirty pounds, but his large frame still put too much pressure on his leg.

He sat down and Chelsea set the mug of coffee before him at the table where he, Chelsea, and Rose had initially formed their little party. Rose's absence was felt in every moment of their waking lives, and Dodd didn't know how Chelsea had been able to carry on after she was killed and David left. She was strong. Stronger than he would have been in her place.

"The physical therapy center called," Chelsea said. "They're moving you on to a new regiment of exercises starting on Tuesday. Your trainer has touted you as her star patient. Bravo, Dodd. You've still got it."

"Not exactly the area I'd hoped would bring renown to my name, but I guess I'll take it, Chelse," Dodd said. "We have any of those blueberry tart things left?"

"Nope," Chelsea said. "No more sweets. Your next goal is to get down from 260 to 245, and I won't be slowing you down with treats."

"Ah, I'm already wasting away here. Doesn't my body need some extra calories to keep healing?" he asked.

"Calories, yes," Chelsea said. "Ones full of amino acids and nutrients. You'll be drinking that blue-green algae, turmeric, and protein shake there, and I'll fill your stomach with some hearty greens and turkey for lunch."

Dodd almost quipped that he'd wished he hadn't made it, but he stopped well short of the starting line of that bad idea. "David called," he said. "He is safe and searching for his father. Keeps asking for leads on the name, but it seems like he's making some progress on his own over there."

"He's still in Israel?" Chelsea asked after a sip of her coffee.

"Palestine," Dodd said.

A scratching sound at the door pulled Dodd's attention, and he was thankful for the distraction from that topic. He stood and waved Chelsea off as she made to protest, then he methodically made his way to the front door, his eyes glancing at the empty space where the hutch had been as he went.

The door swung open to empty air, and Dodd glanced around before finding the source of the sound standing on the stoop. A black bird with shining feathers and eyes so intelligent it unnerved the man stared back at him. The bird held a sealed envelope in its mouth.

It flourished its wings, dropped the note, issued a gurgling croak, turned, and took flight.

Dodd blinked and watched it depart before kicking the note inside with his good leg, where it stopped at the couch. He sat and picked it from the floor, holding it in his hands and considering it when Chelsea walked in.

"Getting your mail here now, are you?" Chelsea said. "Should I phone the priest and confess to our life of sin, or will you be making an honest woman out of me?"

"The last thing I need right now is a night of dancing and drinking," Dodd said. "Maybe keep the drinking on the table, actually." He tore open the mailer and read the message. His lifted eyebrows and the shift from a dour expression lured Chelsea, who stood to look over his shoulder.

"Dunno who it's from," Dodd said.

"Sam?" Chelsea asked.

"If so, he's got a lead for us," Dodd said.

"About David?" Chelsea asked.

"Nope," Dodd said, "but I think everything related to Sam has something to do with David, Chelse. Whoever it is wants us to take a look at an all-inclusive living community and workplace up in Connecticut."

"I can't even begin to wrap my head around an idea like that," Chelsea said. "So, what, you go to work and then live around the same people who clock in with you every day? No friggin' thank you. I have a hard enough time not wanting to kill coworkers after hearing them chew without having to deal with whether or not they're housebroken."

"I'm with you. Only person I ever enjoyed cohabitating with was Ramirez," Dodd said.

"Ahem."

"And you, of course."

Chelsea rubbed Dodd's back. The loss of Ramirez had been overshadowed by Rose's death, but Chelsea knew he missed his partner. "Is your leg up for the road trip?" she asked.

"I think I can hack it," Dodd said. "If I can lean on you."

"Don't..." Chelsea started, but it was too late. Dodd began to recite the lyrics to the classic song in his unassailable baritone. "I swear, Brendan, I will smother you in your sleep with a pillow."

"To be done in by a beautiful woman in bed—what a way to go," Dodd said.

"I'm going to pack a bag and make some lunch for the drive. If you're still singing when I get back, I won't let you have an ounce of egg salad," Chelsea said.

Dodd fell silent immediately. Chelsea's egg salad sandwiches were nothing short of ambrosia—and quite the upgrade from a turkey and cheese number. Plus, he needed all the nectar the gods would be offering to pull this off.

Ω

Ammit's gullet was not the bile-laced slime luge one may have thought it to be, but instead held the quality of a cozy cabin after dusk. The walls weren't comprised of wooden planks, however, but limestone bricks eerily reminiscent of those that might line the architectural achievements of pharaohs like Khufu. Still, the space was dark save for an emanation of light from some corner or another, and the Pericarp spent none of its limited mental faculties attempting to discern its source.

Pericarp, in three parts, bounded about the space, chasing after itself, while the most primitive of the three attempted to regain its hearts. Had Samael witnessed the spectacle, he would have taken note of the fact that the baser instincts of Pericarp had now placed this goal above all other tasks. The sad creature knew it needed its hearts.

Pericarp chased Pericarp who chased Pericarp, until they found themselves in an area with shelves arranged in an open honeycomb configuration. Each shelf held a heart, and the assortment varied in hue from slightly dark red to a maroon so deep it bordered on blackness. The first Pericarp became insane with anguish at not being able to discern which heart was its own, and the others consoled it.

"Oh, you poor little thing," a voice called from behind Pericarp.

"Is it not the worst thing to be torn from your identity and never delivered to revelation?"

The first Pericarp ceased its howling upon hearing the voice within Ammit's gullet and proceeded to move toward the source, a woman of great beauty and splendor.

"That's right, my little one, come to me," she said. The other two attempted to dissuade their baser self, but they did not act fast enough, and their counterpart fell into the embrace of the mysterious woman. "Do not worry about her, she guides you well," she said.

The woman raised her hand to point to the hearts, stacked higher than the eye could fathom. From them, a glow pulsed through the room. A golden chain wrapped around skin as pale and luminescent as moonlight, its source, and the third Pericarp was the only one to notice.

The woman's hand guided her to a portion of the shelves with hearts of a lighter color. The boards holding them did not bulge under the heavier weight that the darker hearts held, but sat flat and plum enough to make any carpenter sigh with delight.

"You're not at all wanting, are you, dear? No, not you. The boy wouldn't have shared himself so completely with anyone who was, I suppose," she said, lifting three identical hearts from the shelves.

"Come, little sister. Let's make you whole once more."

Ω

Chelsea and Dodd traveled east toward Connecticut in relative silence, each pondering the odd nature of their destination.

"What exactly are we looking for when we get there?" Chelsea asked.

"Not exactly sure on that, but I have a feeling the bloodhound in me will guide us, or at least, that's my hunch," Dodd said.

"Any idea how we'll handle it when they ask us who we are and what we're doing there?"

"I fully intend to use the weight of this shield if we get that far, but I'll be satisfied with just having a look for now."

Chelsea pulled off the interstate and found their destination to be only two turns from the exit. She read the large sign out front as they maneuvered onto the access road.

All Century Living and Work Facility: An All-Inclusive and All-American Village!

"Ooof," Dodd let out, cuing her to the fact that he'd read the sign too.

"Looks like they are pretty contained here," she said.

"That's a fancy way of saying they're private. That sign read to me as, *keep out*," Dodd said as he adjusted his leg.

Their car rounded the bend of the winding road, and they observed ticky-tacky condos nestled in loops that branched off from the main artery that flowed through the development. They passed an assisted living facility, an expansive club house, and two restaurants before Dodd nodded to a road shaded by maple trees that led away from the general living areas.

"I'll just bet there's something worth looking into up there," he said.

Chelsea nodded and turned. "I never took you for a betting man," she said.

"Well, you've got to gamble now and again in my line of work," Dodd said.

"True, but you're retired now, honey," Chelsea said.

She didn't often use terms of endearment with Dodd. His name alone felt like one to her and barely using his first name smoothed the coarse strands of this unspoken truth. When Chelsea did use one, it often came on the wind of a tone that was meant to make him feel better.

It was true, he *was* retiring from his gig at Homeland Security, but the deed wasn't officially done just yet, and spotting the security booth ahead made him happy for that. They may need his credentials here, after all.

Chelsea rolled to a stop at the window and smiled at the security officer. She noted his sidearm as being a little off putting for a check-in officer.

"Morning," he said. "Do you have an appointment?"

"Good morning. My name is Detective Brendan Dodd with Homeland Security. I've been asked to come by and report on the general operations of All Century. Would you mind radioing in for a liaison for us? Thanks." Dodd handed over his credentials.

The guard looked them over and picked up the receiver of his phone. After hanging up, he leaned back out of the booth. "Take the drive around and past the employee parking lot. You'll see a domed building and an interior garage. Park within there, and someone will come out to greet you."

Chelsea nodded and drove according to his direction. "Well, that was easy."

"Seems like it was," Dodd said. "What they're doing now is calling my office to figure out what the hell is going on. The office won't know either, so they'll say something along the lines of *humor us or deal with not humoring us*. Most of the time it's a quick sweep, and we're out of places like this in a flash anyway. I'm betting they'll humor us."

Chelsea's automatic headlights blinked on when they entered the garage, and she guessed Dodd was right when they saw a representative waiting for them. She parked and they got out.

"Hello, Officer Dodd. Welcome to All Century. My name is Gloria Lansdale," she said, extending her hand. She turned to Chelsea. "And you are?"

Dodd said, "Her name is Chelsea Dolan. She's a specialist assisting with an outside investigation having to do with the anomalies that occurred in the region some months ago. She'll require access as well."

Chelsea shook Gloria's hand with a smile, feeling sheepish at having been introduced instead of doing so herself, but she knew better than to go off-script when Dodd was in his wheelhouse.

"Right," Gloria said. "I'll take you in to see Mr. Jarvis, who manages our operations. It won't be far, but would you like a chair, Officer?"

Dodd shook her off. "I'll be fine, but thank you for your consideration."

They walked through the garage to the access doors and entered the building. The slight incline gave Chelsea worry, but Dodd handled it without outward sign of strain. The recovering was going well, but she knew he shouldn't push himself.

Mr. Jarvis awaited them in a carpeted lobby that served both the side and main entrances. Workers came and went with the ease that one might expect when they lived on the grounds. Free to head home for lunch—or even a midday nap, perhaps. The convenience was alluring in some ways. Though Chelsea knew she'd find it suffocating in short order. Working from your own home was one thing, but having the workplace permanently tethered to her home and place of sanctuary would have been maddening.

"Welcome," Jarvis said. "I trust Gloria covered who I am already. She's a real pearl, this one." Gloria gave him a feigned slap and laughed before taking her leave, and Jarvis went on, "Now, how can we be of service, Lieutenant?"

Dodd noted Jarvis's knowledge of his rank. "Well, Mr. Jarvis, the happenings from this area are of interest to us. Since All Century takes up such a large plot of land, we were asked to come and have a look. That's all."

"All Century didn't report a single incident before or during the lockdown, Lieutenant. I can't imagine why we'd be of interest," Jarvis said, making no move to show them any further.

"That's precisely why you are of interest," Dodd said. "The surrounding area was something of a hot spot for reports during the lockdown, yet All Century appears to have been untouched. We just want to see if there might be a reason why, and perhaps turnkey that information to help with the protection of civilians in case a similar incident ever happens again."

Clever old goat, Chelsea thought. Jarvis must have agreed, because his smile faltered ever so slightly.

"Well, I do hope we will be able to be of service," Jarvis said. "Please come this way, and I'll show you some of the facility."

Jarvis turned to lead Chelsea and Dodd through the facility, but Dodd lost his balance and fell into the man. "I'm so sorry. Slipped there on a smooth spot. Takes a while to get used to using just one crutch."

Jarvis smiled as he steadied Dodd, and they continued on to find things were much as they expected. People came and went, busy in conversations or with documents in hand. Jarvis explained the various sections as they passed. They quickly learned All Century was a medical research facility, according to Jarvis, though not of the usual type. The company developed various mechanical implants and enhancements to help people cope with disabilities.

"Lieutenant, this section might be of interest to you. Here, we are crafting a mechanical exoskeleton to help allay pain and immobility of the knee and lower leg. One of these puppies will have you dancing a waltz at physical therapy in no time," Jarvis said.

"I'm a salsa man," Dodd said.

"Do any of your medical implants embed directly into a patient's brain, Mr. Jarvis?" Chelsea asked, dispelling the illusion she was nothing more than a wallflower.

"Yes, actually," Jarvis said. "Two of them. One is in middle development, just beginning trials, but the other is nearly ready for FDA approval. It is designed to bridge breakages in neural pathways and nerves themselves to essentially cure paralysis, Alzheimer's syndrome, manage Parkinson's symptoms, you name it. It is called REPATH. We are quite proud of how far we've come with it."

Chelsea nodded, and Dodd made a strained expression. "Well, Mr. Jarvis, we've appreciated your time. I'll happily report what we've learned, and we'll see if the good folks in the think tank can establish a connection."

"Very good, Lieutenant Dodd and Ms. Dolan. Very good. I'll let you see yourselves out. The entrance is just back around the bend there. The structure is an expansive dome, which you've no doubt taken note of from outside. We've nearly come full circle. Be well," said Jarvis as he turned heel and wound back the way they'd come.

The two shared a glance, making to continue to the exit.

"He wasn't kidding. We do have the means to help you recover."

Chelsea and Dodd turned to see an older man with straight white hair. He was a dead ringer for an aging scientist type, but in place of the lab coat, he was wearing sweats.

"You can make a full recovery, even at your age, Lieutenant," he said.

"Might take you up on that, Mister...?" Dodd asked.

"Arnold Piper. I'm the head of research and development here." Piper smiled, and his teeth seemed inexcusably ancient. "Leave your contact information at the front, and we will reach out. Dillydally, and we may lose our window."

"Will do. Thank you for the offer," Dodd said as he and Chelsea turned to leave.

Chelsea glanced back before they rounded out of sight to find Piper was still there, looking after them.

"What's with Dr. Kevorkian back there?" she asked.

"I don't know, but he definitely doesn't smell right," Dodd said.

"God, I know. He smelled like he was varnished by assholes," Chelsea said.

Dodd couldn't help his laughter. "And you're the one who gets on *me* for cursing."

"Sorry, but I don't have your gift for description," Chelsea said.

"That's not what I meant, by the way," Dodd said. "He's off. I mean, they all know we're up to something by being here, but he was on another level."

"Agreed. Let's beat feet," Chelsea said.

The two made their way back to the car after Dodd gave the number of his burner phone to the receptionist. They drove out of the garage and took a look back at the dome in its massive glory. Chelsea had a hard time believing Dodd was able to make the trip around it.

"Not an especially fruitful mission. Sorry, Lieutenant."

"Well, it wasn't for nothing," Dodd said. "We've got this now." He flicked out a keycard that read *Engineering and Development: Class A*.

"When you tripped?" Chelsea asked.

"I don't go teeter-totter often. I had thought you'd made me the second I pulled that stunt. Tsk tsk, Ms. Dolan," Dodd said. "Let's just hope I was right, and there weren't any cameras."

On a whim, Chelsea decided to turn right onto the main road through the community instead of the way they'd come. The layout remained unchanged and unremarkable, but something caught Dodd's eye, and he asked her to turn off to drive around one of the residential loops. Little more than halfway round, Chelsea saw what had piqued his interest. One of the complexes of four condominiums had burned down. It was a boil on the perfect surface of this place. They didn't bother getting out to look around. Chelsea felt eyes upon them and wanted to get back to the real world and away from this eerie facsimile.

As they continued on their way to the exit, Dodd let out an exaggerated, *"Hmmmmmm."*

Chelsea followed his gaze and saw another complex with construction tape and dumpsters in front. This one had burned to the foundation.

Ω

Freja arranged the three parts of Pericarp around the three hearts they'd collected from the shelves. The initial unease at not knowing where they were that caused the first to wander was not present any longer, and Freja didn't suffer the same chore of collecting her over and over.

"This will cause you great pain," Freja said. "The same pain that ushered you to us, I'm afraid, and more. But you will endure, little sister. I've faith in that."

The third found herself uneasy at hearing the warning, but she remained in her place. Freja gently took her golden chain from around her body and began to encircle Pericarp and her hearts. Reaching the end, she clasped the chain, binding it.

"Ooooooh," the first exclaimed as the chain cast a gilded light through Ammit's belly. Pulsing, the light grew in splendor, leaving nothing ungraced by its touch.

The parts of Pericarp began then to join with one another, though the process was slow, and Pericarp became anxious, as though a creeping sensation was taking root and growing within it. The chain tightened, and the space between them became less and less, leaving little room for the hearts between. When no more crowding could be done, the hearts found their way back inside of the Pericarp, and as they did, the three parts wailed with fear and misery. The pain of dying could be heard throughout Ammit's body, and the creature itself became unsettled. Moving its jaws to allay the pressure building within, Ammit broadcast Pericarp's agony to Thoth, Ma'at, and Samael.

"She's having a hard time of it in there," Thoth said.

"She shouldn't be in there in the first place," Samael said. "Her heart was righteous."

"Freja has her, Samael. She is being remade," Ma'at said.

"What? Why didn't you tell me what you were planning?" Samael asked.

"We didn't know you would agree to such a risky trial. The girl may be lost to chaos, after all," said Ma'at, never taking her eyes from the roiling Ammit. "When Freja came to us, we knew of no other way than in the belly of Ammit."

Samael wondered how many more people were involved in Uriel's plan that he wasn't aware of. The archangel of wisdom was thorough, and entrusting Samael with the complete plan would have been dangerous. He didn't begrudge Uriel taking other measures. He would have done the same.

Howls of agony flowed from Ammit with ever-increasing volume. Samael would have expected it finally reached its crescendo when yet another wave rolled out and through him. Within, Freja soothed the third Pericarp—the only of the three to truly understand the pain and malice they'd endured. She knew the process would be a painful one, but to see the girl relive her demise as she was stitched back together caused her worry. Still, worry or no, she was powerless now but to see the process through to the end.

The body of Pericarp was partially fused and no longer existed as three parts of one. The consciousness of the third, now merged with the primal instincts of the second and the first, was nearly combined as well. This proved to be the harshest on Pericarp, as the memories of burning alive dwelt within the first. She howled like the winds over a mountain in a storm.

Then the howls suddenly stopped. Freja saw the process had not yet been completed and said, "You must not stall, dear. You'll surely be consumed by your torment if you do."

The first Pericarp raised her hand and moved to caress the face of the third. A chill shuddered through the amalgam of bodies harnessed within Freja's golden chain, and the screaming ensued, though now it didn't emit as a stream of pure torment. The sound held a grit. Pericarp was willing herself through to the end.

Thoth and Ma'at sighed when they heard the change. Samael, too, felt some hope kindle within him.

The ever-gold light of Freja's chain ceased, and what remained looked tarnished and decayed. It fell from Pericarp as she dropped to the floor. Freja retrieved the chain and tucked it into a pocket of her robes, then she lifted the body of the girl she'd been asked to help bring back from the dead.

"Can you tell me your name, dear?" Freja asked.

Pericarp turned her head to look upon Freja's face, and her gaze danced over skin the color of moonlight.

"Rose."

PART TWO

THE DERVISH
IN THE SANDS

CHAPTER FIVE
PROMETHEUS

Dodd pored over records of the fires at All Century, but he couldn't find a single one where local police or fire departments were involved. He exhausted his law enforcement resources before turning to Chelsea. "A place that size could have a private fire department on site, couldn't it?"

"That, or they just let the places burn," Chelsea said. "Your suggestion seems more likely. I'm still wondering why your friend Sam sent us in the first place. There's something fishy going on there, no doubt about it, but I don't see what that has to do with us."

"Maybe not Sam, and not us, not necessarily. Don't forget about your souped-up son. I wish Ramirez was here. He was always better at kicking the dust off things like this than I was," Dodd said as he closed the lid to his laptop.

Chelsea sidled closer to him on the couch and lay in the crook of his arm, where she found herself feeling small and safe at the same time. "I know you miss him terribly. We've lost so much, Brendan. Such bright lights. Ramirez and Rose didn't deserve to be consumed by some vague conflict between supernatural assholes, and I mean to deliver some comeuppance."

"Hell hath no fury, they say..." Dodd said and leaned down to kiss Chelsea's forehead.

"Jarvis... Jarvis..." Chelsea repeated. "There's something nagging me about that man. It's just out of grasp, but it's there."

"Could you have crossed paths at the university?" Dodd asked.

"That's what I'm thinking too, but he's in engineering, and that's a world away from my field," Chelsea said.

"Could be he switched fields. You know how you sciencey types get flighty when there's a fire lit under—" Dodd stopped as Chelsea bounced from his arm.

"Not the university," Chelsea said. "The museum! He was an affiliate jacking grant money to research spontaneous human combustion. The research was getting nowhere, so they cut him loose. God, Dodd, he must have aged forty years in the span of ten."

"You're sure?" Dodd asked out of habit. He knew Chelsea's intuition was generally infallible. Through their short relationship, he'd gained an enormous respect for his partner that tempered his love for her from a mere attraction into something firm and solid.

"Absolutely positive," Chelsea said, flashing a grin of triumph.

Dodd couldn't resist stealing a kiss before saying, "Combustion research and some big fires signal a red flag. Any way we can look into why he was interested in people going up like kindling?"

"I don't have access to the museum's records any more, but Leonard does," Chelsea said. "I'll give him a call, and we can see just how deep this rabbit hole goes."

"Good idea. In the meantime, I'll take a look into the financial backing of All Century. I have a feeling this thing doesn't end with Jarvis," Dodd said. "There's always some rich asshole."

Ω

Brahman summoned a car for the newly formed quartet, and David instructed the driver to head north into Israel and then east well beyond where any lights from Jerusalem could reach. They'd used the vehicle until the road vectored from their destination and disembarked. David and Brahman led the party on foot, with Acrit and Flueric following behind.

Acrit's ability to weather Flueric's presence had been impressive. David had unmasked the illusion of Brahman being some mystic relatively quickly. He was a tycoon of sorts, and one with ill-begotten gains, David knew, so his cavorting with Flueric wasn't a surprise. But the boy should be writhing in the oily presence of the angel— or whatever Flueric was. David's hunch that Acrit was more than he appeared seemed more solid by the minute.

"Not far from here," David said.

A flourish of movement erupted from the landscape and caused Brahman to fall back to meet Flueric. "He's led us into a trap. I knew it!"

"Not one set by him," Flueric said.

They watched as David continued on despite the chitters and growls of quick-approaching creatures. The sounds ebbed as they neared David. Whatever was attacking simmered down as they approached.

"They're hesitating," Acrit said. "Brahman, you'd better cover your eyes."

Light emerged from David in tendrils of plasma and cloaked him. It danced about, lapping at his body as it grew outward until finally the force keeping it at bay was released. There was a brilliant flash and, in the moment before night gave way to the brilliance of a cruel sun, the faces of their attackers were visible. Monsters had surrounded David, and their rancid mouths were open in howls that had been halted before the sound could meet the air.

A moment passed, and the smoldering wreckage of the children of Lilith floated gently to the ground around David.

"Just brilliant," Flueric said.

"What the hell is he?" Brahman asked.

"He's something unexpected," Flueric said. "Something useful."

"Let's not fall too far behind," Acrit said.

David called back to the others, "I doubt they'll try that again. I don't think very many are here to begin with, so banding together to be annihilated at once isn't wise. They've surprised me with how dumb they can be before, though. Don't let your guard down."

"Dumb or desperate," Flueric said. "These foot soldiers take orders and will follow them no matter the danger. It looks like Lilith has taken to tantrums again."

"You've got a lot of knowledge, Flueric," David said. "I still don't know your angle, either, but I'm wondering if you'll tell me who you are. Normally I wouldn't ask, because I can see through the façade. Like Mr. Silbi there, who has been calling himself Acrit. You, though... You're well concealed."

Acrit stopped his forward motion at David's statement.

"Oh, come now," Flueric said. "Did you think he'd be so dumb? I'd made you from the street, and you were *with* him."

"I didn't think he'd grow so quickly..." Acrit said mostly to himself.

Never in his wildest dreams did he think the product of an angel and a human, a Nephilim, would have such well-honed senses this quickly after realizing his powers. It was unprecedented that one would even have full reign of the celestial power within him to begin with, but to know how to control it was beyond comprehension.

"What is the meaning of this, Acrit?" Brahman looked about the group incredulously. "You've been deceiving me, you little shit—"

"Well, you could have made it a little harder to accomplish, Brahman," Flueric said. "Honestly, when I started advising you, you were sharp, man. Has building sandcastles with the salted earth for years on end given you brain damage? Calm down. This doesn't change a thing. You'll meet the Grigori like you wanted to."

Acrit's gaze remained on David's back, but he made no move to advance nor run.

"I don't mean you harm," David said, "but you can expect some questions regarding my mother. I know you're the one who took her to Azazel. His stink is all over you."

"That is fair, David. I feel you'll find those answers once we reach Dudael," Acrit said. He wondered how things may play out now that he was aware that David knew the truth.

David said, "I hope so. Your future depends on it."

"How did you learn?"

"I pay attention," David said, motioning for Acrit to continue on leading them.

A chill of excitement ran through Flueric. "Don't fret my anomalous little friend. I'm merely an observer."

"Nobody asked," Brahman said.

Ω

Samael watched as Ammit hitched and squirmed about the floor of the amphitheater. "Is he going to be okay?"

Thoth laughed. "Takes more than a tummy ache to hurt that one. Though I do wish they'd get on with it. It pains Ma'at to see him suffer so."

Ma'at walked over to the towering reptile and tried to sooth it. Her presence did have an effect, but Ammit's eyes belied his discomfort.

Within, Freja was taken by the strength of Rose's stare.

"Who are you?" Rose asked.

"I am Freja, my dear. I've come to help you," she said. "Can you stand?"

Rose took a moment before sitting up. "I think so, but give me a minute, please."

"Of course. After all, you've been through quite the ordeal. And there's not even a drop of Heidrun's mead to soothe you."

Rose took a longer look at Freja. "You've a unique name. Even more unique clothes. How is it that I'm in some kind of dusty warehouse filled with organs and a beautiful woman robed like a Roman and named after a Viking god?"

"Oh, these clothes suit my comfort so much more than donning armor and such," Freja said. "The dwarfs could probably craft something cozy and functional, but I much prefer my robes and cloak when the mood strikes, and it often does. I am also the first of this name and more. The Romans you mentioned called me Venus, the Greeks, Aphrodite, but I prefer Freja."

73

"You're telling me you're Freja, leader of the Valkyrie?" Rose asked.

"The same," Freja said. "I'd thought it best to reveal myself to you at our first meeting rather than conceal it as I did with David. He needed to keep his mind on other matters, after all."

"Now that you mention it, David *did* tell me you had met in Valhalla. I'd forgotten. My memories feel like they are trickling in slowly," Rose said. "He didn't say you were the most beautiful woman in existence, though." There was a beat and silence before Rose asked, "Did you spend much time together?"

Freja laughed. "No, not so much. He was preoccupied with finding his way back to you far more than spending time with me, my dear. I found his chivalry to be quite welcome."

Rose began to stand and faltered. Freja steadied her and helped the girl to find an upright stance. "That's good. I'd hate to have to kill him when I see him again."

"Ah, it's good to see your division hasn't stolen your mettle," Freja said. "You'll need it for the journey ahead of you. Come, let's walk out and meet your chaperone, shall we?"

The two found their way through the room and down a long corridor before reaching a door with no handle or knob. Freja laid her free hand on the door, and a light emitted with the force to blind Rose. When she did open her eyes again, she saw three figures standing at the end of a long slide. It took a moment for her to realize the slide was a tongue.

"Uh, I don't think I want to go down that," Rose said.

"It's this, or a residence in the belly of the beast." Freja said no more and waited to see how the girl would act.

Rose tested her knees before letting go of the goddess to plant herself on the tongue, and she pushed herself along until gravity took over. One swooping slide later, and she was at the bottom, considering how to get around the massive teeth of the thing.

Freja tiptoed her way down with the grace of a cat and helped her to her feet. "Sliding through those shouldn't be hard for you. Let us try."

Rose once again went first and slid around the first row of teeth before an exhalation of rancid breath made her cover her nose and mouth. "Ah, yuck."

"Yes, it's rather dreadful. Keep going before he belches," Freja said.

Rose continued on and couldn't shake the feeling of going between pylons at a carnival fun house. She soon reached the end and stepped lightly over Ammit's lip to the ground. Freja hopped out behind her and stopped to check her robes for stains when Ammit closed his mouth on the train trailing behind her and gave a tug. Rose couldn't mistake the expression on the creature's large face. He was playing with her.

"You drop that this instant, you perverted lizard," Freja said. "If you so much as yank my garb down an inch, I'll plant a dagger in a spot that will ensure you never forget your manners again."

Ammit gave another small tug, and Rose could swear it was smiling.

Ma'at said, "Best listen, Ammit. She's not known for bluffing."

Ammit let out a chuff through his nose and opened his mouth. Freja half turned and freed the robe from the point of his tooth before patting his nose. "Good judgment, lizard."

Samael had stood by quietly as he observed. He hadn't exactly known how he would combine Rose again, but he knew it was his charge to restore her. Watching the girl walk on her own out of the beast was a relief as well as a revelation. He could focus his mind on tasks far more suited to him—those concerning the world of the living. "Ma'at, Thoth, how would you endeavor to return her to the living world?" he asked.

"We've given the topic some thought since Uriel happened by, but we won't divulge our counsel without a price," Thoth said. Ma'at turned to Samael eagerly.

"Fine," Samael said and reached into a bag he'd been carrying since liberating Rose from purgatory. "There are seven here, and I'll return soon with more."

Ma'at snatched the treasure in his hands before he could offer it, and she jumped up and down with glee. "There are seven, Thoth, seven!"

Thoth smiled. "It's a wonder you never get tired of those romances."

"I didn't forget you," Samael said, handing Thoth a much larger volume entitled *Infinite Jest*.

"Oh, you remembered when I mentioned the writer having been found just. I do wager he had some time being split before moving on, though. Those who end in such ways tend to," Thoth said as he examined the hardcover.

"He's still there," Samael said. "Shouldn't take much longer for him to shake off the chains of the mortal realm and become ready for the after."

"Thank you for the gifts," Thoth said. "We know you were planning to give them to us anyway. The demand for payment was a quip, you see."

"I wasn't joking! I'd have kidnapped the girl if he didn't give me my precious stories," Ma'at said, looking over the covers.

Samael looked to Freja and Rose, who were observing the spectacle. "She's addicted to smut."

"Who isn't?" Freja said.

Ammit rolled and played alongside Ma'at, who had made her way back over to him.

Thoth laughed. "She so enjoys reading her books while laying on him. The problem is she reads aloud sometimes, and I think she's corrupting the poor beast."

"That would help explain why Pervy the Gecko over there tried to swallow Freja's clothes," Rose said.

"Shrewd and strong," Freja said. "I think we will get along quite well, Rose."

"Strong indeed. I can't believe she is walking. Still, we have no measure of the lasting effects of—" Samael was hushed by Freja and smart enough to know when to let her take the lead.

Freja turned to Rose. "You are quite resilient for a mortal. Perhaps there is more to you than meets the eye, as there was for David."

"Nope," Rose said. "Two parents. Two very vacant parents, but very human too, I was told. I'm no unwitting angel."

"Oh, there are far more ways to be special than that, Rose," Freja said.

"Two sides of the same coin?" Samael said.

"Perhaps," Freja commented as she inspected Rose, who found the attention to be unnerving.

Thoth broke in, "We had both decided we would take her back over the river and through the veil. Before you protest, we've considered other avenues, and there really is no other way in such a short time."

Samael said, "It bends, but to break through is impossible. The veil is beyond tampering, as far as I know."

Thoth shrugged as he read the back jacket of his book. "You'll have to find a way through."

Samael blanched. He himself was tasked with delivering souls from the mortal realm to the one awaiting them just on the other side of the veil between both worlds. From this point to the beginning of his involvement, he'd taken great care to ensure his actions would merit him no punishment. Everything he'd done was well within bounds, and those that weren't were under his purview as the angel of death.

This, though. This was forbidden.

"I may be able to help," Freja said. "Other than you, who else is allowed to traverse the veil with souls in tow?"

Samael thought for a time, wracking his mind for instances where it had occurred. He couldn't think of anyone but himself and...

"Your Valkyrie? But they must abide by the same edict as I do. It's a one-way trip if there are passengers in tow."

Freja smiled and turned to Rose. "You love cats. Take mine for a time, and they'll help Samael guide you back to David."

"How do you know that I love cats?" Rose asked.

Thoth said, "Other than you being the living, breathing embodiment of the stereotypical cat lover, Freja can see people. Even more so than most who have that ken in our realm. She may have even gleaned if you and David will ever meet again."

"Not that. I can't quite see through the murk when it comes to how this will end. That may be because the Fates themselves do not know," Freja said. She gave a quick and sharp whistle, and two black-and-white forest cats bounded to her side. They were much larger than a normal house cat, but not so large as to be confused with a mountain lion. Freja bent down to remove their harnesses. "Drat, I'll be forced to walk back to the Fólkvangr, though I can concentrate on renewing the luster of my chain as I travel, I suppose."

Rose looked at the cats like a child's eyes devour unwrapped gifts.

"Go on then," Freja said, and the cats bounded to Rose, whose hands danced over them in reverie.

For a moment, Samael had forgotten the tortures the girl had just relived. *She is strong.*

Samael motioned for Freja to walk a small distance from the group and said, "I'd like for you to bring Rose with you."

"Oh? I thought she was your charge," Freja said.

"She is," Samael said, "but I have another matter of growing importance to attend to in the world of the living. Uriel would not balk at such an idea, I'm certain of it."

"Well, she is a delightful mortal," Freja said. The way she exclaimed the word *mortal* did not escape Samael's attention.

"So you're wondering about her, too?" Samael asked.

"Yes. She's not so obvious to understand as David and his angelic blood, but there's something to her," Freja said. "I'll take her if nothing more than for the mystery." She walked back to the cats, who'd laid about Rose, and refashioned their harnesses. "Rose, I'll be tending to you directly. I hope you find the idea to be acceptable."

"Um, well, I don't find it *objectionable*," Rose said.

"Very well. We will leave now," Freja said and began walking out of the amphitheater with her cats in tow. Before following after, Rose turned and walked to Samael, disarming him with a hug.

"I know you've done a lot to help me. I recognize your face from the hospital, so you helped David, too. Thank you," she said and hurried to catch Freja.

The three looked after her as she moved away.

"Well, she could have thanked us, too," Thoth said.

"Oh, be quiet you twit," Ma'at said.

Samael stood in awe of the feeling coursing through him. He felt both at perfect ease with the situation and filled with vigor to pursue his purpose. The lingering sensation firmed the idea that Rose was more than he or any of the others knew.

Rose caught Freja as she stepped over a threshold of stones. Before them, sitting just to the left of the entrance, was a beautifully ornate petite chariot. The cats fastened themselves to the front by slipping their harnesses through slender hooks, which Rose found to be a neat trick, and Freja motioned for Rose to stand beside her.

"It doesn't fly, I'm sorry to say," Freja said, "but the cats are swift, and we'll be at our destination before you tire."

"Where is it we're going?" Rose asked.

"My hall, Sessrúmnir, in the Fólkvangr," Freja said.

"I thought the Fólkvangr were your warriors. That's what David told me, anyway," Rose said.

"The realm is the Fólkvangr, as are the warriors, so he's half right or half wrong," Freja said, eying Rose in a way that told the girl this goddess was still curious about her. "He's certainly half something."

Ω

Acrit called David to a stop once they'd arrived at the location of Dudael.

"There's nothing here," said Brahman, whose words were punctuated by deep inhalations.

"All that strenuous exercise for naught, eh, Brahman?" Flueric said.

"Well, I'm not quite twinked with some other-worldly vitality like you three, am I?" Brahman said. "I'd forgotten how much of an asshole you can be."

"Why, thank you! I do love reminding people, especially ones like you, of that very thing." Flueric walked to David's side. "What will you do when you meet dear old daddy. Big speech prepared, I bet?"

"No, just some questions," David said.

"Oh." Flueric mimed a pout. "What a cold first meeting."

"The fact that it's the first meeting is not what will make it cold."

"Ah, something more than abandonment issues. Yes, very sad, very sad indeed. Well, I hope you get to murder him, or whatever it is your heart is truly aching for. You've been through quite a lot to get to this point, after all. Would be a shame to waste it."

David looked at Flueric, and the malice in the young man's eyes conjured a smile from the well-dressed traveler. "I've decided I don't like you very much, Mr. Flueric."

Flueric's smile broadened.

"Acrit, where is the entrance?" Brahman asked.

"It's not easily visible, but I can help with that," Acrit said as he walked on a few yards more and raised his hands. The air about the outcrop of rocks before them began to shimmer, and as it did, what lay behind became diluted. Colors swirled together in a manner to remind David of the portal that helped him escape Leviathan.

The shimmer ebbed, and the firmness of reality once again took dominion over the landscape. There, just ahead, was an opening in the rocks. David walked on beyond Acrit and entered the cave without a word. Flueric clapped Brahman on the back and followed.

"This isn't right, none of it," Brahman said, shaking his head. Acrit glanced his way before disappearing beneath the ground. Brahman sighed and followed.

"Watch your head, Brahman!" Flueric called back. "It's swollen so much you might get it stuck in here."

"Har, har," Brahman called. "Hey, Acrit, how far down does this hell hole go?"

"It's a deceptively short journey," Acrit said. "We're already almost there."

"Can you fools see in the dark or something? I can't see a damned thing in here," Brahman said.

He wished he'd taken more time to prepare before rushing out with this boy. He'd learned quite a lot when they uncovered the first Grigori in the states. For one, the magic—or whatever it was— cloaking the door didn't work if you'd already seen beyond it once or had a guide who had. Finding Dudael a second time would be easy. For another, he'd need equipment and a crew to dig out the sleeping angel. The chains of the first few proved to be deadly to the touch, so his team had been forced to dig out the rock it was tethered to and transport that, as well. The fruits of their labor had been sweet to the tune of hundreds of millions of dollars. Brahman had begun seeking bigger fish nearly immediately after the first Grigori had been placed within the containment facility. He had no idea of how many were imprisoned here on Earth, but it wouldn't take many more to make him billions, a figure he'd lusted after since tasting the power such bounty brought.

"Stop here," Acrit said.

Brahman could hear a discussion as he inched closer, but he couldn't make out exactly what was being said. By the time he reached them, the talk was winding down. "Did you warn them not to touch the chains?" Brahman asked, in an attempt to garner solidarity.

"Yes, and he also instructed us not to wipe our asses with the drapes," Flueric said.

Brahman's silence spoke volumes.

"I'm going," David said. Acrit followed close behind and then Flueric.

Brahman had not once feared for his life on this journey, not with these three spearheading it, but when Acrit lit the vats of oil lining the walls of the cavern, the light showed death situated directly before him.

The angel, bound by chains shrouded in ethereal energy, was awake.

Ω

The facility was dark and indistinguishable from the night. Dodd kept his head down as he surveyed the garage entrance through binoculars from the relative safety of the trees. "Doesn't seem like much by way of security. Remoteness may have made them lax, though we shouldn't count on that. Chelsea, do you remember the route?"

"Yes, I enter the same way we did for our tour, but I don't head round the front desk. Instead, I take the side hall that leads back to the big loop we were on. I'll head to engineering and see if this"—Chelsea held out a metallic object the size of a key card—"unlocks the door to that room. Once I get in, I'll snap some pictures and come right back out."

"That's the whole of it," Dodd said. "Oh, and Leonard is going in with you."

Chelsea looked over to Leonard who was shivering in the late winter chill. "You're up for that?" she asked.

"I am," Leonard said. Chelsea couldn't tell if his emphatic nodding was a symptom of the cold or not.

"He agreed to it, since I can't. The rules here are simple, you two. We're breaking the law by trespassing. That key card code generator will likely bring up the charge to breaking and entering and more, so you get in and you get out." Dodd sighed. "I wouldn't even be gambling like this if this whole thing didn't stink to high heaven. We know something is there, we just need to get our eyes on it. Capeesh?"

"Got it," Chelsea said. She motioned to Leonard to follow her with his head low. They made their way down the slope and walked with a quick nonchalance, so anyone who might spot them wouldn't think they were interlopers.

Dodd watched as they entered the garage and left his view. He sighed and hurled himself to his elbows. It was time for him to investigate the burned condo units under the cover of darkness.

The skull crawl through the brush proved painful for his elbows, but his leg was mercifully unbullied by the underbrush. He doubted the next part of his journey would be so kind to it, though.

Once at the car, Dodd drove back through the sleepy streets of the community until he reached the first of the units that had burned. He liked this location for two reasons. The first being how it was closer to the research compound, and the second was that there was more left here than in the other units they'd spotted.

Dodd parked facing out of the roundabout and exited the car, pulling his crutch out after. The trudge up the walkway and concrete stairs proved more tiring than Dodd had anticipated. The jaunt in the woods must have left him running on his reserve energy. He cast his eyes on the other units and saw the soft glow of interior light blocked by curtains. All were drawn closed. Dodd stepped over the threshold and entered.

Char-laced air met him within the unit, despite it being at the mercy of the wind from outside. The remains of furniture littered a living room, and Dodd took the time to view what was left of a bookshelf.

Nearly everything had been blackened by the smoke, but a single picture frame glinted light. He carefully lifted it and wiped the glass to see a partially melted photo within. It showed a young man standing with a paddle and life vest, the arm of a companion wrapped around him, but the rest of the picture had melted away. Dodd took stock of the engagement ring on her finger and moved on to another photo of the same young man dressed in a smart blue blazer and slacks, smiling in the way only those in their mid-twenties with little to weigh upon their shoulders can.

The kitchen was intact, besides the wood cabinets that had burned, dropping their glass contents to the floor where they'd shattered and blackened. The crutch proved tricky here, as it would slide from purchase if Dodd happened to place it on one of the shards littering the area. Still, he was thorough in his search and found nothing.

Dodd made his way to the bedroom, and his eyes were immediately drawn to the ornate queen bed. This room had burned thoroughly and may have been where the fire started. The walls were cleaned of paper and paint, and he could make out whole sections where the studs were missing. This room also lacked the benefit of natural light that the others were afforded, so he switched on his flashlight and began to peak through the contents. When finished, he went to the bathroom and opened the medicine cabinet. His days as a cop made this stop second nature. You always knew there'd be dirty laundry in here, if some was to be found. He saw three identical small white bottles among the toiletries and took them out. They had the presence of prescription medication, but there weren't any pharmacy codes or drug names. The first label read: *A. Colly. Compound AB-E - Three Times Daily - Take Without Food.*

Dodd placed the bottles in his pocket and made for the exit, but the bed stood out to him again, and he stopped before rounding the corner to exit the bedroom. He walked closer and inspected the remnants. Sturdy hardwood made up the frame and was the only reason it still stood at all. The blankets had been wholly consumed, as had all of the mattress except the springs. There was a peculiar coating on the metal coils that drew Dodd in to inspect them. He saw an oily mess that had solidified enough once cooled to form an ooze. Dodd pulled a kit from his interior pocket and scraped some onto a tray. When he shined his flashlight to inspect it, the material was unmistakable to him— body fat.

He looked about for the remains of a skeleton and saw none nearby before the sound of a creaking floorboard called his attention to the living room. He switched off the light and remained still.

There was silence in the unit and, but as Dodd straightened up to move, he heard the broken glass in the kitchen being crushed. Someone was taking deliberate steps through the house, and Dodd wanted to be the first one to get eyes on the other. He slowly moved himself into the corner adjacent to the doorway and sat on the floor. The large man laid his crutch to the side and pulled his gun. Then, he waited.

Sounds continued as whoever it was moved closer. Dodd couldn't help but think the actions felt somewhat primal, like hearing raccoons plundering a dumpster. The atmosphere had become dense with something, and Dodd couldn't help but feel he was breathing the smell of embers for the first time despite the char all around him. It afflicted his senses as an invader, unwelcome and malignant.

Dodd remained undetected even as a tall figure entered the bedroom. He was able to make out the outline of a sports coat with tufts of fur poking from the open chest, and large legs matted with coarse hair down to the cloven hooves that took the place of feet.

The retired detective, who had taken great care to ensure their stealth to this point, didn't wait to be noticed. He fired three shots at the creature, and each landed at a pivotal area: the knee—or hock, in this case—the shoulder, and the side of the head. Dodd saw his last round spark off a horn jutting from the temple of the creature, and he decided it was time to make for the exit. The creature cleared the doorway as it fell to a knee in the direction of the bed, but it was not down for the count. Not yet.

His slow pace maddened him as Dodd finally breeched the doorway. He turned to see the creature stand and face him. The creature still maintained its place in the shadows, but Dodd saw flames dancing within where his slugs had torn pieces of it open. Dodd tried to reckon the alien nature of this creature with its human eyes. The veridian orbs looked upon him without an ounce of malice.

"Can you speak?" Dodd asked.

The creature did not respond with words, but it reached a hand toward the detective, who took a sliding step backward into the hall. Dodd continued to move, and the creature mirrored his movements but came no closer. He made his way through the hall and into the living room, where a sidelong glance at the pictures caused him pause. The monster was wearing the same jacket as the kid had been.

It was hard to keep his composure, but he did, despite having been able to reach out and touch the thing. When he made it through the entrance and to the stairs beyond, Dodd stopped. The creature didn't cross the threshold of the unit, and Dodd's view of it was becoming obscured by waves of heat dancing in the air. Dodd forced himself to pivot and make his way down the stairs before turning back to see the creature was now completely obscured.

By the time he made it to his car, the curtain of heat was nearly lifted, and nothing of Dodd's otherworldly visitor could be seen.

CHAPTER SIX
PANDORA'S BOX

Chelsea and Leonard had little trouble infiltrating All Century. The duo rounded behind the reception desk and walked gingerly through the corridor to the rear, where they used Chelsea's memory of their tour to isolate their directives. Throughout their progress, Leonard maintained a quiet resolve that Chelsea hadn't seen in him before, as though the little university researcher had developed self-esteem during the past months from being called upon to help.

"There's an engineering department through here," Chelsea said. "I want to see if we can get pictures of what they're really making."

Leonard nodded and pulled the copy of the key card he'd made at the university and swiped the door lock. It disengaged, and Chelsea grinned.

"Neat, isn't it?" Leonard said.

The three had decided it would be best for each member of the party to carry one, since they didn't know if they might need to split up. Dodd even had one in case he needed to come inside, though Chelsea had balked at the notion at the time. She had agreed, but only because she meant to ensure there was no need for him to take the risk.

The two entered the door and resisted the habitual urge to don the white coats hanging from a rack. The department held a sterile look, the same as a meticulously cleaned operating room, and it sparkled even in the dim lighting. Chelsea led Leonard into a workshop where the exoskeletons for necks, arms, and legs were on display.

"It looks like they'll need to use that REPATH technology to make these work too," Leonard said. "It's not so nuanced—the idea I mean—but to see them ready to apply it to trials is something else. This could revolutionize long-term disability and physical therapy treatments."

"I'm not sure I'd want a microchip in my brain that could tell that thing what to do," Chelsea said. "One close strike of lightning, and Brendan would be two stories in the air with my slipper up his ass."

Leonard laughed. "I'm sure they have similar fail-safes as pacemakers."

"They still tell you to stay away from electrical current for those, don't they? That's strike two." Chelsea took a few pictures and eyed the signage before motioning for Leonard to follow her.

"They aren't just planning for REPATH to help with this tech," Leonard said. "It's supposed to have applications to speed cognitive function and to access information through the internet, too. Might change the world if it becomes commercial."

"Oh, screw that," Chelsea said. "That's a hard no on anything even remotely like that. I'll take the seventeenth century life over melding with the machines. I don't even trust the updates coming through my smartphone anymore, let alone linking them directly to my thoughts."

"There are some dire implications, for sure, but the future will come to us whether we balk or not. Don't forget how quickly smartphones changed the world. First, it was internet in a pocket, then social media platforms jumped aboard, and it led to things like the Arab Spring."

The two walked over floor tiles embossed with the now infamous word REPATH before entering the section where the technology was being developed.

"Chelsea, something is off here."

"Well, yeah," Chelsea said. "This place stinks to high heaven. That's why we're performing our very first B and E together."

"No, not just that. Where do the human trials take place?" Leonard asked. "There's no area for a medical stress test or monitoring vitals. No medical equipment at all, actually. Just the engineering tools for crafting such small chips."

"You think they'd do that offsite?" Chelsea asked.

"Not likely, given the level of secrecy. That's another thing. Their security is abhorrent. Why?" Leonard asked.

"Brendan and I noticed that, too. We think it's due to there being surveillance cameras on the whole property. That's why we came up with the strategy of hiding in plain sight. They'd never notice us walking the twenty feet from the tree line to the garage, and Dodd would drive the car out and around like any other resident might. Seems to be working. We're not in the gulag yet."

"It's off, Chelsea. There's something more to this place. We know there isn't anything else of note in that direction..." Leonard pointed his finger up at the domed ceiling. "So look for anything leading down."

Chelsea and Leonard circled back to the hall and looked for any clues that might bring them to a sublevel of the complex. Leonard was inspecting an emergency exit door that didn't appear to be connected to the exterior of the building when he jumped at the sound of a male voice.

"My my, Ms. Dolan. You decided to join us after hours, and you've brought us a new friend. Lovely."

Ω

There was no rage or malice in Azazel's eyes—only tempered steel. The fallen angel was bound in such a way that his knees were tucked in tight beneath him and his arms were pulled out front in a perpetual state of prostration.

David's father's eyes left Flueric and slowly drifted to him. The hardness within them softened.

"So, my son has found me. Welcome to Dudael, David," Azazel said. "What diverse company you keep."

"They're a means to make it to your door and nothing more than that. I have questions for you," David replied.

Flueric sauntered into the room. "Now I feel so *used*. I'd thought we were becoming so much more than acquaintances, David." He turned out his pocket watch and flipped it open. "My my, great champion of the Grigori. You've been here for some time now, haven't you? Driven mad with isolation, no doubt. Poor thing..."

Acrit stepped to the center of the room. "He hasn't been alone. I've been tending to his needs."

Brahman's scowl deepened, but his eyes remained on the chained angel he'd been seeking for years. "Flueric, contain Acrit. We need to get a crew out here by sunup to begin the excavation. I aim to have this specimen placed below ground in our facility as soon as possible."

"No," Flueric said.

"What?" Brahman said. "We have a deal. You, of all people, know you must honor it."

Flueric's eyes blazed. "Me of all people, you say? I'd assumed you were cocksure, but not this blinded by greed. Do you really think our agreement would favor your terms?"

Brahman's mouth moved, but he was unable to speak before redoubling his thoughts. "Think of the power, Flueric. Think of how much faster we can suffice our goals through the world with it." Brahman's eyes lifted to a ledge above the cavern, where two black desert eagles sat. Blood caked their hooked beaks and made the tycoon pause in his arguments.

"I like this better," Flueric said. "This is new and far less boring. I want to see what the boy does."

David walked to the chains that bound his father to the floor and stared him in the eyes. "She's dead because of you," he said. "Whatever you had planned, whatever your motives were, none of that matters. You ground the most beautiful part of my life into dust, and today I will do the same to you."

Azazel maintained his silence but shot Acrit a look that kept him locked in place.

"Did you hear me, *Dad*? She was turned into charcoal because of your petty games. All of them." David threw his hands up and flames ruptured through the tips of his fingers. "All of the demons, the angels, they sacrifice us like pawns. And for what? To play at war!"

"There he is. There's that rage," Flueric said, stepping back to the wall. "Brahman, you may want to find some cover."

David shot a look to his meddlesome traveling companion. "You think I'm so naive as to turn this place into a kiln?" He knelt before Azazel until their faces were inches apart. "I've grown."

David stood and dug his hands into his chest. His expression showed pain, which fueled his rising anger, and a hilt slowly emerged as he paused for breath. More of the sword he'd taken from the sheath at Leviathan's prison came forth, and David uttered a primal cry to shake the very foundations of creation as it emerged.

Acrit gasped and shared the same thought as Brahman—David meant to behead his father, and the tool in his hands was up to the task.

The sword, now freed, maintained its impossible size, and David hefted it with no sign of strain before turning it to a downward stroke in one motion.

"No!" Acrit cried.

The strike did not remove Azazel's head, as Acrit had feared, but cleaved the chain holding the Grigori to the floor. He sat up for the first time since modern man was negotiating the world with Neanderthals and breathed. David slashed the remaining chains.

"Stand up," David said.

Azazel rose to his full height, well above David's, and looked at his son. "We will conclude our business, David, but—"

"I know. Do what you have to do," David said.

Azazel knelt and lifted a fractured link of the chains that had bound him before stalking toward Flueric, Acrit, and Brahman.

"Oh, now this is very unexpected," Flueric said. "I never thought I'd see you walk the earth again, and by the means of *that* sword. Wonders abound."

He didn't move despite Azazel's approach, and he needn't have. The fallen angel walked past him and to Brahman.

"I gave you the means to become great, to become closer to the creator. And all people like you have done is pervert my sacrifice," Azazel said. Brahman stepped back until he hit the wall. He had time to reach his hands out before Azazel stuffed the chain into his open mouth.

David watched on as Brahman's face began to disintegrate into itself. The evil man's body pulled toward the link in a perverse tangle as it was consumed. The spectacle took only moments, and once finished, there was nothing left but the sound of coarse metal landing in the dust.

"Be at peace, man of war," Azazel said.

Acrit hefted a torch and pulled Flueric's sleeve. "We should leave."

"You're right, I'd rather not ruin another suit tonight."

Flueric followed Acrit to the tunnel and outside.

Azazel looked to David. "I don't want to fight you. You're my son, but so much more. Can we speak?"

David replaced the sword within his body and moved toward Azazel.

"I want to feel your body break with my own hands."

Azazel shifted his posture for the attack but was unable to dodge it. His head had shattered the Precambrian metamorphic rock of his tomb by the time the thought of having mercy had left his mind.

Ω

Rose traveled with Freja within the chariot for some time before she commented on the journey.

"We're moving so fast, but I don't feel wind," Rose said.

"You're dead," Freja said. "You can't feel the wind anymore, I'm afraid. It troubles the archers who come to Sessrúmnir, too. They've spent their lives painstakingly studying the wonders of the wind, only to have it stripped away. They do adapt, though, and so shall you."

"Sure, a minor adjustment—"

"You'll find some solace when we reach the hall," Freja said as she lifted the reins to guide the cats through the landscape David had been carried over by Uriel on another journey beneath the veil of reality.

Rose thought of her experiences before having been recovered in the gullet of Ammit. "Why was I split into three pieces in the fog?"

Freja lowered her eyes and, for the first time, appeared something other than carefree to Rose. "That is a place of reconciliation. What you call the fog, we call the murk. It is where those who've died are made ready for the next step in existence. To be truthful, I don't know exactly why you are split, but I can guess that it helps you find a purer form of thought before moving on. Did you experience that?"

Rose shook her head. "No, I felt scattered and lost. Part of me was in pain while the others were trying desperately to help, but they couldn't." She thought for a moment. "It felt like trying to roll water into a ball."

"How interesting!" Freja said. "Perhaps you were making progress without knowing it. Water is rolled into a ball all the time, you know, but most probably don't realize it."

Rose didn't understand and chose to look off into the distance rather than ask for clarity. The forests were giving way to rising mountains, and the eye could reach the summit of each despite their great height. Only when her mind was clear, and she wasn't grasping for meaning, could she find it. "Snow. You mean a snowball, don't you?"

Freja smiled. "You're a wonder, little Rose. A wonder, indeed."

"I don't feel wonderful. Do you know what happened to David, Chelsea, and Dodd?" Rose asked.

"Indeed!" Freja said. "All alive, but David is quite fractured without you, as you've probably guessed. He's liable to do something rash."

"Yes, I'd guessed that," Rose said. "But I'm happy they're all alive. Dodd was broken in front of me before I was taken. I don't remember much after that."

"He was wounded, but I can't see so far as to determine how he is recuperating. As for your memory, best not to try and remember yet. The time will come to face your demise, but we should place our focus elsewhere until then. Look there..." Freja pointed as the chariot rounded a bend to reveal their destination. "That is my hall."

Rose looked upon a vast field filled with wildflowers surrounding an elegant hall adorned with ivory towers and expansive sections of redwood timbers. A shrill cry from above called her attention to the half a dozen winged women flying overhead, their armor casting darts of sunlight around them.

"The Valkyrie welcome you to Fólkvangr, Rose. Come, let's meet them."

Ω

Dodd steered onto the main road to make his way to the rendezvous point. Deep seeds of pain were flowering within his mending bones, and the experience was fatiguing him.

The cones of his headlights vectored around the corner of a sharp turn and revealed that their little mission had been found out. Three unmarked cars blocked the road, and men signaled him to stop. Dodd eased the break and kept his hands on the top of the steering wheel.

"Detective Dodd, would you mind stepping out of the vehicle and coming over here?" a tall man wearing a headset radio said.

Dodd slowly left the vehicle and used slow extravagant movements to reveal his crutch to the men before placing it below his arm and walking in their direction.

"We have the detective, sir. Bringing him in now."

Dodd couldn't make out the reply, but he assumed Chelsea and Leonard had been bagged as well. Still, you never show a card that hasn't been laid on the table yet.

"All right, gentlemen. I understand if there's some confusion, but we've already been given access to the grounds by Mr. Jarvis. I'm sure a call to my home office can clear up any misunderstandings."

"You're being taken into custody for trespassing, Detective. Please come with us. Mr. Piper would like to continue the discussion he began with you a few days ago."

Dodd nodded and lifted his arms as more of the security detail approached to search him. Relieved of his sidearm, they put him in the back of a Suburban with far more care than he'd anticipated. "So, we've swept away some of the fog cloaking this place, guys. Mind telling me what you're really up to here?"

"That's up to Piper, Detective, but I can assure you of the fact that you're in well over your head."

"No shit," Dodd said.

They rode in silence together until the guy whom Dodd assumed was head of security said, "Rest assured, your companions are being treated with as much care as you are."

Dodd's stomach sank. He'd known the odds of Chelsea and Leonard being undiscovered were slim, even if the sound of his gun being fired had led to his discovery by All Century. Still, this statement of fact jarred him.

"They're civilians," Dodd said. "I should hope you do treat them with care until they're turned over to the police."

"Detective, you're a clever man, yes? We both know none of you will be turned over to anyone."

Ω

Chelsea felt a chill seep through her clothes from the metal chair she'd been deposited in. Leonard sat quietly beside her. Despite their circumstances, Leonard appeared to be holding up quite well. He'd even delivered some encouraging remarks and brief smiles as they'd been led through a corridor to the elevators that had brought them down to the catacombs of the facility. Leonard had been correct in his assumptions. She still hadn't been able to spot anything to indicate All Century's depth of operations as they were brought to a room remarkably similar to the engineering departments they'd sleuthed through earlier. All seemed normal but a large circular door with keypads standing as sentinels on either side.

"Ah, Ms. Dolan, it's fine to see you again. And *so* soon, too. You, sir, though, you're new to me. Mightn't you introduce yourself?" Arnold Piper said as he pulled on a lab coat and donned blue gloves.

Chelsea watched with growing anxiety as the decrepit scientist continued to prepare his work station. "He's a friend who came along to help me. You don't need to bother with him."

"Oh, it's no bother," Piper said. "We are always happy to receive new subjects. Volunteers have been in dwindling supply as of late."

"My name is Leonard Barlowe," Leonard said. "I work with Chelsea at the university. We're colleagues. She asked me to come along to ensure the key cards worked, and that's it."

"It's not that simple Mr. Barlowe. You've been sleuthing through our halls, and at this point, I think we can all agree that I'm not worried about you leaking any sensitive trademarks. We're engineering the evolution of the human species here. The public isn't ready to understand that just yet, though. So, it is imperative that we keep any little nuggets you've dug up under, well, *ground*, I suppose." Piper finished his costuming before motioning a security guard over to one of the keypads at the large circular door. "Let's take a look at the bigger picture."

Before Piper could make his way to the adjacent keypad, a buzzer sounded and a red signal erupted near the elevator. Chelsea's panic rose as the room washed over in crimson.

"Ah, it looks like our third guest has arrived. Good. I'd like for him to see as well," Piper said.

The descent of the elevator was as maddeningly slow as it felt when Chelsea and Leonard had been brought down and, despite having time to steel herself for seeing Dodd captured, the sight weakened Chelsea's resolve. Dodd was escorted into the room and arranged in another chair across from Chelsea and Leonard.

"Well, the Hardy Boys we ain't," he said through a smile.

"On the contrary, Detective," Piper said. "Had you not found the remnant in that housing unit, we would have likely ignored your intrusion. These two would never have found their way down here on their own, and you'd all have left as blissfully ignorant as you'd come. It's something of an irony, in fact. Your skill has damned you all."

"Spare us the forbidden fruit of knowledge bit, Mr. Piper," Dodd said. "We've been privy to quite a lot more in the last few months than most people. You're the one who's entering a realm you've no business fooling with."

"Astute, but misguided, Detective," Piper said. "Tell me, what did you fire your weapon at in that house? Did something spooky your way come?"

Chelsea's eyes widened, but Dodd spoke before she could ask. "Chelse, there was some infernal thing in the unit. I think it was been left behind from whatever experiment they did on the guy who lived there. Young guy. Just a kid, really." Dodd turned to speak to Piper. "Whatever you are doing is causing your subjects to spontaneously combust, isn't it?"

One of the security officers handed the pill bottles Dodd had taken from the unit over to Piper, who hefted their weight before depositing them on the table. "Some have, yes. Some have merely died. But some have *thrived*. I believe what happened to Alex Colly was due to a lapse in taking medication, but we're still studying the findings from his combustion event. You never answered my question, Detective. What did you fire at?"

So Dodd had stumbled upon something Piper wasn't aware of when he entered that house. Maybe the Colly remnant, as he called it, was a point of interest. Something new.

"I'll tell you if you guarantee you won't hurt Chelsea or Leonard, and if you let them go," Dodd said.

"I can guarantee Ms. Dolan won't experience harm," Piper said. "Female testing hasn't started yet. A negative fate may befall Mr. Barlowe, I'm afraid. As has come to light from our discussions, some of the subjects expire."

"Use me instead of Leonard," Dodd said. "You said it yourself, I've got a lame leg. Maybe you can patch me up."

Piper paused before responding. His eyes slid down to Dodd's leg. "We have been wanting to increase our understanding of how the procedure affects subjects who are not in pristine health. It has been difficult finding those who are willing to be sickened or have limbs broken before their procedures, and our results have been far more positive in the willing."

"Seems like a no brainer, then. Leonard most definitely is not willing, and I am," Dodd said.

"Brendan, they're not going to let us go even if you let them kill you with whatever they're doing to people down here," Chelsea said.

Dodd's eyes softened. "We don't have any other choice, Chelse."

"Very noble of you, Detective. Very noble indeed." Arnold Piper arranged himself at the door and signaled the other man to swipe his card after raising three of his skeletal fingers and signaling a countdown. A moment passed before the doors slid open to reveal a ramp leading further down into the darkness.

"Let us proceed."

CHAPTER SEVEN
CAT'S IN THE CRADLE

David let go of his father's head and let him crash to the ground with the inertia he'd gained from hurling them both from the depths of the prison. He landed and walked across the sand until he was able to observe Azazel standing.

"It didn't have to come to this," Azazel said. "But your feet are planted firmly—it seems there is no other recourse."

"Tell me why you planned for me to be born," David said. "Tell me why you damned those around me to suffer like this."

Azazel brushed dust from his legs and combed rocks from his hair. "You're necessary. As for the suffering of others, some walk a path paved with pain. Those who travel with them must tread the same road."

David bared his teeth as orange flames surged upon the fallen Grigori. Azazel stood motionless as vehemence enveloped him. A scream raked the sands as the torrent grew in intensity, and the boy finally relented. He may have done so to preserve the life of his father, perhaps having felt a mote of mercy break his will of vengeance, but what he saw stoked his anger once again. Azazel stood tall amongst the smoke, completely unharmed.

"I delivered fire to your kind, David. Did you think I'd be so helpless against it as Asmodeus was?" Azazel asked.

David stepped toward Azazel with short, light steps, remembering Mukhulai's shoes gliding over the floor of the arena. "It wasn't my fire that consumed Asmodeus. It was Uriel's. Another who was taken from me because of you." David used his quick steps to close the distance between himself and his target at a disarming speed and swept Azazel's legs. Once gravity had control over his body, he was helpless against the downward strike that followed. "Besides, I don't need fire to hurt you."

Azazel rolled to his side and heaved a sigh. "That hurt, I'll give you that. I know you've made sacrifices, David, and I am sorry for it, but your road was never meant to be an easy one."

"Sacrifices are willingly made," David said before leaping atop Azazel's back and securing him in a choke hold. "I've *lost*. There's a difference."

Azazel attempted to pry David's arms from his neck before relenting. It appeared as though he was giving in, but then David felt the emergence of his father's amaranthine wings. They flourished and took in the wind to hurl the two skyward before changing directions to lance them to the sand. David leaped from Azazel's back before impact and rolled to safety as his father careened himself to miss the ground by no more than an inch. The tips of his fingers glanced over the grains of sand before he rose through the air and hovered above David.

"You are powerful, but you don't know the essence of your strength," Azazel said. "Without that, you'll never best me, nor any of the angels above me. David, you play with fire like a caveman when you could be dancing within the fabric of the cosmos."

He raised one hand to the sky and pointed at the sand with his other. "How soft and inviting the grains are when you use your hand like a sieve to let it cascade to the earth. But what is sand, David?" Azazel asked. His question was punctuated by a thick bolt of lightning from the sky that blinded David. When his vision cleared, he saw the ground had become fused into thick desert glass. "What is its nature, now?"

"What does that prove?" David asked. "I understand how lightning works. The world has moved on plenty since you were imprisoned thousands of years ago. I'll wager one look at a computer will make you feel like the cavemen you mocked before."

"Doubtful, David," Azazel said. "I imagine it's just another step in humankind's development from the snowball I started rolling down a mountain all those years ago. Have you so little respect for me that you'd think I wouldn't have a trajectory planned?"

"It's not your planning I have no respect for. It's your ethics," David said before reaching down to the desert glass and hurling it skyward as though it were a massive discus.

Azazel dodged the object by inches, but he continued to appear at ease. "You seem to have a good grasp on aerodynamics as well, but how is your understanding of meteorology?"

Clouds had been forming above the desert unbeknownst to David, until their presence was illuminated by electrical currents from within. David looked to them and felt dread fill him as the hair on his arms lifted from his skin. He had a split second to guess where the bolts would strike before he had to move. The ground erupted behind David just after he had leapt to the side, and he continued to move as though the lightning was being placed where he was standing instead of where he might be heading. His guess that Azazel wasn't trying to kill him, or at least leave a lasting maiming, was holding water until a bolt tore through the sky and branched to strike in multiple places at once.

David used his speed to evade the trap, but his arm was singed. He'd cast his cloak to the side as a decoy, but the concurrent claps of thunder and continuous barrage of electricity told him he hadn't yet earned himself the split second he need to leap to the angel.

Azazel clapped from above. "You're doing quite well. Very good instincts for someone your age, but instinct can only prop you up for so long. What you need is knowledge. Here, let me teach you a lesson." Azazel called the wind to his will and threw it at David in straight-line blasts to impede his movement. The lag was proving effective, and David could sense his time to dodge was shortening with each leap.

He was just under Azazel when he said, "You're smart and experienced, but you're underestimating me."

"Oh," Azazel said, "I thought it was my unfavorable opinion regarding the promise of humanity that got me into trouble in the first place. That seems to be how the story is told these days, anyway. So please, illuminate me."

David dodged another lightning strike and threw his hands in the air. "I understand what an accelerant is." Flames erupted from David and met with gale force winds to arc through the air toward Azazel. His expression of surprise before folding his wings around himself was enough to tell David he'd done harm to the angel, but how much? He still didn't know the true nature of the sword he held within himself, but he did feel it drain his energy when he tried to practice with it. It was too risky to fight with unless he was sure he was going to die.

Azazel dropped to the sand, and David continued the conflagration until the winds died down and the lightning ebbed. Clouds above began to scatter as the unique rose-pink wings unfolded to reveal the eyes of David's father boring into him. "*Now* you're showing the promise I'd hoped to see. See past the rage and use that wonderful mind you've been given. Do that and you'll rarely falter, David."

"Stop talking to me like you're Mr. Miyagi, you piece of shit. Tell me why you had me. Tell me why Rose had to die!" David cried. "I swear with every ounce of myself that I will make you suffer for her. For how she *burned*."

David slammed his foot into the glass at his feet, throwing shards into the air before propelling them with fire toward Azazel, who tried to use his wings to propel himself above the projectiles. But the wind was no longer his ally. The shards melted and formed globules of molten glass and, though the angel had avoided the majority of it, his legs had been coated in the biting substance. His cries of agony brought Acrit from the far-off dunes as David approached Azazel.

"It's time to stop this, David," Acrit said.

"I disagree. He's still alive," David said. "Don't meddle, or I'll be forced to deliver you to wherever it is you things go to when you've been wiped off the surface of our reality."

"We go back to it all, David," Acrit said. "In a way, it's a divine mercy. Azazel's punishment, to stay alive and disconnected from the world and beings he cherished so much, that was his hell. No amount of pain you inflict can come close to that suffering. Peace now, and let us talk. If you don't relent, there's also the danger that he might become—"

Red flames rose from the ground where Azazel knelt in the sand. His burns wouldn't subside for some time, not with the energy stored within the molten glass doling it out over time. It was clear that the pain grew, and the Grigori's anger rose to match it.

"You are so proud of that fire, David. It's exemplary for such a young cauldron to burn so intensely, but I've existed within and beyond time itself. We are celestial, we burn for eons, and we grow." Azazel's hair turned the same amaranthine color of his wings, and he rose from his knees.

"—serious," Acrit finished, but he'd already run past Azazel and into the shelter of the inky night.

Azazel loosed a blast of celestial plasma toward David, who covered his face with his arms and braced against it. The heat was unimaginable to him, and he felt it eating into his skin and melting his hair. A shock wave following the charged particles lifted David and threw him into the night air. He relished the cool relief as he was thrown free from the assault before his consciousness faded.

Ω

Dread filled Rose, and she couldn't understand what had conjured the feeling.

"You needn't worry. The Valkyrie are no threat," Freja said.

Rose shook her head. "It's not that. Something just happened, and I don't know what, but it was bad. For a few seconds I felt like I was burning..." She stopped before delivering the final word, *again.*

"Hmm, I see," Freja said. "Kara, go send word to Samael and have him check on David. It's urgent."

One of the Valkyrie peeled from the rest and sped to the horizon.

"Why do you think it's David?" Rose asked.

"I believe you two share a connection deeper than even the depth of your love would forge on its own," Freja said. "He may have wandered a bit too quickly into the deep end of things. Not to worry, though. He's not likely in mortal danger."

Rose pondered this before asking, "Do you think Lilith found him?"

"For her sake, I'd hope not," Freja said. "Lilith hasn't much in her arsenal to stand against a being with such power as David has. He's quite the enigma, that one. Still growing, too."

"How do you know?" Rose asked.

"He's still part human. We can feel his presence amongst the mortals in your world. It's as though a river has become deluged after a storm," Freja said. "It is my guess that he has finally met his father."

"His real father?" Rose asked.

"Yes, Azazel," Freja said. "But let's dispose of this topic for now. We have more urgent matters to attend." She snapped her fingers, and her cats pulled the carriage toward the hall. The Valkyrie flanked them as they traveled.

"I'm sorry, but I can't just drop it," Rose said. "David may have been hurt by Azazel."

"Oh, I'm sure he was," Freja said. "He also likely did some damage himself if he was able to make Azazel fight him seriously enough to wound him. The watchers were never known for their battle lust. More an intellectual crowd, those. But you needn't worry. If I'm correct, and I often am, David's demise would also lead to yours. You're connected to him, Rose. I'm not exactly sure how just yet, but I intend to find out."

"Well, that doesn't make any sense. Then why didn't David die when I died?" Rose asked.

"He's no longer human," Freja said. "Though the portion of him that was once human may have lost half its luster when you died, that is possible, he can't simply die any longer. Not after he met the Leviathan and awakened his celestial power."

"That does track, and in a weird way, it makes me feel a little better," Rose said.

"Let that settle in your mind for now," Freja said. "We have to bring you to life, girl. That's no easy task. I'll need you sharp and focused to accomplish it."

The carriage came to a stop at the entrance to Sessrúmnir, and Rose disembarked to feel the soft grass beneath her feet. The whole area was lush and beautiful in the way a field blossoms after the spring rains. The hall, elegant in its construction, lent itself to its feminine ruler with imperceptibly long curvatures and waving arches. Rose couldn't fathom how stone could be carved in a such a way, but she didn't have time to ponder, because Freja was already striding through the entrance between beds of snow-white lilies, and Rose had to struggle to keep pace. The Valkyrie landed behind her and followed the women inside.

Cries and howls filled the hall at the sight of their leader. "Hail, Freja!" whooped in unison three times with a pause and then was followed by three more. Freja delivered a brief bow before turning down a side corridor. Rose paused to observe the people inside. There were many, and they were all arranged about long tables. Most appeared to be discussing battle plans on large maps, but some were content to dine. The calm demeanor of the crowd felt off to Rose as it clashed with the battle garb of the many occupants.

"Follow, Rose. We mustn't dawdle," a Valkyrie said as she walked past.

"Yeah, sorry," Rose said and moved to catch up.

The halls maintained their beauty with artwork hung about the walls and beautiful statues spanning multiple traditions guarding the doors leading from the corridor. Rose saw Freja lift her skirts as she made to climb a set of stairs and felt out of place in her attire. It hadn't dawned on her that she'd been traversing the afterlife in the discount jeans and sweatshirt she'd thrown on after hearing the banshee's wail in David's room. A shudder raked her as she saw snapshots of memories from that night, and she shook her head to remove them. A hand steadied her.

"Not much longer now, and we will make sure you get some rest."

"Thank you," Rose said.

Freja entered her chamber and the women followed. This room was about war and little else, a stark contrast to the decor of the hall that Rose had already seen. Spears and halberds decorated the walls, their tips and blades in perfect condition. Around them were wall torches with plates of some herb burning beneath that filled the room with a pungent odor Rose couldn't quite place. It may have been the first time she'd ever smelled such a combination of fruit and oil, and though it was unpleasant at first, it quickly made Rose feel sharp, as though her wits had been dampened up until that point.

The Valkyrie positioned themselves at an enormous, marbled table with a circumference to humble the largest wheels humanity had ever conceived. Freja motioned for Rose to stand at the empty place. "Kara is not here at the moment and wouldn't mind sharing her place."

"Thank you," Rose said.

"I'll dash to the point, ladies," Freja said. "We are here to help this mortal woman find her way back to the realm of the living. Do any of you have ideas?"

The Valkyrie looked to one another. The first to speak was a tower of a woman. "I didn't think it was possible anymore, not since the days of demigods traversing the planes of existence. But those are no more, not for thousands of years." She paused to think before stating, "Until, that is, the boy from Walhall came and left through the mouth of Jormungandr." She looked to Rose. "I am Skogul. We are pleased to have you with us, but I cannot for the life of me imagine a solution to your quandary. You are not of celestial power like the boy."

"That is true," Freja said. "But I think our Rose has something special about her as well. I just haven't placed it yet." Freja looked around the table. "Sigrun, Hrund, Mist, Göll, Herja—nothing?"

The remaining Valkyrie stayed silent. Their calm demeanor contrasted their fierce outward appearance, and Rose couldn't help but feel secure in their presence.

"Why is it that you feel there's something more to me?" Rose asked. "Plenty of people have been through trauma and been able to carry on."

"You weren't put through trauma, Rose," Freja said. "You were put through hell, and while some have experienced that or worse, it is not something any of them *fully* recover from. Yet here you are. Calm, collected, and strong. But it isn't just this aspect to you that makes me curious. As Thoth said earlier, I can see people. See their true nature. Yours is utterly unique to me, to the point that I cannot quite place it. We need to define it to understand you."

"How can we possibly do that?" Rose asked.

"Oh, I think we may have a way," Freja said.

She swept her hand over the table and its surface rippled like liquid to reveal an image. It was a house perched on two legs of a bird. One foot lifted in the air to scratch the other before the house cocked to the side ever so slightly. Rose couldn't be sure, but she felt as though it was looking back at them.

Ω

Samael neared the fabric between the world of the living and the veiled. He had been away for too long, and his ability to perceive the events there was beginning to wane. If the circumstances he'd set into motion were playing out the way he'd hoped, David would be returning to his mother after meeting Azazel by now.

He felt the need to check on the detective, too. He knew he was wrapped up in some of this sordid business again and felt somewhat responsible for him. If he had stumbled upon the abominations being conjured in the world of the living without the boy, he'd be in trouble. Uriel was sure David would recognize their creation as a malfeasance and set its destruction in motion, but Samael felt as though things had taken a turn somehow.

He glided over the river of lamentation on obsidian wings. The return always took more effort, as though there was an invisible jet stream flowing from life to death. He dipped lower to make ready for the uncomfortable feeling of crossing over when the sound of a horn blowing stopped him.

Kara, Freja's Valkyrie, who rode the winds with more fervor than all her peers, was bearing down upon him. "I've a message from Freja," she called.

"All right, no need to shout. You caught me in time," Samael said to ease her anxiety. No Valkyrie could cross to the mortal realm, despite their reputation and main charge of ferrying the souls of felled warriors to the fields of battle and exalted halls of Freja and Odin. They were relegated to picking up the chosen from the shores of the Styx. Restrictions such as this commonly came with a smear of lower status, but the Valkyrie tended to exist outside such prejudice. Their ferocity and skill in battle was well known to all, and their fealty to Freja spoke to an unseen aspect of the goddess. One that Samael often thought of when considering her capabilities.

"Freja wishes to inform you that David has been wounded," Kara said.

"Azazel—" Samael said. "I've another urgent matter to attend to. I'm not sure I can go to him."

"Freja gave no advisement to what you should do, she simply wished for you to know," Kara said.

"Sweet Mardoll doesn't *simply* do anything, Kara. We both know that," Samael said. He thought for a moment that dragged through the darkness of the cavern. "I will continue on my original course. Let Freja know that I believe David is not in any danger he cannot overcome with his will and his mind."

"Very well," Kara said, and turned to leave with her message.

"Wait, Freja has sight beyond sight, but not to pierce so far—or so I thought. How does she know this?" Samael asked.

"She didn't inform me, but she was with the girl, Rose. Perhaps she learned from her," Kara said.

"Thank you, Kara," Samael said and watched her leave on silvery wings that sliced through the darkness and the murk beyond.

Uriel had informed their small circle of the chance that Rose and David may share a connection beyond just that of lovers, but he himself hadn't seen any evidence of it. Perhaps Rose had gleaned David's predicament from so far into the world beyond the living and through the murk as well. If that was true, Samael surmised, then she was far more unique than any of them could have possibly predicted.

Samael turned and dashed through the membrane separating realities and endured the spectacular feeling of being scattered that always followed.

Ω

David awoke to the flickering light of candles and sat up in his bed with a start.

"You've recovered fast," Acrit said from a cozy corner of the room. "But I knew you would. The stories seem to be holding true, David. You are something rather unique among your kind. A half mortal who can command his celestial potential with the same dexterity of the angels who were forged in it."

"Where is he?" David asked.

"He is in the next room, thinking about the situation," Acrit said. "He means you no further harm unless you force him to bring it upon you."

"I'm not so sure he'd land that trick as soundly the next time. I'm a quick study," David said. He'd awoken with a sense of reason and fullness to his mind he hadn't felt since Rose's death. The feeling added a calmness to his rationale and somehow helped him to look past his anger.

Acrit stood to pour water from a kettle into two cups at the small table next to him. "Hubris doesn't wear well on you, so drop the bravado. You didn't want to kill him—even I could tell that. You simply wished to unload your rage upon him, and so you have. I bet you even feel better now."

David knew he was right, but being seen so clearly by those who'd manipulated his very existence wouldn't allow his edge to dull. "So, what are we doing now? Having a tea party together like nothing happened?"

"No," Acrit said. "We are sharing comfort *because* something happened. It is common and it is healing, David. Don't forget, you are very young. Let the wisdom of those who've experienced millennia and beyond reach you from time to time. It will firm you to endure all of this."

David opened his mouth and then closed it before asking, "Is Flueric with him?"

"No, not in the moment, and not in any other way either. Flueric is not welcome in Azazel's presence. He left shortly after you lost consciousness. Likely to continue meddling in the affairs of your world."

"Is he an angel? He feels like one, but there's something off. Uriel and Azazel's heat feels like warmth radiating when they're at rest. Flueric feels like a wildfire."

Acrit brought the cup to David. "That's an apt description. We will speak of Flueric when the time comes, but the waters needn't be muddied for the conversation you must have with your father."

David held Acrit's stare before taking the cup. He measured this thing masquerading as a boy to have mettle, and he sensed no malice in him. The lip of the cup felt gritty against his lips as he drank.

"Come, it's time."

David followed Acrit into the room adjacent his temporary domicile, where he'd been laid to rest and heal. He observed Azazel seated cross legged on the floor at a fire built atop a modest hearth.

"I'd have thought you'd had enough time to think by now," David said.

"You weren't unconscious very long," Azazel said. "It's a wonder, isn't it? We cannot sleep, but we can lose consciousness against our will. Besides, there's not enough time in any of the realms to complete the contemplation of a devouring mind, David. You're likely coming to this notion." His body no longer postured toward conflict, but his eyes maintained their beautiful rosy color.

"I haven't been bogged down with much up until recently," David said. "Truth be told, I feel like I've lived ten lives since that bridge collapsed and I'm still pissed off at you, you know that, right?"

"Obviously. Rage doesn't completely quell after a fight, though it tempers some. I've seen great men come to blows and embrace in friendship afterward. Women tend to keep their rage a bit longer. Not sure why that is."

"You won't be the first to not understand the subtle nuances of the feminine," Acrit said as he sat on the floor.

The posture and vulnerability of the two looking up at David made him feel awkward until he took a seat as well, but he kept his silence.

"I am sorry for what you've lost. I can't bring her back to you, but I can at least answer your question of *why*," Azazel said.

David looked on at the fire and used his nails to grind the stones beneath him to dust.

"A long time ago, well after I'd been created, I was charged with watching over the development of mankind. I had many under me to aid in this endeavor. We, the Grigori, were the watchers. I stood vigil as man toiled in the muck, more like a beast than the image of the creator who'd cast them into existence from the spoils of stars as old as the universe itself. They raged and coveted rather than find the sparks of enlightenment, David. They wallowed in the shadows and fell to the whims of the devil."

David looked to Azazel and Acrit at the mention of the devil. A figure he'd not worried on much since finding out that the world beyond the living contained the beasts and figures he'd thought were only birthed from the imagination of humankind.

"Lucifer hates humanity," Azazel said. "The very thing he'd rebelled against. Something from within the creator made flesh and vulnerable, that is what your kind is. What better way to exact his revenge than to corrupt and pervert them? Well, he was less cunning and more ruthless back then. And, with us branded as watchers, there was little we could do. The edict was to not meddle unless explicitly instructed to do so. Yet, I could not obey." Azazel reached to the pile of dust David had created from scratching the stones and threw some into the fire. The minerals crackled and popped, delivering a pretty display suitable for a kid's science show. "I gave them fire."

"It's the vermiculite in the stones that does that," David said. "There's no magic there."

"There's no magic anywhere, David," Azazel said. "I gave them the tools they needed to uncloak the truth behind the magic. I gave them the frameworks of *science*. Engineering, the wheel, agriculture, societies—more and more until they thrived. I was not alone in my work, either. More than two million of us mentored your kind until we were cast down for defying the oaths we'd once made to watch."

"It didn't help that scores of them were having sex with the women," Acrit added.

"No, it didn't," Azazel said. "I myself did not lay with a woman until your mother was brought to me. And by then, I'd already figured out the potential for a human with celestial power. Not the bastardized Nephilim that once walked the earth, terrorizing the weaker humans, but a champion to help them rise above themselves and stretch for their true potential, one they will never find with Lucifer's influence upon them."

"And that's supposed to be me?" David asked.

"Yes, in part," Azazel said.

"Well, I'm not sure why. You bested me out there. Some angel should step up and do it," David said.

"You don't seem to understand. You're far more powerful than I am," Azazel said.

"Oh yes," Acrit chimed. "I'm not sure a single member of the Host can match your potential."

"I don't understand," David said.

"Consider what you don't know about your power," Azazel said. "Yes, you've learned quite a lot on your own, but you have ages of exploration ahead before you could ever master it. You were beaten by wisdom and experience, not strength."

Acrit pointed to the fire. "Do you know of light, David?"

"Yes, of course. It's a particle without weight, and it moves faster than anything," David said.

"Exactly right. Though there were moments as you dodged the lightning that *you* moved faster. How is that so?" Azazel asked.

David looked to Acrit, but he shrugged. "Don't have a clue myself. I'm not that high on the pecking order."

"You're high enough to know this, Acrit. Speed is affected by gravity and—"

"—and David is massive," Acrit finished.

"Still not clicking up here, guys." David tapped his forehead.

"Angels are representatives of celestial power, David. Stars. What better to bend the fabric of time than we?" Azazel said. "At times, you were able to slide over the curve your power can make in time. Well, the weight of it, anyway."

"And when you did, you outpaced light itself," Acrit said.

"I see what you mean about wisdom and experience now. I have a lot to learn, but that tip will help a ton right away. I know a lot about science," David said. "Applying that to the energy I feel inside will take some time, but I have a few ideas already."

"Just be careful," Azazel said. "Those who burn the brightest and hottest are the shortest lived amongst us, though your hybrid form of human and angel does hold secrets. Still, I wouldn't overdo things until we know more."

David thought for a time, and the three enjoyed a silence before David changed the tone of the conversation.

"Why did you choose my mother?" David asked. Acrit tensed, but Azazel kept his composure.

"One part opportunity, and another her nature. Acrit masqueraded as Arthur Silbi for some time before finding Chelsea Dolan. He surmised she was made of the right stuff to carry you for me."

"Oh, and what stuff was that?" David asked.

Acrit cleared his throat. "She was a person of science who relentlessly pursued truths she knew to be just beyond her perception. The perfect person to raise the amalgamation of humanity and celestial being. I do not think I was wrong in my assessment, either. Not after having met you."

"We needed you to *strive*, David. It was poor luck or planning by fate for Lilith to see you as a danger to her existence. You weren't—at least before she crossed you," Azazel said.

"I didn't strive for anything before her either, though. I was planning a simple life with Rose," David said.

"You wouldn't have settled for that," Azazel said. "I'm sure of it. One way or another, you'd have noticed your potential and saved humanity."

"Save them from what?" David asked.

"Themselves," Acrit said.

Ω

So long. Too long. Can't wake up. The world is always black. Don't want to go back there. Cold there. No more alone. Alone is hell.

The creature with two identities wandered inside the apartment as a specter to those who hadn't a notion of the world beneath the veil. They may see it, or feel the mercury rise as it wafted by, but they would never quite perceive its presence in the manner that Dodd had. It was alien to their senses in such a manner as to be ignored by the mechanisms of the human mind that govern such things.

Where is man? He saw me. He knew me. Must find him. He can save me from alone.

What had once been Alex Colly stood in front of the threshold he'd dared not cross since becoming a smoldering ember of lamentation. The mere thought of crossing often caused the pull from the void to become stronger, and he dared not chance flipping back to it. A place not graced with the light that birthed all things, it conjured fear from him at the most primal levels. But the void wasn't calling now. It was Dodd's presence that was screaming to him.

"Never alone again," Alex whispered to himself as he stepped into the night outside of his small prison. The breeze caressed his face for the first time since his death, and he felt alive even for a moment before feeling himself pulled toward the All Century building. The security guard at the gates wouldn't be able to place it, but for a fraction of a second, he could have sworn he smelled a smoldering camp fire nearby before the thought passed into a memory.

Ω

Dodd felt a pang of fear for the first time since realizing the danger Chelsea was in. The spike in worry wasn't from a place of love for her, but from the place people bury with layers of bravado and denial since their time as children.

The feeling of being in trouble.

"What abomination have you assholes conjured up down here, Piper?" Dodd asked as he surveyed the operating table. It was a chaos of metal and tubing which funneled into a larger cable wrapped in what Dodd assumed was some alloy. All crafted with the purpose of conducting whatever was in the especially large holding tank at the center of the pharaonic room.

Piper laughed. "You're not the first to react to it this way. Detective, what you see is the bedchamber of one of the most beautiful and intricate creatures ever known to mankind. It is a little daunting, I'll capitulate to that point, but is it not also *beautiful*?"

"I think the concept of beauty is being twisted a mite bit there," Chelsea said.

"Agreed," Leonard whispered.

"Ms. Dolan," Piper said, "I'd almost forgotten you were there. If I remember correctly, you dedicated quite a large fraction of your life to the excavation and study of this exact subject matter. Surely this is exciting to you."

"I feel like Dr. Ian Malcolm at about the halfway point of *Jurassic Park*. You'll remember he wasn't exactly thrilled," Chelsea said.

Some of the staff chuckled at Chelsea's comment, while Piper muttered about never having had time to read such frivolous things. Two men hefted Dodd up to sit on the edge of the table, and the gravity of the situation finally loosed Chelsea from the daze she'd been in since they'd been captured.

"I swear, Piper, if you hurt him, I'll make sure you don't have time for anything ever again," Chelsea said. She shook off the grasp of one of the men holding her arm and made her way toward Dodd. Piper waved off the security who were moving to secure her.

"You're worried, but you needn't be. What we do here, Ms. Dolan, is heal people," Piper said.

"Except those ones that burst into flames, you mean?" Chelsea said.

Piper cleared his throat. "Yes, except those who neglected their regimen—and a small pool of those who did not. There are no breakthroughs without sacrifices. Surely you, a woman of science, know this. Where would we be with cancer research now if the eugenics program was not conducted in Germany during the Great War?"

"We still haven't cured it, asshole," Chelsea said before Piper nodded to the guards and she was pulled back to her seat. "And science doesn't need to leap ahead at the speed of light. We caress the earth and find artifacts with such care and delicacy that it may take months to uncover the truth, but we reduce the danger of perverting it. That's what your little gang doesn't understand."

"Quiet now, or we will have to gag you. This part hinges greatly on timing. One part skill, and one part luck. Would be a shame for you to rattle me in my work and kill him. His last memory would be of you prattling on from your high peak of morality. Not good, not good. Shush now," Piper said, never once turning to face her.

The scientist saw to it that Dodd was dressed down and properly secured before inserting the intravenous tubes into his arms. "Now, Detective, I must warn you about this injection. We place this as an intra-arterial tube, and there is more pain than a usual IV. Substantially more, by the measure of our other patients' experiences. Please do not squirm, or the special plunger will not clear your blood before the substance is injected into your radial artery."

"Why does it need to go to the artery? They all cycle back to the same place," Dodd asked.

"We haven't quite figured that out yet, but some think the substance must go directly to the heart lest it lose its bonding ability," Piper said.

"What is the substance?"

"Not quite sure of that either, not for lack of trying."

"What is it bonding, then?"

"Well, that I do know. It's going to infuse you with the fires of creation, Detective," Piper said as he pressed a button on his console.

The tank beside them began a laborious unveiling of the contents within. With each inch of movement, they were able to see more tubes running to something situated at the center, like an urchin at low tide. Chelsea pitched an audible gasp when the contents came fully into view.

Within the container was a large man, nude as the day of his entrance into this world and interlaced with hundreds of tubes the color of obsidian. He floated suspended in a viscous liquid that held his limbs and hair in a stasis. His head, perfectly formed in the manner a man like Piper might wish his own to be, pitched backward, and they observed it from opposite vantage points. What had caused Chelsea to start was not the existence of a man in the chamber, but his eyes. They were propped open and unmoving despite the new stimulation they must be receiving. Their color was a blood orange that denoted a ferocity within.

"He is beautiful, isn't he?" Piper asked. "This is the second of the fallen that we've collected, and he's been very fruitful to the project. Very well suited to the bonding, his energy is."

"How can you sap the life from him like that?" Leonard whispered.

Piper laughed. "These are the beings that have laid waste to cities, gambled with the lives of mortals, and murdered our children at the whim of their master. I find it hard to conjure pity for him. Isn't that right, Baraqiel?"

Chelsea and Leonard exchanged glances at the name. "And what if he wakes up and decides to bring justice upon you for these deeds?" she asked.

"They are the ones who gave us science, Ms. Dolan," Piper said. "Why shouldn't they enjoy the fruits of their labors from a closer vantage than the perch from which they once surveyed us? And he cannot break free. His bonds are to the earth, and they've been transported with him along with the ground to which they were affixed."

Chelsea observed the black and purple chains leading from the angel's wrists down to the bottom of the tank. Their angle let her guess that the large columns of metal holding the tank also housed these chains, and their root must be beneath the floor.

They've built the entire structure around him.

"Well, there's no time like the present," Piper said.

An assistant placed a bite plate into Dodd's mouth as Piper reached to one of three levers and pushed it forward. A hum initiated from the tank and caused the suction effect Chelsea knew would be needed to draw whatever material from the angel. An empty cylinder between Dodd and the tank began to fill with a mist of the same color as Baraqiel's eyes and, with more time, the density caused the cylinder to look as though it was filled with a liquid rather than what Chelsea and Leonard knew to be a cosmic essence.

"Now comes the tricky part. Bear with me, Detective, as this will be rather uncomfortable."

Piper feathered the second lever up and initiated the transfer of the essence into Dodd. His eyes went wild, and his veins bulged from his skin. Chelsea was certain they were going to rupture, and he would die right before her eyes on the table, but he held. He even managed to look at her and give a wink before shuttering his eyes to manage the pain.

Piper read a meter of Dodd's vitals and tensed to move the third lever no less than three times before looking back to the cylinder that was draining the essence into Dodd. His brow wrinkled, and he threw the third lever to its full level.

"My God," Leonard said, as they watched a slurry of the same color as the binding chains make its way into Dodd's artery. He strained with all his might when the substance entered his body, curling his lips back from the bite plate to reveal a snarl reserved from all but sustained torment.

"And... *now*," Piper said as he fully engaged the second lever, draining the remaining essence of Baraqiel into Dodd.

He stepped back and watched Dodd. Chelsea saw the rest of the staff similarly retreat and said, "You fucking cowards. How many people have you razed on that table to back away as instinctively as that, huh, Piper? Not even man enough to take the heat. Figures."

"You mind your mouth, or I just may forget my promise to dear Romeo there," Piper said.

"Like I give a damn what you decide to do with us. There's no way you're letting us out of here after we've seen *that*."

Chelsea gestured to the tank, the doors of which were now halfway shut. She stared at the eyes of the angel ensconced within, wondering if those eyes could see, feel, and perceive the anguish of all those who'd laid on the table before Dodd.

Red light bathed Piper's features, causing Chelsea to think he'd become the devil himself, before she realized the siren for the elevator was illuminated and throwing light down the corridor at them. Piper smashed a button on the console, and the doors they'd come through just minutes before slid closed, yet Chelsea felt safer.

"Leonard, be ready to move," she said.

Leonard nodded and kept his silence. He was probably also smelling the sulfurous smoke drifting to them from beyond their sealed chamber.

"Prepare Gabriel's prayer," Piper said to his security, and two men double-timed to a box affixed at the periphery of the room and took from it items bundled in a tan cloth. They fussed with it, but their bodies barred Chelsea from seeing the contents.

Piper, concentrating on Dodd, said, "Don't worry, Detective, it's all smooth sailing from here." He initiated another sequence and monitored Dodd's vitals. Dodd had stopped struggling, and Chelsea felt a surge of relief.

He might live—

"Chelsea, the door," Leonard said.

When she looked, she saw two glowing orbs on the door, and they were growing. The thought that it might be welders breaking in came to her mind before she wondered if sulfur was a conduit for welders.

Something told her that it wasn't.

Ω

Colly meandered through the corridors of All Century, and the familiarity clasped his mind and will together. Fear of the void propelled him to find the man, and newfound purpose invigorated him beyond the shade of what he'd become since his death. During moments of clarity, the tether binding him to the world—and the sheer fragility of it—was abundantly clear to him. He could sense that he had become a perverse anomaly, an alien, and whatever mechanic was in place to purge such things from the fabric of reality would soon come to expunge him. Soon after, he'd slip into the wandering stupor that claimed more and more of his existence before the void would claim him.

A spark was what would wake him from the void, though he wasn't asleep. Sleep would have been too merciful. In the void, he was a dumbed and deaf facsimile of something else. Then the tether would whip itself tight for a moment, and he'd be back, if for just a short while to await the cycle once more.

But the man had made him *feel* again for the first time. He'd been *seen* again.

A sense of drawing pulled him deeper into the facility, and he knew that he must head down if he wished to be seen again. Alex Colly was terrified by the notion of returning to that place, remembering such pain that he'd wished for death a thousand times, only to be denied by Piper's desire to harness the power of the gods. The beast, though, was unafraid. It was drawn to the very thing that had given him life in the first place, and it held the reins for the moment, with Alex's will to join Dodd helping it.

Two guards at the door to the elevator managed to see the beast, but it had been too late—they laid in smoldering piles on the ground, gone from the entity's memory the instant the doors slid closed and the elevator descended. A feeling of wholeness continued to build, and the drawing had quieted Alex Colly's screams from the back of the entity's mind to leave this place of torture. The beast only became more frantic to reach the chamber. It slammed the sealed door with its growing might, but it could not buckle the metal with brute strength alone. Laying both palms on the door, it siphoned the frenzied feelings of Alex. Heat flowed from within the demon and into the metal alloy of the door, and the beast pushed with all its might.

Chelsea was the first to see the clawed hands reach through the molten metal and became frenzied in her effort to untie her bonds. Leonard observed the display with great scrutiny right up until the very moment he fainted.

The small group of security protocol, now enshrouded in robes that appeared as though they dated to before the first millennia ticked over to year one, worked themselves into position and made ready to deliver Gabriel's prayer. Chelsea might have laughed at everything from the costumes to their little gift box of demon banishing goodies, had she not been so certain she was about to die alongside Dodd and Leonard.

The beast pressed through the door, glowing alloy meandering down its body as it surged down the corridor toward the tank. There was a disturbance from within, as though Baraqiel had made a sudden movement, and Piper took his eyes from Dodd's vitals for the first time to look to it.

"You're on your own now, Detective. Godspeed," he said and turned to view a monitor displaying the angel. He saw no movement other than the liquid swirling in a manner as though there'd just been a motion, then Baraqiel's eyes shifted to the camera. Piper felt unease for the first time since taking the reins of this project after having been appointed by Brahman himself. He knew the angel was watching.

The beast entered the room with less fervor than it had used to breach the portal enclosing it, but its tense demeanor made Chelsea believe this relaxed state would be short lived. A low hum caught its attention. It was followed by another at a different pitch. Chelsea looked to the security guards, who didn't lift their eyes from the parchment they were reading. They'd begun the prayer. She shifted her attention to Dodd, who'd started moaning, and she remembered her task to wrench her wrists for some leverage to remove the bonds.

Alex Colly's fears of this place abated when he recognized Dodd's presence by his moans of agony. He surged forward into the mind of the body he had slowly been losing dominion over. The beast placed its hands on its head and roared, emboldening those delivering the prayer. They pitched louder and increased tempo.

"In the name of the Creator, the Most Gracious, the Most Merciful, I seek refuge in You, the Most Generous, and by Your Perfect Words, the boundaries of which cannot be exceeded by anyone, whether he be devout or a criminal, from the evil that descends from the heavens, or that which ascends to it, and from the evils that are sown within the earth, and that which comes out of it, and from the trials of the night and the day, and from the visitors of the night except those that come in goodness, O Most Gracious."

On they chanted as the beast contorted a mere ten feet away, until the moment Alex was able to obtain full control. He paused and looked quizzically at the chanting men, which caused them to flick their eyes to demon—its very human expression sowed confusion into their resolve.

Colly turned to Dodd and stalked to the table. Piper, who was transfixed by the stare of Baraqiel, noticed the hulking form approach but made no effort to move.

Chelsea watched as the beast loomed over both. She, just moments ago so certain she would watch her newfound love be torn to shreds and be unable to help, was shocked to see tears form on the cheeks of the creature. Dodd had become motionless—likely having lost consciousness from the pain of his procedure.

A large hand gently removed the sensors on Dodd's body and pulled the needles that had delivered their ill-begotten substances into the man—who'd never wandered far off the path those who are good and true tread.

A certainty that Dodd was destined to become like him increased Colly's sorrow. He had never met any others like him, not here, nor in the great void that he knew awaited him. He was certain of his impending isolation in the cold nothing once the beast took full control of him again, and the anguish and terror of this conclusion slowly transformed into anger at the understanding that his small glimmer of hope lay broken on this table.

A minute amount of space had broken between her skin and the rope of Chelsea's bonds, and she began pulling her hand into a tight roll with her fingers pointed down to force them through. Even the beast's tears, turning to steam as its skin rose from dark brown to burgundy, did not break her rhythmic resistance as she alternated hands, feeling slight give at each effort. Over and over, she pulled until her skin gave way and slick blood coated her wrists and the bonds. The vital liquid allayed the friction of the rope just enough to deliver her freedom, and she turned to a waking Leonard.

"Get your wits up," she said. "We need to figure out how to lift Dodd."

Leonard's swooning head filled with images of Dodd collapsing atop him and mashing his little body aside, and he giggled before spotting the beast, enshrouded in waves of heat. His head cleared of humor and filled instead with terror. "Chelsea, that's an ifrit!"

"I thought so, too," she said. "It's probably going to kill us, but we have to get Dodd."

"I don't have any idea how..." Leonard trailed off when he saw the legs of the table. "There are wheels on the inside. We can push him up to the door."

The ifrit, now fully formed from Alex Colly's anger, turned from Dodd and loomed above Piper before the chant caused it enough discomfort to hurl the panel of controls at the security monks.

One had managed to dodge out of the way in time, but the other took the full force of cragged metal and vanished between it and where it met the wall. Piper didn't bother turning when the beast stepped over him to wrench the metal slides from the chamber and break through the glass to reach Baraqiel. It lifted the angel from its bonds and felt how lifeless the form had become. A howl pierced the chamber as the ifrit vented its rage and sorrow at the state of that which had given it life. It curled itself around the angel as though to protect it as the temperature rose in the chamber.

Leonard and Chelsea kicked the wheels down on the table and pushed it toward the ramp, then up to the door. Leonard tested the temperature of the slag that had resulted and found it had cooled enough to cross without serious injury, but the floor was covered in mounds of the hardening alloy. The wheels could not pass over, and they'd need to try to carry Dodd.

Chelsea strained to lift Dodd and yelled her frustration in unison with the melodic cries of the ifrit when the futility of their combined efforts became more and more apparent. Just as her bellows were changing to wails, Dodd floated up as a feather might on a light breeze, as though he weighed nothing at all, and Chelsea and Leonard's hands followed him into the air. It took them a moment to see the person standing behind them who'd reached in to assist.

"I can carry some of your burden," Samael said and ushered them through the portal as the room behind them saturated with flame, reducing any and all within to ash.

CHAPTER EIGHT
SEEDS

Rose and Freja arrived at the small clearing in the trees where they had earlier spied upon the house. Freja had elected to take the chariot no farther than the fields of battle, and the women walked the remaining distance, which didn't feel far, despite how small the goddess's hall had become from their perspective when they'd entered the trees.

Rose asked about the landscape, the battles, and more pointedly, this wise woman she was traveling to meet.

"How does she know more than you? Haven't you been around since basically forever?" Rose asked.

"We have births the same as you, Rose," Freja said. "Some were birthed by the cosmos, some by the thoughts and actions of humanity, and some were forged by the very hands of the creator. While our existence may be defined as immortal or infinite from your perspective, we are all at the same whims of the ever-flowing wheel of time, even me. This woman is far more ancient than I can conceive of. You might say it is a good comparison that I think of her in the very same ways you think of me. Timeless."

"That's excruciatingly hard for me to wrap my mind around," Rose said.

"You will process it well enough, as you have everything else up until now," Freja said.

"Yeah, David always said nobody rolls with the punches like I do. I don't see it myself," Rose said.

"You don't see it because it is natural for you," Freja said. "The pretenders are the ones who pay constant attention to their so-called virtues."

Rose rolled this concept around as her gaze explored the red vines crawling up pristine tree trunks. The forest, a picturesque display of nature at its apex without being hampered by the dealings of man, was a blessing to the senses.

"Did you take David here?" Rose asked.

"I didn't take David anywhere," Freja said. "I looked in on him to ensure he found his way into the hall at Valhalla, and then once again to ensure ingress to the serpent's mountain. I'm afraid we had precious little time together. He was too driven to have had time to truly drink in this place, at any rate. He only wished to return home to you."

"I miss him, but this time, he's there and I'm here. He doesn't even know I'm here, does he?" Rose asked.

"No," Freja said. "He's not been told. That may change if Samael deems it necessary, but I doubt he will. Otherwise, David will likely manage his way back somehow. It's not a far stretch to imagine. He likely needn't even bribe the ferryman, Kharon. Fast friends, they were."

Rose wondered at the mention of a ferryman and suddenly remembered him not just from David's recount, but her own experience. He was very gentle and reassured her that she was in good hands. Rose found his appearance as Fred Rogers to be unsettling at first, given the surroundings, but took to its calming effect soon enough. She hoped she might see Kharon again under better circumstances.

"I imagine David will kill Lilith if he can find her. I don't want him to do that," Rose said.

"Why?" Freja asked. "She nearly killed him, and if not for

Samael's role as sentry, she would have maimed many and butchered you for her erroneous whims. Death will be a mercy compared to what I'd lay upon her."

Rose felt as though she was standing in the shadow of a colossus for a moment. Freja's attunement to war and conflict rarely showed through, but when it did, her persona grew fearsome.

"Not for her," Rose said. "Screw her. I don't want him to head down that path, Freja. He's good by nature. It doesn't take much ink to taint a well, you know."

"Wise statement, to be sure," Freja said, "but don't forget that as people grow, they become more complex—and so too does the solution to most problems. David has grown more than he'd ever imagined he would, and in such a short time. Don't begrudge him if he chooses to taste the nectar of vengeance. It is not always the wrong path. Take my word on that."

Rose thought better than to argue the semantics of murder with a Norse goddess of battle and death, among other things. They walked on in silence, which suited them both for a time, until an upcoming clearing became apparent to Rose. She could make out the outline of the house as it walked about in the trees and saw it flutter its wings when it noticed their approach.

"Be mindful of what you say when we enter," Freja said. "Baba Yaga has often turned her anger on unwitting travelers and cursed them for the most minor of offenses and missteps. I see no reason why she'd make an exception for you, even if I am present."

"She doesn't fear you? I thought everyone was smart enough to fear you..." Rose said.

"Fear answers to the whims of the crone, Rose," Freja said. "She commands it."

The women entered the clearing, and the house cocked to the side to survey them much in the same manner of a chicken. It had the legs of one, after all, with wings to match. Rose could see that the doorway was nestled within an open beak, the top serving as an odd transom, and the bottom a makeshift ramp, complete with crudely constructed stairs they'd no doubt have to ascend soon.

"I'm not too eager to walk inside of another living thing after having been in that alligator guy," Rose said. "How do we get to the door anyway? It's fifteen feet off the ground."

"This little house is not a thing like Ammit. Don't worry. I can assure you it's rather cozy inside," Freja said and strode up to the chicken. She held her open palms out to her sides and committed to a half curtsy before saying, "House of brown, please sit down."

The house came forward a few steps and nestled itself into a sitting position atop its legs, going so far as to jut its door toward the women before laying its beak on the soft pine needles carpeting the soil.

"Remember, mind your words, Rose. Especially if you're answering a question asked by Baba Yaga," Freja said.

Rose mimed crossing her heart, and Freja smiled as she led her into Baba Yaga's hut.

Ω

Acrit led David outside as dawn ushered in a new day.

"Do you see how the light changes color there as the sun moves higher on the horizon?" he said, pointing beyond the structures and land forms nearer to he and David.

"I do. It's refraction, and how the light bends as it enters our atmosphere," David said.

"Right you are. The science is there in your mind, but I wonder how you are applying it," Acrit said.

David adjusted his clothes before closing his eyes and looking toward the sun. Rays of light warmed his skin and reminded him of what it was like to be younger and free, outdoors all the time.

"I don't really need to apply it," David said. "I don't work with the subjects daily."

"Ah, but then where's the wonder? Do you know what happens inside of the blades of those leaves the instant the radiation of the sun reaches them? They spring to life, David. An explosion of activity hinging on the evolution built over thousands of years. That's nothing

128

short of a miracle, yet you don't wonder on it. And look there…" Acrit pointed to the shadow cast by the large leaf of jute hanging away from the center of its parent plant. "We call this molokhia here. It provides nourishment to many of those who call Syria home."

"I see it," David said. "I had no idea we were back in Syria. Why did we come here?"

"There are many lessons to be learned where war churns the sand over and brandishes the destructive wiles of humanity. Focus your attention and look at the leaf." Acrit tickled David's forehead with the blade of plant.

David realized Acrit had been planning on instructing him when he'd asked David to partake in a morning stroll.

"What do you believe is happening on the ground facing side of that leaf right now?" Acrit asked.

"I'm guessing its cooler in the shade and will warm up a little slower than the side facing the sun," David said.

"So short sighted," Acrit said. "You're right, but that's obvious, and you shouldn't be content with the obvious. Beneath that leaf is a world wholly different than that above it, as is one side of the earth when it turns from the sun. Hundreds of organisms and millions of cells are being affected by that difference and behaving accordingly. There is a resonance to them as they dance within the shade, the light above, and the subtle lines that divide both worlds. We are seeing a microcosm that treats the passage of time in a wholly different manner than the one you experienced as a mortal—and now as a celestial being. Finding the meaning of the resonance is key to understanding your power."

David took time to understand Acrit's meaning before he said, "I see what you're saying about being short sighted, but I don't understand how that relates to my power so well yet."

"David, you have the potential energy of a star many millions of times larger than the sun within you," Acrit said. "There is no end to the possibilities of that energy. A star will churn through its cycle and radiate the energy needed to bring about *life* on the planets surrounding it. It will collapse in a massive display and birth the elements required to create *life*. You are now a product of that process and the source of it all at once. Understanding how the universe works is paramount to mastering yourself. As we said earlier, you have already innately bent space time around you when your will propelled you to move faster than light itself. If not for that, you may have been consumed by Azazel's attack."

"I thought he wasn't trying to kill me," David said.

"The heat of battle and an angel who hasn't practiced with his power in some time can lead to some nasty outcomes," Acrit said, kicking a rock over with his leather babouche. "Under here, you have sand and soil, water, nitrogen, magnetite, traces of zircon, and on and on. All comprised of elements forged in the stars that watch over us every night. Those same twinkles of light merge the elements and lay the foundation for life to form. All specifically designed and placed by our sentient creator for the purpose of your existence within this churning universe."

"I hadn't really thought of it like that. The elements are made by the stars, and so are we..." David said.

"The resonance, do you feel it in you?" Acrit asked.

"I don't."

"Keep it in your mind, David. You will when the time is right."

Both watched Azazel appear, carrying a bucket of water to their temporary sanctuary from a hand pump somewhere in the middle of the small community. David observed the people of this place as they appraised his father with brief glances. A stranger to them, yet he was welcomed at arm's length based on the unspoken agreement of live and let live.

"Water for tea?" Acrit asked.

"One of the few pleasures we have, eh? I'll never understand those of us who have a taste for spirits. Nasty stuff," Azazel said and placed the water on the ground, splashing some on the parched soil. "Tea is a communion."

David watched as Azazel placed his finger into the dampened earth to create a burrow, and Acrit reached into his pocket to produce a single seed, which glinted in the sunlight.

"A communion between who?" David asked.

Azazel waited for Acrit to place the seed into the ground before gently covering it and placing another palm full of water over top.

"Life," he said simply and beckoned David to follow him to the top of the hill overlooking the village.

The three walked to the hilltop and looked out over the area before David broke their silence. "You know, you must not have ever tried Heidrun's mead if you're so dead set against alcohol. It's probably the closest thing to ambrosia to ever exist."

"Ambrosia does exist, and I didn't know you'd become so nestled into the mead hall to be allowed to sup at Odin's table." Azazel looked to Acrit as if to say he'd delivered him bad intelligence. "That's not a feat many can boast."

"I never met Odin. I've wondered about him, and why he wasn't there. A Viking named Bulwyf was running the show during my time in Valhalla. A little coarse at first, but a good guy. Sarena, too. Well, Joan of Arc, I guess. It's hard for me to keep straight sometimes. Anyway, I was given the mead by Mardoll. She's a bit of a lush, that one."

"Freja?" Azazel asked and repeated his look to Acrit.

"Listen," Acrit said, "I could only relay the rumblings that came my way. There's no private detective to be found who can cross the membrane between worlds, so I'd appreciate it if you'd cut me a little slack."

"Freja is a wonder, and she is far more welcoming than Odin. You were lucky her eye fell on you. Uriel's doing, no doubt," Azazel said.

"No doubt," David said and looked at the people going about their business below as the sun beat on their backs. "He saw things a lot like this. From a higher vantage."

"Indeed," Azazel said. "He was the best of us, even when I was in high regard, but you wouldn't know it from asking him."

"Is he really gone?" David asked.

"Perhaps," Azazel said.

"It's possible, but not certain, David," Acrit said. "The creator isn't one for ultimate destruction. That is one of the reasons there is a high edict not to destroy in the first place."

"We kill all the time. There's killing occurring as we speak," David said.

"Killing is not destroying," Azazel said. "You've learned that firsthand. Everything goes on to some form or another. A log leaves smoke and ash after it burns. But to wholly consume something and bring it to nothingness? To extract matter and spirit from this world? That is forbidden. That is what Uriel did to Asmodeus to save you from doing it yourself. This is how your story was written so you could live on, David, lest you'd be the one gone, and our hope for your kind would further dwindle."

"What hope is there if we're all scattered? You say Lucifer is to blame, but how can he wholly corrupt so many people? It seems like a tawdry excuse for humanity's sake, really. Maybe they aren't worth saving," David said.

He watched three children spill out of their home to join others who were playing a game of some fashion in a clearing behind some of the houses. It must have been well practiced, because they fell into the rhythm quickly and formed squads on either side, seemingly to protect their areas from invading marauders from the other side.

"We had the luxury of watching your kind before he was left to corrupt them," Azazel said. "They weren't so eager to lend their ears when it was clear who the message was coming from. But the devil is no fool, and he adapts. Now, the megaphone is large and hard to discern. Acrit has told me of the advancements of the world. Of the lengths those who stymie critical thought would go to control those who'd let their guard down. Not everyone is lucky enough to have been born when and where you were, and to have had the resources you've had. Strip those away, and it's no longer a coin flip as to where your kind leans. I've seen it."

The children had reached the endgame of their play. One team, stacking more captures than the other, had far more players left on the field. A large girl from the losing side bent down to clench a rock, a move hidden to all but the three watchers on the hill. The children played on.

"I don't disagree," David said. "Things have been accelerating for people at breakneck speeds. Change is confusing and scary. Those who can benefit from the confusion are definitely trying and largely succeeding. Just look at social media and you'll see the divisiveness between us now."

"Your kind is at a crossroads, much like the one you passed to find Valhalla. It's nearly time for them to choose their path," Acrit said.

"We don't know which way they'll choose, but the writing on the wall looks dour," Azazel followed.

A swift boy with an ivory smile darted for the enemy base and was met with a tag to the temple that sent him into the ground in a heap. The girl who'd struck him ran on to block any other invaders and masterfully dropped the rock behind her into the dusty soil. The boy tried to regain his feet and fell once more. Blood on his head revealed foul play.

"Maybe we will collapse on ourselves like a star does," David said. "Maybe it all needs to end to start again."

"That has happened many times," Acrit said, "but you've now found a touch of the stars, haven't you? Something to bring about an ultimate end."

"Nukes?" David asked.

"And not just those, though they'd do fine on their own. Biological weapons abound, I'm sure, and more demented concoctions to usher you all to Kharon en masse. That would be an end to your chapter, I fear. After so much meddling, I'd doubt the creator could find you worthy of continuing. A scrapped project that started with great promise and all hope but became too tainted to endure."

"I wouldn't be so sure to assume the creator's intentions," Azazel said. "It's never been clear since I've existed. We stand closer to it than humans, and by leagues, but I've never been so bold to assume as you do."

"Different strokes for different folks, I suppose," David said.

The children from the losing and winning team converged on the boy and lifted him to his feet, another used his own shirt to stop the blood flow from his recent adversary on the field of play, while others chastised the assailant who'd tried so hard to hide her deed. Some turned and left with her, but they were few. Far more stayed with the boy, and soon the children were immersed in another game. One with less resemblance to war.

"She's to be the scapegoat, then," Azazel said.

"And they press on," Acrit added. "See? There is hope to be had."

The three walked down the hill to steep their early afternoon tea and discuss David's path. As they walked, David observed the golden sapling that had already begun reaching toward the sky from the gift of moisture Acrit had laid upon it.

Ω

The fire had continued to spread and consume the complex, despite a flow of emergency personnel who had streamed past them as they made their blatant escape. With a little luck and good fortune, they were able to locate their car and drive out of All Century. Chelsea had insisted that Leonard stay with them instead of dropping him at home. The task of monitoring Dodd needed filling, and soon Leonard stopped his protests. The idea of men in black storming his condo while he watched *Doctor Who* was not one he enjoyed contemplating.

Samael sat quietly in the passenger seat, feeling minute in scale to Chelsea compared to when he'd first appeared to heft Dodd from the table. His presence still weighed upon Leonard, whose anxiety would have it no other way. Chelsea appeared to have no trouble in that regard. She had no problem berating him as soon as they'd made it to the highway.

"Why would you send us there if you *knew* what we were walking into?" Chelsea said.

"I didn't send you. I was informed—*recently*—that you were involved with that facet of things now," Samael said. "My guess is that you two were the only ones who could and would uncover what was happening here in your realm with fidelity. Being affiliated with David is likely the reason. Uriel placed many things in motion before he left us. It's possible the same messenger informed us both."

"Who was it?" Chelsea asked.

"Haven't the foggiest, to be honest. I must say I would have chosen you two as well, had it been me. My short list of capable people has grown shorter as of late. Most of my acquaintances are quite brief, sadly."

"Birds," Chelsea said.

"I beg your pardon?" Samael asked.

"Were the messengers birds?"

"Oh. Yes, actually. Well, a single bird. A raven in fact," Samael said. "An interesting method of sending."

"We aren't pawns to be shuffled and struck from the board, you know," Chelsea said circling back to her gripe.

"Of course not. I hope you don't think I feel that way."

"Well, how else should I think you feel?" Chelsea asked. "Rose is gone. David is off on some vendetta, and now Brendan has been turned into a science experiment and may die."

"He is in trouble. I don't know what medicinal support they were using to keep the humans alive after the injections, but I do know what happens when they don't take it," Samael said, turning to the backseat. "Detective, can you hear me?"

Dodd remained unconscious, though his features strained, showing he was still in a great deal of pain.

"If I may, Chelsea?" Leonard asked and pointed to the domed light in the car.

"Sure, Leonard, sure," she said.

Leonard turned on the light and produced a number of bottles from his jacket pockets. He began reading them with great consternation.

"Where did you get those?" Chelsea asked.

"I snagged them on the way through the lower room, just outside of the chamber where they did this to him." Leonard glanced to Samael. "He was carrying Detective Dodd, so I had time to ransack the container, but I still don't know what they are. They're cryptically labeled."

"Oh, a crafty one. I do like crafty ones," Samael said, staring at Leonard, who refused to look up at him.

"We have four that say Compound A with no directions, and six that say Compound AB-E. That one says take three times daily," Leonard said and rattled the bottles.

The car began to feel warmer, and Samael switched on the air conditioning to high. "He's heating up. We should try one of those," he said.

Chelsea thought of the two medicines. The one with the directions seemed more prescriptive, like what you'd take to maintain long term illness or disease. Her intuition told her they should try the vaguer of the two first. It was more likely they one prescribed for directly after the procedure and may work to keep Dodd from turning into the Human Torch on them.

She grabbed a half-full bottle of water from the console and held it for Leonard to grasp. "Are the Compound A pills capsules?" she asked.

Leonard opened the bottle. "Yes, fairly large, too."

"Okay, I want you to empty that bottle down to a quarter and then mix the insides of two of those capsules into it and help him drink it," she said. "Can you do that?"

Leonard didn't answer but opened the window and nearly lost the bottle trying to empty it to the level Chelsea had directed.

"Ah, only nimble of the mind," Samael said. "That's still good."

"You aren't helping," Chelsea said.

"Sorry, I think aloud. It's a bad habit from being on my own all too often," Samael said.

"Sad story, truly," Chelsea said, "but you still haven't given me any inkling of why we've been put in the crosshairs of some pretty heavy dudes, Sam. What was going on there?"

"They're building some sort of army, by the looks of it," Samael said. "Something to edge out the drones they've seeded throughout the world already. Something that can withstand unbearable heat—that's what we were thinking. Without the watchers, there was no way to know for sure. Uriel didn't leave any clear directions on the matter. He trusted me to flush it out and to help humanity deal with it, so here I am."

"We're so lucky to have you, too," Chelsea said. "Leonard, is he drinking it?"

"Almost done mixing it. The particulates are not very keen to become a solution, so it's taking some time," he said.

"Leonard, honey, you have to pour that down his throat before he blows up and kills us," she said.

"Well, three quarters of us, anyway," Samael said. "I'm pretty sure I'll be fine."

"You really aren't helping," Leonard said.

"Ah, he's overcome his fear of me already. That's very good, too," Samael said as he looked out over the highway through the windshield.

Leonard pulled Dodd's head back and opened his mouth. He poured a little of the water into his mouth and hoped he wouldn't choke and sputter it out, but Dodd instinctually gulped it down and received the rest shortly after in the same manner. He slumped back into the cramped head space between the door and ceiling before muttering, "More of that."

"He spoke. That's great," Samael said.

"When you're done narrating, can you reach into the glove box and grab the bottle of water I've got there?" Chelsea said.

Samael passed it to Leonard, who plucked it with two fingers by the cap and then poured it into Dodd's gullet.

"Do you think he'll make it?" Chelsea asked.

"I do," Samael said. "He is quite well insulated in virtue, that one. Those types of people tend to do well in circumstances such as these, though that is not always the case. That said, he will probably be fine. That's my bet."

"And what does 'fine' look like?" Chelsea prodded. "Hopefully not the molten behemoth we had the pleasure of meeting earlier, who scorched his way through a titanium alloy door."

"That wasn't Behemoth. Truly a massive creature, that one," Samael said. "Not quite as large as Leviathan, but massive, nonetheless. I believe what you crossed paths with was an ifrit. Much easier to handle, but quite unpredictable. I also don't believe the fellows experimenting with celestial power back there knew they'd conjured one."

"That was my hypothesis as well," Leonard said. "Ifrit, I mean."

"That's a worst-case scenario, by my measure. While people have been becoming demons of that kind for millennia, they are exceedingly rare in the..." Samael pondered for a moment. "Wild. He is likely being put into an equilibrium by the substances in those pills. As long as he has that, there should be no chance for immolation, and certainly no ifrit using him as a portal to this world."

Chelsea cast a glance to the back and saw Dodd's facial features relax, at least to some degree.

She stepped on the accelerator and pushed toward home.

Ω

Rose entered the mouth of the chicken house after Freja and moved to stand beside her. The goddess noted the lack of fear in the girl she'd cautioned just moments ago. She hoped that trait wouldn't lead to her undoing here.

The interior was indeed cozy, as Freja had said it would be, but it had an earthen feel, promoted by the presence of herbs hung to dry and mud-kilned bowls adorning the shelves above a large fire. A cauldron befitting a performance of Macbeth mottled by orange tongues lapping from beneath released a fine steam into the room. Life breathed through every corner of the home, though it should have felt muted by its earthen decor.

"Guests," croaked a toad so large and fat it looked as though it could swallow Rose whole.

"Who comes to my little home?" Baba Yaga asked.

Rose was startled to see the old woman turn. She'd been standing with her back to the women, and her cloak was so like the forest floor that Rose had taken it as a mound of sticks and leaves for kindling.

"Freja and Rose have come," Freja said. "We are looking for clarity from you who are so wise."

"Flattering me, Freja?" Baba Yaga said. "Why not discuss my

endless beauty? We ladies are always told that's far more important than wisdom."

"You're quite a far cry from any semblance of beauty, and you won't catch me in such a witless trap, forest witch," Freja said.

Baba Yaga laughed as she approached the cauldron and broke dried herbs into the brew. "You always were a boil on my rump, Freja. Glad your spirit is still as strong as ever," she said. "And what of you, tiny flower? What brings you here with such a prestigious escort?"

"I've come to find out some secret about myself," Rose said. "You've a lovely home, by the way. I can't imagine how you keep it so tidy while it's walking around like that."

"Oh? Well, likely magic, little dear. That'll be the answer to most of your questions about this house and those who dwell in it, right, Princess?" Baba Yaga asked of the toad.

"Bitch," Princess said.

Baba Yaga's cackle filled the home, and she produced a large rat from her pocket and threw it. Princess hopped once and caught the scampering creature on the tip of her tongue before consuming it.

"Princess here was once a flattering maid, you know. Quite the pretty little thing. Stumbled on me in the wilds surrounding Alexander Palace. Pity for her that she was so crude at the time, though she's made nice company over the years," Baba Yaga said. "I'd imagine she'd very much like a companion sister to pass the days, Rose. Any interest in staying awhile?"

"None, but thank you for the offer," Rose said. "We have some things to do before I can stay anywhere for long."

Freja was thankful for her tactful response. "Rose isn't an ordinary mortal, at least not by my reckoning."

"Any tarot totting snake oil salesman could tell you that. She's something, all right. Untapped, at that." Baba Yaga approached Rose quickly and grasped her hand to inspect it before producing a needle from her garb. "I'll borrow this, little flower." She pricked Rose's finger. The girl flinched but didn't pull away and earned a smile from the witch. "You're a sturdy sort."

"Been through a lot," Rose said.

Baba Yaga snorted.

"What will you do with her blood?" Freja asked.

"See what it does. What else would I do with it? Drink it?" Baba Yaga said.

She turned and grasped a glass from a nearby table and blew the dust from it before squeezing Rose's finger to coax crimson ichor into it one drop at a time.

Rose looked at the spectacle before catching Princess staring at her. She couldn't be sure, but the intensity and narrowed eyelids evinced contempt.

"Very good. Here." Baba Yaga pulled a bright purple leaf from her pocket and chewed it to a mash before spreading a generous helping onto Rose's finger. "Don't fiddle with it for a few minutes, and it'll be good as new."

Freja did a poor job of hiding her disgust, but Rose listened and kept her hand out to avoid having the slurry slide to the floor.

"Do you have any guesses as to what Rose's mystery might be?" Freja asked.

Baba Yaga returned to her cauldron and swirled the glass, but she didn't empty the contents inside. Instead, she sorted through her herbs and shook them while observing the floor. "Who are your parents, Rose?"

"I don't know," Rose said. "I was taken into foster care as a kid and jumped around a little before landing with my long-term family. By the time I was old enough to ask anyone where I was found, nobody knew."

"Makes sense, since you weren't born of a natural woman's womb. At least, I don't think you were." Baba Yaga's eyes widened. "There we go." She reached down with great effort and plucked a brown seed from the floor and placed it in the glass with Rose's blood. "There. Shouldn't take long to find out what we've got here. Now then... How'd you die, little flower?"

"Is everyone here besides, well, your types, dead?" Rose asked.

"No, there are exceptions, like Princess. She's from your world. Spirited away in her prime, no less," Baba Yaga said. "But you're as dead as they come. Death isn't the end of most stories, though some probably wish it were, and I am well certain it isn't the end of yours. We all come to an end in some form or another. Time and perspective matter in that regard."

Princess hop-walked to the corner and laid her head down.

"She passed in great pain," Freja said.

"A victim, then?" Baba Yaga said. "Certainly an odd fit to be in your hall, playing chess with the rabble-rousers of Valhalla..."

Rose hadn't been sure of the circumstances required to gain entry into the Fólkvangr, but she'd heard David explain that those in Valhalla were there at least partly due to having sacrificed themselves in some way.

"I was taken by a demon so he could lure out my boyfriend and kill him," Rose said.

"A supernatural killer, eh?" Baba Yaga asked. "None too lucky. But our types rarely have an easy time of things."

Freja was surprised to hear Rose recounting more details about her death. She'd wondered if the girl had been reconstructing the last moments of her life as they'd traveled, but she expected Rose might ask questions or divulge her experiences to allay her trauma.

"I wouldn't consider having my wrists and ankles shattered and being set on fire to be lucky, no," Rose said. She held the stare of the old witch in a moment that somehow felt gentle.

"You're made of sterner stuff than he was," Baba Yaga said. "No doubt your little boyfriend came and wiped the demon off the face of the earth. That's how these fairy tales go, though the damsel in distress usually lives in the stories."

"Something like that, with a few tweaks here and there," Rose said.

"You're no damsel in distress. There's a tweak to start with. Look there." Baba Yaga pointed to the glass which held a sapling of some botanical remedy or ingredient Baba Yaga had purpose for. The plant was growing so quickly that the women could observe it if they kept their eyes on it. "The problem is, unlike so many out there today, you're designed to give life and growth as opposed to taking it, Rose."

Freja moved to the sapling, now twice as tall as the glass containing it, and cut the plant in half with a dagger she produced from her robes. The plant continued to grow despite the damage, and the roots pressed out on the glass to the point of cracking the vessel.

"She's a seed of Gaea?" Freja asked.

"Terra, Rhea, or as so many have called her, Gaea—whichever name we'd choose. She's likely a gift from the life bringer," Baba Yaga said.

"I'm a seed?" Rose asked.

"Looks that way, or some other derivation of the same," Baba Yaga said. "I am a seed of Gaea, Rose. We are capable of a great many things, but no two are quite alike. Rarely do we surface, and rarer still do we find ourselves in the veiled world of the living, though it is possible. You're the proof."

"How can you be a seed of life when you have killed so many people?" Rose asked.

Princess opened her eyes and raised her head at this. Freja took her eyes from the still growing plant and looked to Baba Yaga, who'd ruined the lives of many for less pointed statements.

"I have a temper. Though the stories can sway the mind to conjure all manner of ideas of me. Don't worry. I am not always boiling children or turning feeble minded princesses into the forms their actions deem worthy. I commune with the natural world in a way that's foreign to most, mortal and immortal alike." Baba Yaga caressed leaves newly sprung from buds just moments before. "Sometimes a spider jumps from a hole and snatches an unwitting snack. The key is, who is in the wrong—the snack for being witless, or the spider who has use for it?"

"She's a person, too," Freja said. "One with a vast knowledge of the how life behaves, but one with her own whims."

Rose inspected her finger after removing the cloth from it. "That makes sense. I guess we're predisposed to stereotyping where I'm from, even if there's no bad intentions behind it. Thank you for explaining."

"Such a polite little thing, no false faces, and tougher than baobab bark," Baba Yaga said. "To think, you've been hiding out there without notice is not terribly astounding, but to have missed you would have been a such a tragedy. Rose, there's not much for you here in my little house, but I do have a direction to deliver. Freja, take her down the way behind my hut. It leads to a lake that will be difficult to overlook. Make camp there until the light has turned long and departs."

"What will we find?" Rose asked.

"An opportunity," Baba Yaga said. "Best be quick. With luck, we will meet again, though luck's been brittle as of late."

"Let's go," Freja said.

Rose made to leave and stopped.

"May I take this?" Rose's eyes pointed to the plant.

"I don't see why you'd want it. Nothing special to that sapling," Baba Yaga said.

"It probably isn't, but it's got a part of me in it now," Rose said.

Baba Yaga smiled and showed her teeth of crooks and cranny.

"Take it and go now, little Rose. Let's see if you'll stumble on a missing piece or two to your story."

"Thank you," Rose said and turned to follow Freja, who waited at the threshold.

"Oh, and mind the mandrakes down the way—their screams will drive you to the grave."

Ω

Dodd roused to a darkened room, which his mind recalled instantly to be Chelsea's parlor. He stirred and turned to the table to see a glass of water next to a pill bottle. Reaching with hopes of drowning his thirst, his fingers raked the wooden table to make up the ground between and grasp it. A slender hand slid it closer, and Dodd covered it with his own.

"Thank you, beauty," Dodd said.

"It's Leonard."

"Well, you're beautiful in your own way too, Lenny. How'd we get out of there?"

Leonard slid his hand from beneath Dodd's. "We had help. Your friend Sam showed up and carried you for us."

"Sam is here?" Dodd asked. He sat up and emptied the glass of water before making to stand. "Where?"

"I don't think you should get up yet. Why don't you lay back down?" Leonard said. "Chelsea, Dodd is awake."

Chelsea flowed into the room with the grace of a well-practiced caregiver. "Sit your colossal rump right back down on that sofa, Brendan. We have to check you out first."

Dodd waited for her to get within arm's reach and snatched her into a hug. Chelsea's arms found their way around his waist, and they embraced until Leonard cleared his throat.

"Where's Sam, Chelse?" Dodd asked.

"He was in the basement looking through my stuff," Chelsea said. "I'll go get him."

"Let me," Leonard said. "You two should have a second."

Leonard scurried from the room and made the short walk to the top of the basement stairs. His understanding of the events that occurred here were muddled, largely by his own refusal to hear a detailed account and the pain it brought to Chelsea to relive the event, but he'd learned enough to know he was standing in front of the hell mouth that had allowed Asmodeus's ingress here. He paused at the stair, unwilling to make the first step, like a child imagining specters from shadows.

"Come on down, Leonard," Samael said.

Somehow, this made Leonard's anxiety worse, but his compulsion to please outweighed it. When he rounded the corner from the stair to the basement, he saw Samael postured in Chelsea's chair, looking over a molded recreation of a rectangular stone shrine.

"Do you know where this is from, Leonard?" Samael asked.

"It's from a dig at Gath, the city over Elah," Leonard said. "That piece was one of many found there while they were looking for evidence of the Philistine giants, if I'm not mistaken."

"And there were many." Samael turned the mold to its side and placed it down.

"Yes, it was a great find, and the archaeologists did an amazing job preserving the artifacts at the dig," Leonard said.

"I mean giants. It wasn't just Goliath and his brothers, you know," Samael said. "The earth was rife with half-breeds then. They pillaged and plundered, for the most part, and were the bane of all. Even demons and creatures of legend abhorred them. It was no small feat to quell their advance, but humanity can endeavor to rise to most challenges, even if the occasion is felling giants."

"Why do you think they were so brutish?" Leonard asked.

"Power corrupts," Samael said. "It's a cancer on most, even my own kind. When one finds themselves risen above others, the sheer thought of losing that vantage will drive them to embrace the vilest notions. Just look around you at the world of the living."

"I always saw that through the lens of black and white dualism. Some are good and some are bad," Leonard said. He hushed when Samael turned to look into his eyes.

"Every being with a consciousness has the ability to choose, no matter the odds stacked against them. This isn't idealism, but the very nature of free will. No person or thing is born evil," Samael said.

"Will David become evil, do you think?" Leonard asked.

"This is why I like you, Leonard. You're afraid of everything but the truth," Samael said. "We won't know what David's choice is until he makes it. He is good, inherently, and has grown to love much, but true loss and sorrow can topple even saints."

"He killed Asmodeus," Leonard said, "but he deserved it, so that's not the best metric."

"One cannot kill an angel or half-breed so easily, especially one like my son, who commanded his celestial power more artfully than most," Samael said. "David would have had to destroy him, which violates the laws of physics, as well as divine law. Matter was not forged simply to cease to exist, you see. David was saved by one of our brothers, at any rate, who stepped in to do the deed in his place."

"I know of the poems stating you fathered him, but I didn't take too much stock since it wasn't canon," Leonard said. "I'm sorry for your loss."

"Don't worry. I'm not offended, and I am not his father. That designation is for those who mold their offspring. I did no molding of Asmodeus," Samael said. "I've fathered many. There's a whole pantheon of deities in existence because of me and my offspring, but I don't count Lilith's son as one of them."

Leonard considered Samael's demeanor and presence. He found him enlightening for the first time, but his intelligence would not allow for him to forget the angel's frightening job.

"Who is carrying the souls of the departed while you're here with us? I've been wondering since you arrived here," Leonard said.

"Well, I'm not just here right now, if that helps," Samael said, "but you've a hungry mind, so I'll explain it like this. We are bringers of light. Think of light hitting a prism stone, and that should help you visualize how it works."

Leonard thought of light scattering across the earth to cherry-pick the dead from this realm to the next, and a shudder ran through him. He remembered his grandmother having a light scattering stone set at her window sill, and dancing amongst the rainbows as a child, but something didn't add up.

"You've black wings, correct?" Leonard asked.

"Correct."

"Well, I'm making the connection between the color of stars, and the angels embodying those stars. Blue burns bright. Red can too, but it's fleeting as red stars are at their ends. But what does black mean?"

"Well, Leonard, even stars die, don't they?"

Leonard's eyes widened in surprise.

"Let's check on Dodd. He will need some coaching now," Samael said, gesturing for Leonard to walk ahead of him. The two climbed from the basement to the first floor. Dodd and Chelsea were in the kitchen, and the scent of tea filled the air.

"How are you feeling, Detective?" Samael asked.

"Pretty good, thanks to you. I'll take alive over six feet under any day," Dodd said.

"I told him not to push it, but his leg is already firm enough for him to walk without his crutch," Chelsea said.

Leonard pulled up a seat next to Dodd and poured himself and Samael a cup of tea. "That's good. I'm glad you're on the mend."

"I don't want to kill the mood, but you'll have more to worry about than that leg," Samael said.

Chelsea clicked her tongue and set a fresh container of milk on the table. "Pun intended?"

The angel smiled. "The witticisms never dull in this house, I see."

"So, lay it on me. Am I going to become a fire fricker like Colly?" Dodd asked.

"I don't know for sure. This is the first revelation of humanity directly meddling with celestial power. Though we do have some information. Those pills, for starters, seem to keep the power tamped down and manageable for mortals while also delivering some of the benefits of being one of my kind." Samael reached to the cup of tea and pulled the hot liquid to his belly greedily. "That is the sweetest ichor I've had in some time." He refilled his cup and turned back to Dodd. "Your wounds are gone. That is something to celebrate, as you'd certainly have been hobbled for life otherwise, but there's a caveat. You're now tantamount to a nuclear reactor. Without care and maintenance, you'll melt down."

Dodd nodded, and Chelsea rubbed his back while Leonard stared toward nothing the way he did when he was deep in thought.

"What's in those pills?" Dodd asked.

"I'm not sure, but it's probably a mixture containing a very diluted form of the chains that bind the fallen," Samael said.

"What are they made of?" Chelsea asked.

"We don't know that. I suppose that's by design, since it's what is used to put us in time out, after all."

"It has to be an element of some sort. We can reverse engineer it. I've been thinking about this a little bit, and we should head to the lab before going to find David," Leonard said.

Chelsea's head snapped at this, and she turned to Samael. "You know where he is, don't you?"

"He found his father. They're getting acquainted—"

"Please don't be cryptic with me, Sam. I appreciate what you've done for my son, and what you've done for Brendan, but you won't get another sip of tea in this household again if you don't tell me if he's all right," Chelsea said, snatching the teacup.

Dodd and Leonard gave one another a knowing look and shrugged at Samael, who had glanced to them.

"I know they battled, and I was going to him to ensure he was safe, but I had to come to your aid instead. I hadn't expected the operation at All Century to have been so perilous. It wouldn't have been right to allow you to perish. I'm not certain of any more than what I've already told you, but I do know Azazel. I don't think he'd kill David."

"The paternal type?" Dodd asked.

"Not especially. But he's the practical type, and he sought to create David for a reason other than escaping his prison in Dudael. Uriel believed he was planning to help humanity overcome the calamity of knowledge they've been given from the fallen watchers. David is probably vital to that plan. Wouldn't do to kill him in that case, though he's certainly capable. It's unlikely David has reached even half of his potential as of yet. It takes time to understand the fabric of reality well enough to fully yoke celestial power, with all its wrinkles and idiosyncrasies, but Azazel has that knowledge. He's one of the most powerful among us."

Chelsea's faced looked dour, and Dodd took a turn consoling her. "He's no dummy, Chelse. He won't get in too deep over there."

"I should note that David is insurmountably more powerful than any combination of angel and human that has come before," Samael said. "Never has one such as he rivaled a ranking angel's power, not to mention surpass it. He stayed Michael's sword, and that speaks volumes. I still don't understand how he has such potential, but I'm sure it will reveal itself in time."

"He's still a boy. My boy. He shouldn't be manipulated by someone's plans because he's so distraught over Rose," Chelsea said.

"Oh, Rose! She's doing very well," Samael said. "I left her in capable hands before coming, and I've no doubt she'll be uncovering her own mysteries soon enough."

Dodd, Chelsea, and Leonard looked at Samael with wide-open mouths.

"I took her from the place of cleansi—ah, *purgatory*—and helped her to reclaim herself, though it seems Uriel had a plan in place for that, as well. His ability to think so far ahead is confounding in itself," Samael said.

"She's alive?" Chelsea and Dodd said in unison.

"Not quite, but she is quite capable," Samael said. "If there is a way back to the living world, I'm confident she will find it."

"David did it. I bet she can, too," Leonard said.

"Very different circumstances, but yes. If there's a will, there's a way, I suppose," Samael said. "The process of flipping with a body is unheard of. David didn't do that. His journey was largely inward. Rose is wholly on the other side, but she's special. I do believe she might be finding out just how special right about now."

"What do you mean by that?" Chelsea said.

"Well, it's nothing I was informed of, but she's hard to see for those of us who can read people. That happens when someone has a touch of, well, *us* in them. She's not of the Host—I'd be able to see that. She's something else. And she might be vital to David in some way other than just being his love."

"How's that possible? She's just an ordinary girl. I've known her since she was little," Chelsea said.

"David was just a boy, and the world was normal before demons and monsters popped out of closets all over the northeast. It doesn't seem too hard to grasp now," Dodd said. "What do you know about her parents?"

"Rose was in foster care from a young age. Her foster parents, the long-term ones she landed with, were good people, but they've been aloof lately. Traveling and such. They came for her memorial, but they weren't even equipped to plan it. Brendan and I did that. I don't know a thing about her birth parents, and I don't believe she does either. That's what she's told me and David, and she's a girl who—"

"—Doesn't lie," Dodd finished.

He stood and flexed his leg before doing some half squats.

"It's great to hear some *good* news for once," Dodd said. "Let's ride the thought of seeing her again and go find out what I'll need to be snorting for the rest of my life so I don't have a flare up."

"Such a crude statement from a dedicated peace officer," Chelsea said.

"Hey, when in Rome, snort what the Roman's snort," Dodd said. "Sam, you coming?"

"Oh no, he's not coming," Chelsea said. She turned to Sam. "You go get my baby and bring him home right now, and then you get over there and figure out how to help Rose. You can come out and play after you've done your homework, Mister Samael. Now shoo."

Samael smiled at Chelsea again. "I can't figure out who you remind me of, but you are fierce, Chelsea Dolan. I'll see to David now, but remember to keep Dodd medicated, and don't overdo it. Too much may be worse than too little."

"I'll keep myself stable, Sam. Thanks again for everything," Dodd said.

Samael drained his tea and stood to leave before turning back to Chelsea.

"It's Attila," he said.

She stared at him quizzically as he turned toward the door. His wings appeared, and Samael finished his thought as he took flight.

"You remind me of Attila the Hun."

Ω

Acrit, Azazel, and David sipped tea and discussed the nuances of creation and the laws of reality for some time before Acrit stole away to retrieve a laptop.

"You think we have Wi-Fi here?" David asked.

"Satellite link. Remember, I've been living through the technological revolution just as you have," Acrit said. He powered on the computer and busied himself with it, seemingly removed from the room.

David stared at his father, who cupped his tea in both hands and raised it to his mouth to drink. His eyes were as striking in their beauty as they were fierce. "Why are your eyes and wings matching colors? It was the same with Raphael and Michael, too."

"It's my essence," Azazel said. "I was forged in fire. All the elements in me are fusing to form others. My color represents that. That's what we've come to believe, anyway. Most all of my subordinates had a similar color. Perhaps the elements in us were thought best for a watcher."

"Were Uriel's eyes blue when he had them?" David asked.

"I never saw Uriel's eyes," Azazel said. "It's thought that he may have still had them at a time while I was already in existence, but he is much older than I am. One of the first. He could have blinded himself long before."

"He tore out his own eyes?" David asked.

"'Gave them up willingly' would be more a more appropriate description. The cost for his extensive wisdom, so we let ourselves to believe. He believed in the creator's vision, but thought it was mired by something and susceptible to failure. I agreed. His sacrifice was to save that vision."

"You know the creator's plan then," David said. "Good. That will probably be helpful."

Acrit chimed in, "He doesn't know an ounce more than you, me, or those gnats flying there. What he means is he agreed *you* would fail as dumbed beasts, clubbing each other over the head. I agreed with that too. Then we decided to help and ended up giving you bigger clubs."

Azazel look at David and sighed. "Oops," he said.

"Pretty big screw up on your part, but that's not the whole story, is it?" David asked. "You're playing 3D chess on this one."

"Wise indeed, the boy is," Acrit said.

Azazel wagged his finger. "Not all my secrets in one dose, dear boy."

"Kharon told me I wouldn't have the particular nomenclature of 'boy' any longer, since I'd seen through the murk while riding with him," David said.

"Well, the thoughts of the river man and my own diverge on that one," Azazel said. "Maybe it's just that I've loftier goals for you in mind. Either way, to me, you're an infant."

"That infant gave you one hell of a fat lip," Acrit said.

"That's not what I mean, and you know it. The years have made your humor turn sour, Iblis," Azazel said.

"I knew it. Silbi is Iblis. You're a jinn, Acrit," David said.

"Guilty as charged," Acrit said. "Your father and I have been in league with one another since before the watchers fell. Perhaps it was my influence that led him astray, who can say for sure, but we see eye to eye on most things."

"It will be easier for David to understand if you explain why you were cast down. He already knows my story," Azazel said.

Acrit ignored the request to divulge his history and turned the computer monitor toward David. "This is an aerial view of one of the facilities run by Brahman's company. Well, *one* of his companies. It's nestled less than thirty miles from where you grew up, David. Take a look and tell me what you see."

David observed the satellite image on the screen. "It looks expansive. There was a fire at the domed building there, up the road from the residential area. It must have burned hot to take out that much infrastructure. Maybe it's a chemical plant."

"They were harnessing the power of a fallen Grigori here. A massive mistake must have occurred for this level of destruction," Acrit said.

"Samael—" Azazel started.

"I doubt he torched the place," Acrit said. "It wasn't the imprisoned angel, either. Brahman moved the chains with it to the location to ensure it stayed incapable of resistance. They conjured something here. Something born of fire and psyche. Something not unlike me."

"He had a hand in it," Azazel said but offered no more.

"Brahman was making Nephilim?" David asked. "But why?"

"He wanted to use the power on himself at first," Acrit said, "but was content with experimenting on others beforehand to ensure he'd live through the experience. Then his business mind took over, and he thought to sell them. What country wouldn't want a lovely army of obedient half angels to do their bidding?"

"He planned to use my power for himself. That's why he was holed up in Palestine like a gym rat. Acrit was keeping close to get an idea of how far along he was," Azazel said.

David clucked his tongue. "Seems further than you'd like."

"It is," Azazel said. "It's also not me I am worried about. It's your kind that will feel the brunt of this affront to natural order, not mine."

"May I see that?" David asked and pointed to the laptop.

Acrit slid the laptop to him. David manipulated the image to look at the full scale of the project and guessed it would cost billions to have facilities like this in multiple locations. He looked at the residential area outside of the facility and saw evidence of living quarters having burned as well.

"Can we see images from earlier, around when the fire was raging?" David asked. "I'm curious if this was an explosion, since there's damage in other sections."

"We can, yes," Acrit said and directed David to pull up a menu with timestamps. "You're pretty good with that, almost like it's an extension of you."

"I grew up with these things. Used to have to cobble them together to play any new games that were coming out. I guess it just sank in," David said. He found a section of the timestamps showing the facility on fire and confirmed the living area had been separate blazes altogether. It was curious, but he spotted something that intrigued him more. "I need a phone."

"We can get to one, but you'll be better off using that to make the call. We don't have much else handy," Acrit said. He considered David's fervor in asking. "What did you see?"

"My mom's car is parked near the facility in this one, on a side road near the woods," David said. "She was there. Probably Dodd, too."

"How can you be certain it's her car?" Acrit asked.

"She has a big *Twin Peaks* bumper sticker on her roof. Why she put it there, I'll never know, but it's been there forever," David said.

"It's likely they destroyed the facility. She is a capable person, your mother," Azazel said.

"Yeah, take it easy lover boy. She's got a new main squeeze now," David said. He searched for any internet calling software the laptop may have installed when he noticed that the mouse wasn't moving across the screen.

"Hey, that's a neat trick. How are you opening windows without clicking?" Acrit asked. "I thought I'd gotten this thing pretty much figured out by now."

"I... I didn't mean to," David said. He relaxed his fingers and concentrated on the instrument under his palms. The operating system began moving faster, and David had a call going to his mother's cell phone and then house line. No answer.

"I have to get back home," David said.

"David, are you sure?" Azazel asked. "We haven't begun to peel back the layers of understanding your power yet."

"I'm not so sure about that," Acrit said. "David's understanding of this age far supersedes our own, and I think he's just realized one way to apply it."

"The seed of an idea, yeah," David said. "I couldn't do much with this because I am limited by the CPU and other factors. I need something bigger to see how far I can go."

"We will set you up with passage home, but it won't come without peril," Azazel said. "Lilith will be trying to kill you."

"She's weak," David said.

"Don't succumb to hubris. It's felled many of the mightiest of all our kinds. She still has teeth—" Acrit began.

"I'll have to deal with her nonsense as it comes. I can guarantee she won't survive if she shows herself to me," David said.

"Hey! Look at that," Acrit said. "You got angry, and the room didn't fill with heat. You *are* improving."

"A toddler learns to walk, and Acrit wants to submit him for a relay race," Azazel said.

"I get that I'm not ready for whatever it is you two seem to have planned for me, but it'll have to wait. I'm not losing anyone else," David said.

Azazel and Acrit looked to one another but said nothing. "We will book your trip," Acrit said.

"Already done," David said, and Acrit smiled. "I'll stop at my lodging and get my papers on the way."

"We will meet with you soon, David," Azazel said. "Keep yourself safe in the meantime."

David stopped before leaving and approached his father, pulling him in for a tight embrace, and then he left through the door without a word.

"Well, that was unexpected," Acrit said.

Azazel looked after David as he walked into the distance.

CHAPTER NINE
NEWTON'S LAW

Night's chorus sounded as pure here as it did when Rose was a child, chasing fireflies through the gloom of a faded day. It overtook the forest as Rose and Freja navigated the sloping path. The sun had begun to set far more quickly than either woman had expected, as is often the case when hampered with a timely goal, and they were soon stepping through shadows.

"She wasn't so bad," Rose said.

"The witch most commonly returns a person's persona onto themselves. It is told of time and again in the stories," Freja said. "It's also a blessing that she was enamored with you. Make no mistake, Baba Yaga's bad side is not something you want to see."

"Princess was evidence enough for that," Rose said.

"Yes, she's one example. I'll also point out that she is an example of one who received a *light* punishment."

Rose saw dancing lights ahead. "What are those?"

"Faeries," Freja said. "And not those that'll make you fly with a dash of their dust and happy thoughts, either. Mind any circular rings of mushroom you see, and we should be fine by avoiding them."

The women left the shoddy path through the woods and trailblazed over water-fat foliage until the lights danced well behind them. Once back on the path, it wasn't long until the trees cleared and the lake became dominant on the landscape.

"It's beautiful," Rose said, drinking in the view. The lake shore meandered about in a manner that felt both lawless and orderly at the same time. The surrounding forest encapsulated it as though a dollop of water had been dropped from the heavens to fill its basin. The clear water kept no secrets, and creatures swam in full view under its surface. Frogs of a much more reasonable size than Princess stood sentinel on lily pads and measured the intruders with winks and croaks.

"Truly, it is," Freja said. "Mind where you step. Baba Yaga's advice is never without use. If we step on a mandrake root, I'm certain we will regret it."

"It would help if I knew what one looked like," Rose said.

She walked to the shore and knelt down to feel the water. She lifted a palm and dribbled it down her neck to lift the heat from her body. The sensation was muted, reminding her of the fact that she was no longer truly alive.

"Here we sit, and here we wait," Freja said, taking up residence next to Rose and placing her perfect feet into the water.

Rose observed the golden chain, which had recently lost its hue. "Your chain is becoming golden once more. I'm happy you didn't ruin it by helping me."

"It's not easily ruined. This chain is Brísingamen, a gift from the most talented of the gilding dwarfs in Miðgarð. It has a beauty that lives outside the confines of time, so it will never tarnish, and it can take in some of my power. This is the power I used to restore you to one from three. Had I not had Brísingamen, I would likely have had to extinguish myself to save you. We cannot expel all of our essence. To do so usually spells the end of us, at least in this form."

Rose looked into Freja's eyes. "You would have sacrificed yourself for me?"

"I don't know," Freja said. "We never know how we will act until the time comes. I like to think I would have. You are important. Just how important remains to be seen, but I've a nose for these things."

"Thank you for all you've done," Rose said. "I feel like I'm a sponge for all the good will everyone has lately. I wish I could give something back."

"You will, Rose. I'm certain of that."

Full night consumed evening while Rose and Freja watched the moon through the reflective glass of the lake. Fireflies drifted by the frogs who eyed them listlessly.

"There," Freja said. "Coming on from the middle of the lake."

Rose had no trouble discerning what the goddess had spoken of with the help of light of the moon. A stag walked toward them on the surface of the water. It was astonishing in size, but that could be said by most anyone who hadn't seen a full moose or elk in the wild, and had a pelt of brown and gold that seemed to illuminate the area around it.

"It's walking on water," Rose said.

"Yes," Freja said. "Its aura is brilliant." The statement confirmed Rose's thought that the creature glowed.

"It's walking to that point there. Let's go and meet it when it reaches the shore," Rose said. The stag walked with its broad side to them and seemed intent on reaching a tree with particularly bulbous low-hanging fruit.

Freja stood without a word and stepped lightly with Rose in tow until they found themselves shaded from the moon under the canopy of the tree. The stag, less brilliant from this vantage, neared and showed no signs of noticing the women.

"I don't think we will startle it," Rose said.

"I've hunted great beasts and average game for longer than your ancestors have existed," Freja said. "It knows we are here. It's simply unafraid."

Rose reached to a piece of hourglass-shaped fruit and pulled it free. She stepped into the water to meet the stag with it stretched out in her palm. It dawdled out of the shadow beneath the canopy and stood in front of Rose. She heard Freja gasp behind her as they both came to the truth simultaneously. The stag's left side, the one they'd seen when it had first appeared, was the picture of vitality, while the right was a grotesque menagerie of rotting flesh and bone. Rose resisted the urge to wince at the sight and kept her hand outstretched. She could see the animal's lung fill and expel the air as it sniffed the fruit from where it stood far above her.

"Steady, Rose," Freja said.

The stag reached its neck down and opened its mouth, one side a permanent grin of bloody teeth, the other perfectly aligned ivory. It took the fruit and ate, one eye twinkling at Rose as it ground the fruit to pulp and juices, which fell from its half-formed stomach into the water to stain its purity.

"We don't know why we are here, but we think it's to meet you," Rose said. She reached to run her hand along the animal's fur, and it greedily accepted the touch.

"I don't know what this is, Rose, so be careful," Freja said.

She made to take a seat and reached down for purchase, but the root she'd hoped would anchor her came loose in her hand. The goddess had one moment to realize what she was holding before flinging it into the forest and plugging her ears. Her warning to Rose was drowned by the screams of the mandrake she'd freed from its slumber.

The guttural sound it produced raked Rose's mind, but she found she could bear it, if just barely. The stag reared on its hind legs and flailed its head in response. Parts of its remaining flesh sloughed off and plunged into the water as it sank from the surface to stand in the shallows in front of Rose. Whatever balance had held its stasis between life and death had been disrupted, and the remaining pelt fell away in slabs.

"Run, Rose!" Freja said as she ran into the woods and feverishly used her heel to dig into the soil, creating a hole to kick the mandrake into.

Once in, she pulled the soil over the top of it and tamped it down, all while keeping her fingers in her ears. The cries softened and became whimpers before stopping, but the stag remained in torment.

Its other eye, now a dead socket to match its counterpart, emitted a red mist as it bore its stare down at Rose.

Freja didn't like the angle of gnarled antlers comprising the large headdress. She'd seen this posture before. "It's going to gore you, Rose. Get out of the water!"

Rose disobeyed, instead sliding below the surface. She swam parallel to the shoreline, hoping the water would slow the stag if it tried to catch her—or maybe forget her altogether. Water welled from behind her to indicate it was moving, and she correctly surmised the force was made by the stag giving chase.

She changed tactics and aimed for the shore, but the stag had caught her already. Its hoofs, having been aimed at her head before she turned, landed inches from her side. Rose turned her body to face skyward and looked to see the belly of the animal through the clear water, its heart beating slowly as if to signal it would soon be nothing more than an animated set of bones caked in gore. She could hear Freja's voice trying to ward the stag off her, but the water dampened the words of the goddess.

As though rising from a dream, Rose planted her feet and pushed herself up and out of the water, reaching just high enough to grasp the stag's ribcage from below. She hung on as it thrashed in the water to free itself from her.

"Hold on, girl," Freja said as she heaped soil atop the mandrake.

Rose instinctively gasped for air and thought of what to do. If she dropped, she'd be back in the same position to be trampled into the sediment of the shoreline. She couldn't hope to climb the animal, and even if she could, what good would riding on its back do for her? She looked up into the chest of the great animal and saw its heart give a stuttering beat before it stilled. Rose couldn't place her reasoning, but she was compelled to reach up and touch the stag's heart. There was something about the arrhythmic nature of it that called her to action.

As Rose's palm found the stag's vital organ, the beast went into a frenzy, but she held fast to its rib with her left hand.

"I want you to live," Rose said before finally being flung free of the stag and landing in the soft mud of the shore. Freja hurried over to lift and pull her to the denser trees nearby while keeping her eyes on the ground for more mandrakes. Rose planted her feet and refused to be easily moved.

"Freja, look," Rose said.

Freja gave one last tug, dragging Rose five feet up the bank before curiosity called her attention to the stag as Rose had bid. It no longer flailed but simply stared up to the moon. The sound of a newly beating heart reverberated through the forest, and flesh grew to hide its good work. Muscle grew and tendons appeared to tether them to bone while its pelt canvassed them at remarkable speed. Even the headdress of antlers reoriented from its chaotic riot of points into an elegant form befitting the creature.

"Don't you dare go back in there," Freja said.

"I don't need to. I think we figured out what Baba Yaga wanted us to," Rose said.

The stag looked to Rose and Freja and dipped its snout to the water to drink before stepping atop the surface once more and returning to its goal of eating fruit from the tree beside them.

Rose and Freja watched for a short time before leaving to return to Baba Yaga's hut. They made sure to mind the ground for mandrakes, but they made good time through the forest. Upon breaking into the small clearing where the witch had been just hours before, they were met with no sign of the little brown house stilted on chicken legs, save for displaced soil and flung undergrowth from it having taken flight.

Ω

Lilith commanded her remaining tengu to stand vigil outside of the gaping mouth of the cave she had claimed. Her nursery, nestled within the system of caverns in rural Kentucky, served to shield her children while they matured into the capable servants she required to press on.

Tchakyen had informed her long ago of the dire news that those she'd sent to the east had met with slaughter.

"Our numbers dwindle," he said, "and we've nothing to show for the losses. The shaitan and David spared none that ventured to the desert to destroy him."

Lilith skulked in the darkness and mulled the certainty that the boy she'd worked so hard to eliminate would soon come to extinguish her for her transgressions against him. He appeared unhampered by edicts governing the Host—as she was, after all—and what mortal would allow such transgressions against them to go unanswered?

The sounds of claws scraping stone and teeth rending flesh gave her ease despite the vulnerable state she'd found herself in. Buried beneath the churning mound of flesh her belly had become, Lilith struck a less intimidating figure, but Tchakyen maintained his bowed posture and received his commands with dignity before leaving the nursery.

After, she made the laborious journey to the night outside and lay breathing deeply of the cool air—the stirrings of those inside her ever present. Their number within this brood was large, perhaps the largest she'd ever held, and Lilith looked forward to the pain of delivery. Agony, always, and drawn out for what felt like eternity, but with each passing child, her power would grow.

It was here, while helpless, that the serpent came to her.

Lilith felt him there long before his tongue reached out to flick her skin. "And now he comes to lead me astray like he did my replacement. A pity, but I've already wandered off, little snake."

"How crass a welcome from the so-called mother of demons," said the serpent.

"Not so crass as you deserve, Lightbringer. Tell me, do you fulfill your namesake much these days?" Lilith asked.

The serpent held its tongue.

"At a loss for words? Why mock my name, then? I have countless children ready to be born into the night, but you dwell in the darkness these days."

"You will deliver tinder for the half-breed and his allies and little more," said the serpent. "We both know legions of yours will do little to even stall him if he comes for you. And why shouldn't he? You murdered his love, and it was your actions that led to the destruction of his mentor."

"What is your reason for coming?" Lilith asked. "I am tired. Tired of games, and tired of running out of life soon after stealing it from those who never deserved it."

"You're right. They don't deserve life," the serpent said. "They don't deserve their station within this creation, either. So let's you and I work together to finally let them find an end to their existence. Many will welcome it, no doubt. Pitiful things, they are. I'm sure you've seen the wonderful mess they've made."

"Oh, and you certainly didn't have a hand in that, did you, deceiver?" Lilith asked. "How will joining you bring me any closer to redemption?"

"We won't be redeemed. Redemption is a fairytale for children and the guilty. This is reality. What we *will* find is power," said the serpent. "He's quiet now, Lilith. The creator doesn't speak to the Host any longer. Their power has passed."

"Two derelicts don't make a right. We will simply fall together instead of apart," Lilith said.

"I've born sons. Yours found his power from my lineage," said the serpent.

"When I climbed from chaos to the veiled world, forging a path for the very first time, I encountered Sin," said the serpent. "We struggled then— Sin with the ignorance of my existence, and I with my resentment of Sin's power. Only after our struggle did we both find the merits of the other's existence and have been allied ever since. From that alliance came Death. And from Death, you bore Asmodeus."

"But he wasn't strong enough," Lilith said.

"Imagine what you, one half of the archetype of humanity, and I, the once brightest star of the Host, could forge," said the serpent. "Let us create another. One stronger than anything creation has ever seen. The antithesis to David's existence."

"To think you fathered Samael," Lilith said and realized Samael's strange power came not from the churning forge of a star, as it did for all other angels, but from the ever-devouring singularity born from one's collapse.

Such power was unfathomable. With it, she could overcome all adversaries.

"I accept your offer under the condition that the child will be mine to raise," Lilith said.

"Of course. A child needs its mother most of all," Lucifer said.

Lilith looked into the snake's black and unblinking eyes before he slithered away, but she was unable to see the smile he wore under his scaled lips. Soon, her screams of agony would rake across the surrounding hills as the precursor to her new children.

Ω

David stepped out of the terminal and spotted Chelsea leaning on her car, waiting for him amidst the usual bustle of people at the arrivals area of LaGuardia Airport. He noted the similarity of purpose between these travelers and the people he had been among overseas. No matter the culture or location, the world was filled with endeavoring humans.

Chelsea jumped up on the curb to embrace David. "I'm so happy to have you home," she said.

David returned the hug and gave his mother one more squeeze before letting go and entering the vehicle. "It feels good to be back together. How is Dodd doing?" The condition of the detective had been on his mind as he traveled.

"He's holding up, "Chelsea said. "There's still a lot we don't know about what's going on in his body, but the medication seems to work. We just need to find a way to get more, but he has a supply that should last him months. He's safe for now." There was a pause as she navigated her hatchback through the throngs of moving traffic to the expressway before she dispelled the silence. "He heals, David." Chelsea looked across to her son. "He heals like you. It's kind of a miracle."

"Seems so," David said, "but everything comes with cost. We just need to make sure that he is in the best position possible when the tax man arrives. And he *will* arrive."

They drove north through the trees and away from the city and discussed in more detail what each had been through over the past weeks.

It was after another lull in conversation that Chelsea decided to broach the subject of Rose. "Samael—well, Sam—he told us Rose is traveling where you were. You know, over there on the other side."

"She hasn't left my thoughts since she died," David said. "No matter what plan I tried to concoct to go over and get her, I didn't think there would ever be a chance to see her again before I died attempting them, but this feeling in me always left me somehow knowing I'd be together with her again. It's almost a pull. I need to find a way to get her back, if she's wandering in the veiled world."

"Even Samael would have trouble with that, or so he said. I'm still not so sure how much trust to put in these angels, but he seems to be trustworthy. Plays his cards close to his chest, though."

David raised his arm to grab the handle at the top of the window. It was a posture he had grown used to when he was a boy and had a lot on his mind. It reminded Chelsea of just how small David really was, despite what he'd become.

"I think I may have a way to get her," he said. "I'll run it by you, Leonard, and Dodd when we get back."

It didn't take long for them to arrive at Chelsea's home. David walked in to the sight of Leonard and Dodd busy in the kitchen, preparing an early lunch.

"Looks like your condition hasn't affected your appetite," David said. "It would've saved you and Mom a lot of money if it had."

"Looks like your travels haven't sapped that good humor of yours," Dodd said. "I'm glad."

David was pulled into a mighty hug before being released to shake Leonard's hand.

The four sat down at the kitchen table—Chelsea, Leonard, and Dodd with their breakfasts for lunch, and David with his tea. In keeping with their budding tradition, they discussed in more detail what they'd discovered before David said, "I learned something from Azazel out there. Something about how to harness the power inside of me."

Leonard listened with intrigue, and Chelsea could see the cogs turning in his capable mind.

"I also learned that I have an innate ability to alter time around me."

"That tracks, considering the tenants of relativity," Leonard said. "When you approach the speed of light, your mass increases, and so too does the gravity around you. This slows time some, but the inverse is also true. A massive object affects the space time around it. If what we've cobbled together about the source of power of the angels is true, then it's likely the gravity represented by the star you're housing or representing is somehow affecting the laws of physics around you."

"Explain it like I'm five, Lenny," Dodd said.

"Uh, David's power is super heavy and heavy things slow down time," Leonard said. "David can slide along that bent time to go between two points faster than physics should allow."

"Not all the way there, but I have the gist, thanks," Dodd said.

"Yeah, and if I can bend time enough, I might be able to recreate that portal that brought me back from the Leviathan's lair," David said. "It seems like it will take a lot of energy, though, and I was cautioned to keep myself from overdoing it. Iblis and Azazel are worried about that. Apparently I can burn out."

"So we will want to be sure we know where she is before you pull this stunt," Dodd said.

"That seems to be the skinny, Detective," Chelsea said and then looked to David. "What's this burning out business?"

"We can overdo it and explode," David said. "I wouldn't worry about it, though. I'm new and haven't tapped much into my potential energy, which is apparently pretty high."

"Young stars don't often go into supernova states, this is true, but be cautious," Leonard said. "At the end of the day, you're drawing upon the power of nuclear fusion. There's potential for an imbalance to occur, and that will spell trouble for you. Likely us, too."

"*Us* as in humanity?" Dodd asked.

"Yes," Leonard said. "You pose a similar risk, as well. Don't forget the meltdown at All Century."

"I didn't witness it, but it sounded pretty intense," Dodd said.

"If by intense, you mean Chernobyl, then yes, intense." Chelsea blew out a sigh and ran her fingers through her hair. "I'm put off by a lot of this, but I know if there's a way to get Rose back, we will be taking any and all risks. David, this isn't a situation where you plan to swap places with her, right?"

"No, because then I don't get to be with her, Mom," David said. "I'm planning on taking her back."

"This is not without precedent. Heracles ventured to Hades and returned. As did Er and Odysseus," Leonard said. "With myth coming alive around us, we shouldn't discount those stories. This may work."

"This feels more like Dante scouring hell for Beatrice, or maybe Persephone being liberated," David said.

"Boys, it doesn't matter the specific katabasis, what matters is the plan we have," Chelsea said.

"Kata-who?" Dodd asked.

David changed the subject. "Where is Samael?" he asked.

"He's off looking for you, apparently," Dodd said. "My guess is he got wind of where you were and is having a chat with your father."

David remained quiet for a bit before looking to his mother. "'Father' is an interesting word. It denotes a love or caring that the word 'dad' doesn't really hold. I thought of him as a dad when I was heading there to kill him. What I found in that lair wasn't an uncaring demon like Asmodeus, though, but a father. And not just mine. I truly believe he cares about humanity. Iblis, too."

"I don't remember much about my time with them, David," Chelsea said. "Arthur Silbi was a charming man—it feels weird that he presented to you in the form of a young boy. I suppose projecting an aura might be something of a specialty for that jinn. I have no recollection of your actual father, and I wish I did."

"He used you for his own means," David said, "which is very on-brand for an angel in my experience, but he seems to be attempting to right a wrong. Azazel is Prometheus. He gave us the means to destroy ourselves, but he also gave us the means to strive for more. Kind of like trusting a teenager with a car. It can go either way. He is trying to offset the meddling of the devil now, partly because he doesn't believe the pendulum of influence shouldn't swing both ways."

"What if the big guy upstairs finds out he's out of his prison?" Dodd asked.

"Uriel said the creator has been silent," David said. "I think it's just hanging back and leaving us to our own devices now, but who knows. I'm sure the angels will keep operating as they'd been before. They fear punishment."

"Rightfully so," Leonard said. "Crossing those orders has landed many in chains, or worse."

"And left some to freely meddle in the matters of humankind. I'm not a big fan of that decision," Chelsea said.

"Meh, people can be corrupted, or they can resist," Dodd said. "I saw all kinds during my time in law enforcement, Chelsea. We always have a choice."

Leonard was struck by how similar Dodd's opinion was to Samael's. Perhaps it was why the angel was enamored with the detective.

The four ruminated on this for a bit, until David stood to set the kettle to boil once more.

"Looks like the deck is being stacked more with every passing decade," David said. "War on education, war on reason, war on freedom of thought... They're winning. I say we help Azazel and kick things back in the other direction for a change. People need help."

"Spoken with all the fervor and ignorance of youth," Chelsea said.

"And the resolve of a hero," Dodd added.

"Don't encourage him," Chelsea said.

"Why not?" Dodd asked. "We have two bona fide supernatural heroes sitting right here at this weather-worn wood table, Chelse."

"You're still in the liability category, big shot, and he's still a boy,"

Chelsea said. "We aren't going to venture out anywhere to save the world."

"I never took you for a pessimist," Leonard said.

Chelsea leveled a heavy stare on the man, but he didn't blanch.

"Realist, Leonard. Not a pessimist or a fatalist, but a realist," Chelsea said. "Let's focus on getting Rose for now, shall we, boys?"

"I think I have a plan, but it won't be easy for us," David said. "I feel like you've kicked a hornet's nest with All Century, and knowing Brahman was involved with them points toward a much larger adversary. We will have to watch our backs for Lilith's horde *and* All Century now."

"I wouldn't worry," Dodd said. "We have an ace up our sleeve."

"I keep telling you not to rely on David as a trump card," Chelsea said.

"I'm not talking about him," Dodd said, shooting a glance at the end of the table. "I'm talking about Leonard. Guys like him are always saving the world."

PART THREE

A BURGEONING

CHAPTER TEN
BACKWARD PAWN

W e've got them under surveillance?" Blakely asked as he and Barbara neared the war room. His counterpart gave him a look that implied the question was almost stupid enough to go without answer.

"Of course they're under surveillance," she said, "but there's other things at play here—other pieces on the board."

"We know about Azazel's escape from the report on Brahman's death, but nothing about the boy. I know," he said.

"That's what this briefing is about," Barbara said. "We have to pivot to stave off any pushback."

Blakely laughed. "It's going to be about more than pushback. We've unleashed a celestial, Barb. This is going to change the world, and I doubt for the better. Moving forward, All Century will be focused on survival."

A set of double doors at the end of the corridor signaled the end of their private discussion on the matter. Barb gave Blakely a quick look as if to say *ready or not* and opened the door.

The table was filled with the usual people from within their organizations around the globe, with some in attendance virtually.

Two empty seats were available near the head of the table, at which stood a svelte man in a smart suit who held court using little more than a broad smile that unnerved both Blakely and Barbara.

"Mr. Sullivan and Ms. Cole," he said. "How good of you to join us. Please have a seat, and we will begin."

Blakely and Barb did as they were bid and exchanged one glance that transmitted the question on both of their minds: *Who is he?*

As if reading their thoughts, he spoke. "Some of you are curious as to who I am, and some have already made my acquaintance. My name is Flueric. Think of me as the former silent *silent* partner of All Century, who has been brought to the surface by the recent tragedies befalling our beloved Erik Brahman and Arnold Piper. Sordid affairs both, and the fallout from which could be quite damning for our organization."

"We're likely to be imprisoned if this makes it to the court of public opinion," chimed a director from Russia, being channeled from far away through a computer screen.

"That's one mindset, sure. A strategy comes to mind where we choose a patsy to take most of the flak and enter federal prison for the majority of his remaining life, only to be pardoned in a few years by a sitting president whom we will largely control." Flueric looked to Barbara. "Or *her*, for that matter. Wouldn't want you to feel excluded by your gender or have you thinking I'm not progressive. Hashtag NotMeToo." Barbara writhed under his broadening smile, and Flueric circled back to his point. "But that seems so boring, doesn't it? Does any one of you want to fall on the sword for the rest of us? I know I don't."

Another member of the meeting said, "Let's take that option off the table."

"Good," Flueric said. "I believe I have a better plan than the cowardly way out."

"What do you propose?" Blakely asked.

Barbara was somewhat surprised at his willingness to engage Flueric so soon after entering this space. Even the air in here felt smoldering, and Flueric reeked of something that was more off putting than his swagger.

"I'm so glad you asked, Mr. Sullivan," Flueric said and laid his palms on the table.

"Call me Blakely," he said. "I was the assistant to the president of operations in Connecticut."

"I know each and every one of you, Blakely," Flueric said. "What your functions within the company are and were, your greatest aspirations and hopes, the secrets you keep buried at the very bottom of the deep wells that you think are hidden inside of you, and what your function was in the development of the High Output Variant Attack Soldiers."

The statement was met with silence from the members of the conference and had no doubt been taken as a threat, though Barbara felt it was delivered as simple fact.

"We won't run from the news of Azazel's escape while we attempt to confine him. In fact, we will break the news ourselves. It's more than a matter of national security, after all—it's a global concern. There will be questions, of course. Heads of nations will posture and showcase their might to assure their people that they can deal with the threat, but they'll be lying, and most know it. Azazel could wipe out humanity in an instant if he chose to. There's no chance using conventional weapons against him. The fallen angel delivered those blueprints to them anyway, in a manner of speaking."

The members of the meeting sat in rapt attention.

"But what we can do is showcase our own soldiers and their ability to tamp down the threat. The HOVAS of All Century, who were commissioned by the heads of state in no fewer than three countries, could be used to defend humanity against the celestials. With this, we could turn the tables of perception to favor us. It was *us* who found and identified the threat. *We* are the only ones who may neutralize it."

"Do you think that will work?" Barbara asked. "Anyone with internet could dispel that notion and place us in the cross-hairs again instantly."

"True, true, but they won't. Has anyone been successful in making such an instant lobby for the truth work in recent memory?" Flueric's smile broadened, and he flourished his hands in the air like a carnival announcer about to pull the curtain back on a new monstrosity to wow a hushed crowd. "No, that won't work. We will have our own information flood social media and muddy the waters enough to keep anything from gaining traction. Let's take a lesson from some effective recent tactics we've seen."

"This could work," said someone far down the table from Flueric. It was followed by murmurs of agreement from others.

"We will need to work fast," Flueric said. "The completed HOVAS will be mobilized and brought together immediately so that we can showcase their abilities."

"Where?" Blakely asked.

"Well, right here in Virginia. Where better?" Flueric answered.

"You believe Azazel will attack here?" Barbara asked.

"No, but we can lure him here and neutralize him publicly. After that, the people and the world will realize our organization holds soldiers so terrifyingly capable that nuclear weapons will become obsolete. Imagine channeling the power of a celestial with the precision of a surgeon's scalpel, we'll tell them. *That* will change the world, my friends, and that is what we will do."

"How many soldiers do we have in total?"

"Roughly five thousand total, with only about twelve hundred of those being what we'd certify as battle ready. Though that's not considering meltdown complications, which will arise, Flueric," Blakely said.

"Easily explained away as Azazel's doing. Nobody knows the truth but us. We will keep it that way," Flueric said. "Ms. Cole, you will handle any issues that crop up within the US government. They tend to balk when wrested from power or the limelight. Expect them to move against us in some way, though I doubt that'll occur when they consider what the soldiers are capable of. They have some inkling already. After all, they've been heavily financing their development."

"Any questions from the stakeholders?" Blakely asked.

The room was silent.

"You'll all receive your assignments for this operation shortly. Do take care to avoid slipping up. Liabilities in this company seem to keep finding themselves dead," Flueric said and left the room.

Ω

Azazel and Samael sensed one another long before making contact. Each was known to the other and had been for long enough to dispense with pleasantries when Samael entered the small abode Iblis had maintained.

"He's off, then?" Samael asked.

"In more ways than one," Azazel said. "Likely been back with his group for the better part of the day by now."

Samael nodded.

"Growing tired of being a soccer mom for them yet?" Azazel asked.

"You'd think so, but they're remarkably unpredictable and some of them are quite funny. I'm rather enjoying it," Samael said. "How has David progressed?"

"He received some guidance, left with a crude plan, and likely he's steeped both in some vinegar on his travels," Azazel said and offered Samael a cup of tea. "I'd imagine he will be trying to recover Rose before confronting Flueric head on."

"That tracks with my thinking, too. Will he succeed?" Samael asked.

"In which endeavor?"

"Either."

"It's hard to say. His knowledge of contemporary science and the use of computing far exceeds ours, I'd say, and he'll be using that as a catalyst to reenter the veiled world, so I'd bet he has a good chance of retrieving Rose. As for Flueric, has anyone truly succeeded in dealing with him since he fell?"

"Fair point. I'd wager the odds are in the dark one's favor, and by a large margin," Samael said.

Azazel stirred the liquid in his cup. "He won't get far when Flueric becomes serious. It'll be a stroke of luck if the boy lives."

Samael stayed silent on the matter. "I believe I'll be venturing to Freja and Rose now. They need to be briefed on David's plan."

"Do you know it? He hadn't shared the details with me," Azazel said.

"No, I haven't seen him. Just his mother and her troop. But I've lived long and met many. I can patch together what David will do from knowing his capabilities and his vector. He will likely attempt to commandeer a powerful machine to be the conduit for opening a gate into the veiled world to retrieve Rose. That will be his first step unless Flueric or Lilith manages to confront him prior." Samael drained his cup of tea.

"I'm glad to be working with you again, old friend," Azazel said. "Good luck on your side of things."

"And you on yours," Samael said.

Ω

Rose turned her sapling plant around in the mead cup while she sat in her room at Sessrúmnir Hall. It had weathered the chaos of their encounter with the stag quite well, though there were some damaged spots on the leaves toward the top. This may have been the cause if its slower rate of growth compared to the remarkable germination, but Freja surmised that Rose's influence was only in effect for a short time, and the plant was now on its own.

The hordes from Valhalla and the Fólkvangr routinely clashed and returned, clashed and returned—a cycle that first appeared interesting but quickly took on a feeling of forced repetition.

As they tussled, Rose worked with Freja and some of the Valkyrie to try to gain a better understanding of her abilities, but, by appearances, it seemed there wasn't much mystery left. She could ignite a spark of life in things both big and small. Thus far, she'd seen no negative returns to her wellbeing by doing so. Being a seed of Rhea appeared quite straightforward in its nature—as did Rose herself.

It wasn't until Samael made an appearance at the hall that Rose found herself pulled from the monotonous routine.

"It is fine to see you grown whole again, Rose," Samael said. "You had us worried for a time."

Freja delivered the details of Rose's true nature to him, and it appeared the two had been speaking for a time before Rose had joined them. A feeling of being considered small and in need of protection enveloped her, much like when she chanced upon Dodd and Chelsea discussing her back when her normal life was just beginning to shatter.

"I am having an easier time rationalizing everything than I thought I would," Rose said. "It doesn't take long to adapt to things anymore."

"Not for you, anyway," Freja said.

Samael nodded. "You seem to have a tendency to glance past your strengths, Rose. Be proud of how resilient and resourceful you are. It's not common."

Rose returned a nod, and Samael smiled at how in character the gesture was.

"We've been hatching a plan in here," Freja said. "One that seems viable for getting you back to the other side."

"Oh, I thought that was impossible," Rose said.

"It is in the context of how many times it has actually happened, and how it's explicitly forbidden by the highest power we know, but the creator's been out to lunch for some time, and we think this will work out for us," Samael said. "It doesn't hurt that doing so *appears* to line up nicely with the creator's wishes. At any rate, all involved are prepared for retribution should we be found guilty of wrongdoing. That's the level of our resolve under Uriel's wisdom."

"I appreciate how much you are all risking for me and David," Rose said. "When we spoke the night I was taken, we talked a lot about feeling so small compared to this cosmic framework we've discovered."

"A single butterfly is small compared to the massive ecosystems on Earth," Freja said, "yet its influence is immeasurably important. Never forget that."

"I won't," Rose said.

"David is aware of your situation and some of your experiences in the veiled world, Rose," Samael said. "He aims to bring you back, and I think he has the capabilities to do so. Should you consider taking this journey, understand that it isn't without perils."

"That doesn't matter. I feel drawn to him more now than ever before. There's something growing within us, and it is crying out to bring us together. And Samael?" Rose said as her eyes leveled upon the angel of death's own. "Thank you for asking me instead of telling me."

Samael nodded. "This is your story, after all."

The three discussed the merits of their plan to bring Rose to the most probable location where David's portal would open when he managed to conjure it. They'd all agreed it would be nearest the edge of the field of battle, where the boy who was not just a boy had confronted Leviathan. Samael surmised that this would be a weak point since David had already ripped through there once prior. The sole remaining aspect that appeared to vex both Freja and Samael was the consideration of when to be there, to which Rose had simply said, "Don't worry much on that topic. Fate seems to be giving me a nudge when I need it. I'll know when he is ready."

Ω

David milled about at the end of the tour group while their guide spoke about System X.

"A state-of-the-art system when she went online in the early 2000s, System X—or System Ten—was among the most powerful computation systems in the world at the time. Now it has found a new place among our hybrid system of unified computers under TinkerCliffs, which we will see shortly," the guide said.

David reached out with his mind to find the computer and explore its abilities. He found that it was as vast and exceptional as the guide claimed. Comparing it to what he'd previously accessed since establishing a better understanding of his capabilities was akin to feeling the waters of a babbling mountain stream compared to a swiftly moving river.

"Are you getting what you need here?" Chelsea asked.

"Oh yeah," David said. "That and more, if TinkerCliffs is even half as exceptional as they say."

"Good," Chelsea said. "It looks like we have things figured, then."

"I'm not so sure about that," David said. "I need more power if I don't want to draw upon my own, and the nearest nuclear reactor is hundreds of miles away both east and west. I have to find something to tap into if I'm going to pull this off without risking sapping myself."

"Does it have to be nuclear?" Chelsea asked. "We're near coal country, after all. Power is power. I think we can get away with not going green on this one, kiddo."

David laughed. "It's megawatts I'm thinking of, in this case, but you're right. My mind settled on nuclear because it's much closer to how my power is generated than simply burning fuel. Fission and fusion, you know the deal."

"Somewhat, yeah," Chelsea said. "I get the idea. You'll have an easier time harnessing it."

David considered his problem, and how he hadn't figured out how to draw the power from a source even if he was closer to one, when a voice entered his mind.

Tesla was an eccentric, sure, his physics teacher had said, *but I defy any one of you to think of a great inventor who wasn't considered at least somewhat strange. It takes a unique perspective to see things the way they do, and that uniqueness appears foreign to many of us. Consider Tesla's plans to use the frequencies in rocks to deliver electric current wirelessly throughout the world to conductors that would then transmit the energy into viable power. Genius in its novelty then and now, but found to be unfeasible due to the high dampening in the earth itself. It would simply need too much startup power to get going.*

The concept had resonated within David, much like it had intrigued the world decades after Nikola Tesla had died.

The tour meandered to a large collection of servers in front of what appeared to be the apex computing system, and the guide said, "And here, everyone, is TinkerCliffs—itself a supercomputing system, but with a slight twist. This revolutionary computational marvel combines with the processing power of five other systems, and this is on top of its massively increased capacity compared to its peers and predecessor, BlueRidge. Simply stated, TinkerCliffs allows for unprecedented speed and utility for research and calculation that promises to propel our researchers to new heights."

David reached his mind toward TinkerCliffs and found himself swept within a raging torrent. In a matter of seconds, he was convinced of the merits of Tesla's theory and exploring how to pull electricity from the vast distances he required. Chelsea looked at his expression of concentration as the tour group glanced to the lights that flickered above their heads.

Ω

A cacophony of chirps and cries filled the southern network of Shenandoah Caverns in central Virginia. One after another, they took turns feeding at Lilith's engorged bosom to drain her of the vitality she had stored there. Some were quick to grow, and their feeding needs grew with them. These were left to explore the caverns and park beyond for other sources of food, but they all returned to the caverns and waited with their mother for when the time was right to venture out and find the one who'd destroyed their beloved brother.

She looked upon the horde skittering through the caverns and felt it was amongst the most powerful she'd delivered, if not the least diverse. There was a time when she'd birth few at a time, but their attributes and character made them easily distinguishable from one another. This brood lacked those traits that one day found their way into folklore and legend, but in its place was sheer numbers. For the first time since having dared to venture beyond the shadows, Lilith felt as though she was strong enough now to stake her claim on this realm and fend off the Host, should they choose to stand against her.

Tchakyen emerged from the darkness and knelt beside her. "They won't need much more time before they're all grown."

"I know," she said. Tchakyen cast a wary glance at her belly, and she added, "This one within me grows strong, as well. His power radiates through me."

The tengu pivoted in his stance and looked Lilith in the eye—a posture he took only when he was about to risk her rage. "Can you trust the one who sired it?"

Lilith continued to rub her belly. "No more than we can trust anyone besides ourselves. He has his agenda, and we are part of it. Count yourself lucky to have been scooped up into the fold of one so capable as he is. Otherwise, you'd likely be reduced to ash."

"I've put thought into that. The Host has left us alone even after we left the shadows to meddle with the mortals. I believe all we need worry about now is the boy. And after considering him, powerful though he may be, he has not sought us out even once. Might it be wise to leave him and his alone and continue on as we always have?"

"From the shadows?" Lilith asked.

"Yes," Tchakyen said. "The last millennia have treated us as scourge, but we were safe within the equilibrium of it all. Why risk our existence for more?"

"Because I was not made to serve, and I was not made to reach for crumbs left by the children of Adam. I am my own, and you are of me. We deserve more," Lilith said. Her round belly emitting a light that pulled the eyes of her children to her.

"I understand," Tchakyen said. "I will bring the horde to the meeting place soon."

"Not too soon," Lilith said, never taking her eyes from the glow coming from her womb. "Make sure their bellies are full before they move."

CHAPTER ELEVEN
DRAWING THE CURRENT

That one's easy. Clark Gable," Dodd said as he struck the stake into the ground with ease.

"Really, that's your choice for best lead actor of all time?" Leonard asked. "Brando, Wayne, McQueen... I'd even say Cary Elwes beats out Gable."

"Okay, first off, did I drive that stake in enough?" Dodd asked.

"Yup, it is the right depth we marked off on it. You can see the mark right above the ground here." Leonard pointed out the line they'd etched into each stake. "Let's drive to the next site."

The two walked to their mid-sized rental car and made their way to the next X on a map that Leonard and David had pored over for the better part of the afternoon while they fine-tuned the plan to draw electricity to an area where he wouldn't be risking people with his plan. One that involved tearing a hole in reality itself.

"Gable doesn't blow the others out of the water, but he has a presence on screen nobody else can match," Dodd said. "Maybe Brando, but he's always postured in his own way. Gable was a natural. And Cary Elwes, really, that's your rebuttal?"

"Oh, absolutely," Leonard said. "Even if it's just the one film, he owns it, and it's a masterpiece on par with *Gone with the Wind*."

Dodd gave him a crosswise glance before returning his eyes to the road. "Maybe I put too much stock in your IQ, good buddy."

"The next site is about three miles ahead and down that side road there," Leonard said as he pointed to the phone's GPS after referencing his map. "Pacino. He alone wins my argument."

"Same problem as Brando," Dodd said.

"Oh, I think he crushes your choice. Could Gable have elevated *Scent of a Woman* to the heights Pacino did? I think not!" Leonard said with a fervor he rarely expressed.

The two were interrupted by an incoming call from Chelsea.

"Hey, Chelse," Dodd said as he answered.

"How are you two making out?" Chelsea asked.

"Well," Dodd said. "We are just three stakes shy of being done."

"Have you taken your medication?"

"I doled out his dose an hour ago, Chelsea," Leonard answered.

"Good," Chelsea said. "Glad you're there to watch over him, Leonard. Sometimes I wonder if Brendan could don his socks properly without help."

"Let's take it easy there, darling," Dodd said. "I'm doing just fine. And don't put too much stock in my babysitter. His recent take on the legends of Hollywood has me questioning my stance that he's a genius."

"Pacino crushes Gable, hands down," Leonard said.

"Agreed," Chelsea answered.

"Okay, you two always gang up against me," Dodd said. "Go ask David if he's seen *Gone with the Wind*, Chelsea."

"I have. It's great, but they're right," David could be heard saying from the background.

"You're all terrible," Dodd said. He turned the vehicle down the side road and rolled to a stop when Leonard gestured for it.

"I'd love to continue this debate, but we're wrapping up and need to concentrate over here," Dodd said. "We should be rolling back into the hotel in a few hours."

"Good. I miss you," Chelsea said.

She'd been worried about Dodd's condition after his experience at All Century, but she had to admit, it was fantastic having him at one hundred percent again. She felt that twinge one gets when a lover has the energy to lift them until their head is in the clouds.

"I miss you too," Dodd said. "Love you, speak soon."

"Bye, Chelsea," Leonard said, and the two swung open their doors.

Dodd collected another of the stakes they'd constructed together with the help of a metallurgist eager to make a quick buck. The design was simple in concept, though Leonard's choice of metal shocked Dodd. Silver wasn't cheap, and David had said it was barely a better conductor than copper, but Leonard insisted. It took some of David's energy to churn enough of it up to coat the aluminum and steel rods they'd made prior.

"Right here should do it," Leonard said, pointing to an area free of debris.

Dodd lifted the stake and struck it into the ground to the mark with ease. His strength had taken some time to get used to and paled in comparison to David's, but he had to admit it felt great to wield many times the strength he did at the apex of his youth. Time between his medication showed that his strength only grew up until he took another dose, though he didn't experiment with this. The danger of losing himself was ever present, and the tiny voice in the back of his mind, so easily managed when he took the pills, grew along with his strength. That voice knew him, and he had a feeling it could be very persuasive if he let the volume get too high.

"Good job. Just one more to go," Leonard said.

"As you wish," Dodd said.

Ω

Sigrun and Mist flanked Rose on both sides as they marched to the mountain. At one time, it seemed perceptibly meager in the distance, but it now loomed incomprehensibly large as they neared it.

"Do you think this plan will work?" Rose asked.

"No," Mist said.

"Yes," Sigrun said.

"Okay, well then, which one of you is smarter than the other?" Rose asked.

The two Valkyrie laughed. "I'd wager that Mist edges me out in wisdom," Sigrun said.

"Ah, nuts," Rose said.

"Don't worry. I don't ever think the plans of mortals will pan out well," Mist said. "It's how they pivot when the dominoes fall astray of their path. Staying true when the chips are down is what decides victory. I have nothing but hope in my heart for you, Rose."

"I know," Rose said. "You've all been so kind since I arrived. Thank you for that. And I won't fold when the chips are down."

She had been in awe of the Valkyrie since having first laid eyes on them, but it was learning of their kind nature that made Rose love them. The winged women were fierce, but their essence derived from wisdom. Mist herself had helped Rose to practice using her gift for seeding life, though she was still unable to bring a living thing back to life once it had fully perished.

A feeling within herself told her that the power wasn't truly meant for that purpose, and she had given up on that pursuit. Instead, she cultivated her ability to *foster* life by helping it start. In this endeavor, she grew quickly, and under her care, the gardens at Sessrúmnir flourished like never before.

"Been some time since the last horn," Sigrun said. "We're due for a conflict."

"Aye, and we'd best keep Rose from it, should they pour into the field from the hall," Mist said.

Rose had witnessed many battles from afar when the warriors of Valhalla and Helheim presented themselves nearer the hall of Freja. She even thought she may have spotted Mukhulai dashing through the fray with the elegance David had described when he'd recounted his time training under him. Never once did she venture out to get a closer look, though. The Valkyrie had forbidden it, and Rose agreed. She'd doubted she would find herself resurrected at the hall if she was killed. Though technically dead herself, she was not of this place and had left her planned trajectory through the veiled world. It was too much of a risk to satisfy a silly curiosity.

"Where is Odin?" Rose asked.

The Valkyrie exchanged glances.

"The All Father has not shown himself in ages," Mist said. "It is not known if he still exists within our world at all anymore."

Rose stopped. "How could that be possible?"

"Keep moving. We will explain," Sigrun said, casting a glance at Odin's Hall in the distance.

"Long ago," Mist said, "Freja and Odin met near this very mountain and discussed terms for the warriors who would be chosen to dwell within their respective halls. Hel too was to receive a third, but she was not in attendance."

"So the story goes," Sigrun said.

"Yes," Mist said, "so the story goes."

"Why do the warriors come?" Rose asked. "David had his ideas about this being a place where they could dissolve their remorse over how they died and make themselves ready for whatever comes next, if there's anything."

"I have a similar theory," Mist said. "They are not ready to move on with the unfinished business they've been saddled with. A warrior's death seems so noble at times, but it is a harrowing experience to find one's self at the tip of a sword. Some die valorously defending others, while some exhibit extreme bravery and fall proving their own strength against another. Still more have been misguided into believing they are fighting for the correct cause, when in reality, they are the instruments of merciless destruction. All find their way here by the wings of we Valkyrie and must churn on through this construct conceived by one far beyond our ken."

"Beyond Freja's and Odin's, as well," Sigrun added.

"It just seems so cruel," Rose said.

"It does, but we've seen them merge with one another and grow," Mist said. "I take this as a good sign."

Rose clucked her tongue. "Like Bulwyf?"

"Yes," Sigrun said. "Many from our hall have had similar

experiences, as well. The numbers of warriors will even dwindle some until another conflict emerges in your world and delivers fresh warriors to feed the process."

"Odin struck his deal with Freja and then left?" Rose asked.

"No, it was sometime later," Mist said.

"Ages," Sigrun said.

"Well, at least an age, if we are considering it in terms of what an age is to us," Mist said. "Best to describe it to you that it was a long time since the agreement that he disappeared."

"Odin did leave some in charge of the hall for his absence, so I believe he left of his own accord and not due to something terrible having befallen him," Sigrun said.

"What could possibly threaten Odin?" Rose asked.

"Oh, the stories you know tell of immortal gods casting bolts of thunder and fostering civilizations, but we are all in this hierarchy of beings living in the veiled world, and we are all susceptible to being destroyed. It is merely the balance called for by the creator that keeps many of us from destroying one another."

"I see," Rose said. "The gods can die."

"If you choose to consider them gods, you may, but do not consider them to be beyond obliteration," Mist said. "Sigrun could heft her mace and lay me through seven layers of soil right now, and I may continue to exist—or live, as you might put it—but should she lay me low with enough fury and intention, I would perish."

"So too is it for me and all the gods, angels, and demons you have learned exist," Sigrun said.

Rose looked at the false sun that floated above the mountain as it struck its summit through the clouds like a spear through the ribs of a titan. She wondered about this and the meaning of the details of this place, the one she'd been plucked from, and the countless more that must exist out there at the ends of the many paths through the veiled world. *Is this all to get us ready for what comes next?* The thought loomed so large in Rose's mind that she chose to scrub it aside and concentrate on the task at hand.

"I hope I can see David again," she said.

"I've changed my mind," Mist said. "I do think this plan will work."

Rose smiled.

Ω

David settled himself between a large black oak and the honey locust tree nestled within its growing shadow. The sun made a final dash for the horizon at his back as he watched the colors of night invade the sky before him.

"You seem too smart to be planning an ambush," David said.

Tchakyen remained still. "We, too, enjoy the merits of a sunset."

"You also enjoy murdering innocent girls," David said. "We are not the same, son of Lilith."

The tengu released the branch and flourished its wings to land softly beside David. The boy didn't move. "My brother's actions are not my own, but I did not come to beg your forgiveness. I came to tell you of what has come to pass."

"Informing the enemy?" David said. "My friend Leonard speaks highly of your kind, the tengu, but I have my doubts you care so much for my safety that you'd tell me your mother's plans. Judging by your energy, you're in Asmodeus's seat now. Why visit me?"

"I am allegiant to Lilith. It is in my blood. But I am not acting against her by coming to you. She knows not what grows in her belly. It may consume her, you, and all of us."

"I highly doubt that," David said. "She'd need to have confided in someone more powerful than Samael to even have the chance to birth something like that."

Tchakyen took up a handful of dirt and let it sift through his rough fingers but said nothing.

"I see. I won't ask who, because I think I may already have a good idea."

"I thought you might," Tchakyen said. "I mean you no benevolence, David. I will continue to work to destroy you once we part ways, but should you find yourself in a position to destroy what grows in my mother's belly, do so—and I will do the same."

"Even if it means you'll be torn apart by your brothers and sisters?" David asked.

"Yes. She's my mother," Tchakyen said and took to the sky in the direction where night had risen. "I must look after her needs."

Ω

Blakely checked the numbers on his transfer reports and then checked them again. "We have enough medication for all of these units?" he asked.

"No," Barbara said. "There should be more shipped to us in two days, which is just before the shit will hit the fan when the units overheat, but it's what Flueric called for.

"Silent *silent* partner—I hate this bullshit," Blakely said.

"Didn't pipe up during the meeting, though," Barbara said.

"Neither did you."

"Shit no," Barbara said. "That guy is terrifying. Could you feel it? And the smell of him! It filled the whole floor. I'm quickly becoming of the opinion that Brahman made some deals with people far worse than he was."

"Like it or not, he's in charge, and we don't have any choice but to fall in line. It's not like we didn't know the stakes when we got started with All Century," Blakely said as he adjusted his glasses.

Barbara pulled a cloth from the breast pocket of her jacket. "Wipe that smudge off, or you'll be fidgeting with those things all night and driving me crazy." Blakely took the cloth and ran it over the lenses as the fog from his breath receded from the edges. "And it *was* and *is* for the money. That's why we do this. I don't think you'd claim different."

"No, I wouldn't," Blakely said. "Not many places we can make what we do at our ages. Angels and demons be damned, I'll retire clean when I'm forty-five."

Barbara nodded. "Do you think Azazel will really attack us like Flueric said?"

"Good question," Blakely said. "He might. It's his generals

and soldiers we've been sapping to make the HOVAS, but I can't understand why a fallen angel would choose to come to the woods in northwest Virginia, of all places, to strike an area where we have no facilities."

"No facilities we are aware of," Barbara said, "but you may be right. I do have a piece of juicy intel in my back pocket that points in a different direction."

"Put this back in your pocket and spare me the theatrics," Blakely said and handed her the cloth.

She took the cloth. "You're not as fun as you used to be, you know that?"

The two struck an odd contrast to the people walking by them in the small coffee shop at the late hour. Blakely, dressed in a smart, charcoal two-piece suit and wearing transition lenses tinted against the glow of his computer screen, and Barbara, wearing a two-piece clergy suit that clung to her figure in such a way as to belie a conservative nature that was offset by her outward sensuality.

"Well?"

"Chelsea Dolan, Leonard Barlowe, and Brendan Dodd are in Virginia," she said.

"Woah... Are you serious?" Blakely asked.

Barbara sipped her coffee. "Yup. Verified to be true. The troublesome trio is up to something out here. What a colossal fuck up it was to let them escape."

"Not so easy to stop someone who has been processed like Dodd was," Blakely said.

"Are we not mobilizing hundreds of them right now?" Barbara asked. "I think it would have been quite easy to pull off."

"Thousands actually," he said, "and that's a good point. There's something else at play here, and we aren't in on it."

"Thousands—but how?" Barbara asked.

"Overseas facilities have been producing like mad," Blakely said. "You've seen the state of the world. Our shareholders want to cash in when World War Three takes off."

"Yeah, after they've largely laid the groundwork for it." Barbara drained her cup. "Will we be ready so Flueric doesn't have us murdered? That's all I really care about, since we're pot committed at this point."

"Looking at these numbers, yes," Blakely said. "The units are mostly in position with a much smaller secondary group being positioned as we speak. But something's up. Never seen this code before. Take a look."

Barbara followed his finger down the list reading *Centuria HOVAS1, Centuria HOVAS2, Centuria HOVAS3*, and on. Near the bottom, just below *Centuria HOVAS 102* was the code *UHOVAS 1*. "What the hell could that be?"

"I'm not sure, but there will be up to a twenty of them positioned and ready to deploy on US soil within the hour. I sure hope Flueric knows what he's doing."

Ω

The angel of death found his seat on a high vantage overlooking a valley in Shenandoah National Park. He surveyed the positioning of containers housing the units of abominations Flueric intended to loose upon the world on this night. Freja emerged from the trees and found her seat beside him. She wore shining plated armor in lieu of her beatific robes. The golden chain running its way through a groove from her neck and down to the top of her boot radiated light upon the feathered cloak clasped around her neck.

"I see you've come dressed to play in the game tonight," Samael said.

"And you're as drab as ever," Freja said. "No sense of pageantry at all."

"Not my style." Samael nodded to the ants marching below. "They seem to have a flare for it, though. Very shiny."

Freja watched the vehicles complete the offloading of containers and enjoyed the symmetry of a well-organized effort. "There is true power in those glinting boxes. Especially that one." Freja pointed to the larger UHOVAS1 container. "That one would cause another flood from Ymir's corpse if the creator was watching."

"I think the creator *is* watching, Freja," Samael said. "Closely."

Freja nodded. "I'd bet Uriel would agree, were he here with us."

"His plan is with us. That's all we need," Samael said. "Is Rose ready?"

"Yes, she waits where the fabric is weakest," Freja said. "And I've another contingency plan, should we find that Flueric has tipped the odds too heavily in his favor." She tapped a bejeweled horn at her hip.

"Oh, I do love a good contingency," Samael said. "Can't wait to see it."

"Let's hope you won't have to," Freja said.

Samael smiled. "Flueric always tips the odds too heavily in his favor. He was the brightest amongst us for a reason. He contains the attributes of every archangel within himself."

"He doesn't have your power, though," Freja said.

"My power doesn't shine," Samael said. "It devours."

Freja laid a hand on his shoulder. "You've given humanity the chance to see another sunrise, my friend. There's light in that." She shifted her posture to see headlights nearing from a winding road to the west. "So they've come. I have wondered what David might be like now."

"I've thought about this, too," Samael said. "Through all of this, I still haven't met him properly. Uriel placed tremendous responsibility on the boy, and Azazel believes he will meet the challenge. We will see soon."

"Yes, tonight we will see."

CHAPTER TWELVE
SINGULARITY

Dodd drove their car to the point on the map, with Leonard directing from the backseat. He held Chelsea's hand in his right and slowed the vehicle to a crawl.

"We getting close?" he asked.

"Almost there. Another minute or two," Leonard said. "You should remember this from a day ago. We were already out here."

"We were also in a hundred other places planting metal sticks, buddy. I don't catalog things in my head like you do, remember?" Dodd said.

"Aw, all that angel juice in your veins, and you're still my big lug," Chelsea said.

Dodd smiled. "Not sure how to take that one, Chelse."

"It's a compliment," David said. "Stay alert, Dodd. Lilith's out here somewhere, and she's got something up her sleeve that's not on my radar."

"10-4, old sport," Dodd said.

They drove for a few hundred more yards before stopping at Leonard's word.

"Okay, it's time to make the donuts," Dodd said.

Chelsea watched her son leave the car and couldn't help but worry over his serious demeanor. He'd changed so much in such a short time—often listless and weighed down by the world. She walked to him and took his hand as they approached the large stake Dodd had slammed into the earth. "This will work, baby. She will come back."

David looked down before returning his eyes to the stake. "I can't anymore, Mom. I can't do this without her."

"I know," Chelsea said, pulling David into a mother's hug. "Leonard, get on over here and let's get started."

Leonard walked over with his hands in his pockets. "Well, it's like we talked about. You're going to sync up with the computer over at North Anna Power Station and set it to generate at full capacity. The overflow will be immediate, so you'll have to try to channel it through the ground and the stakes to come this way. I'm not sure how you'll do that, but you said you had it figured out."

"Yeah, I think I do," David said. "I practiced on a much smaller scale. I can see how the energy will run, and I can coerce it toward the next stake. Luckily, my father gave me a great crash course in conductivity when I met him."

"I bet," Leonard said. "After you've made sure you aren't melting down North Anna, channel from the Mitsubishi plant in the north. That, combined with what you have inside of you, should give enough power for you to do what you do. Though bending time to move faster than light and opening a wormhole are seemingly quite different things."

"They are," David said, "but it's like the difference between using a slingshot and shooting an arrow from a bow to me. Once you've had it in your hands, the subtle unnamed details become known to you somewhere in the subconscious, I guess. It's like throwing a ball."

"Ol' Lenny is more of a Minecraft guy, David, but I think we get the point," Dodd said. "I'll keep a lookout. You get started."

David nodded, and Chelsea and Leonard retreated to an area Leonard deemed safest atop some rocks a few hundred feet away. Grasping the stake, the boy who was no longer a boy reached out with his mind and met the radio signals of the North Anna Power

Station's computer systems. He rode through frequencies and dove through open ports to access the engineering and then control centers, flexing within the system. Feeling comfortable, he increased power generation within the pressurized water reactors. The system attempted an automatic shutdown when it noted an unprompted increase in power output, and David found that this had also occurred in 2011 when there was an earthquake in the area. He overrode the command and met no more resistance.

David then focused on channeling the power to the first stake. He felt it enter the soil, traced its path, and made it resist its natural inclination to disperse. The current became a serpent arching its way to the stake and moved on, as David willed it, to the second, and third, and fourth.

"It's a good sign that he isn't straining," Leonard said.

"Mmmm," Chelsea replied.

David increased the plant's power output to the maximum safe level the plant could handle and pulled the current along the path behind his first surge, as he'd planned. Safety was of paramount importance, and he refused to retrieve Rose at the cost of a nuclear meltdown that threatened tens of millions.

The speed of the electricity was barely affected by the odd course of conduction and Dodd, Chelsea, and Leonard saw the first current arc through the landscape and join the stake David held. The surge in power they expected never occurred, and David did not react as though he was strained by it. Chelsea and Dodd let out a sigh, but Leonard held his breath until the second—and larger—current reached through the hills to David. The stake glowed brightly under its power, but their design held, and David once again remained unmoved.

As if sensing Chelsea's concern, he shouted, "I'm fine, Mom! Everything is working. Dodd, don't get distracted!"

Despite David's worry of him watching the spectacle of current, Dodd had been focused on an oddity within his own mind. He didn't sense any of Lilith's children nearby, or at least not close by, but the voice in his mind that nagged at him grew louder despite him having taken the medicine on time. It sounded muffled but manic, as though it were shouting to the world outside. Dodd concentrated his senses on the surroundings to find out what was causing the uproar.

David measured the power he was pulling into himself as a conductor and knew it wasn't enough. He reached his mind to the Mitsubishi plant and began the processes to draw from it, now straining from being in seemingly three places at once and grappling with the will of the electricity. Still, he was within his bounds, and it took a mere few minutes for the first current to arc to him from the dark night beyond, and the second followed soon after.

Sensing that the plants would only handle the strain for so long, he shouted, "I'm ready. If you see any sign of me not having full control over this, you get in that car and drive like hell."

"Won't matter," Leonard said. "If he creates a singularity and it goes out of control, we will all be sucked into it along with what will amount to the entire solar system and those beyond. It'll grow and grow until it merges with the one at the center of our galaxy."

"Oh, quiet now, Leonard," Chelsea said, giving her friend a small push and then wrapping her arm around him to hold him close. "David will do it. He can do anything. Always could."

David reached his mind from where he stood to the point he remembered in Valhalla. Outwardly, the journey took him little time, but the retracement of his journey from Kharon's dock to Leviathan's mountain prison felt as though it took an eternity. All the experiences he'd had and knowledge he'd gained poked out from his memory banks, and he wished he had spent more time thinking of them.

Soon, he found the thinness in the fabric by feel rather than his imagined sight, in the same way a person could feel a canker in their mouth with the tongue while it eluded their finger.

Just a little closer to the fringe, David thought and pushed to the boundary so he didn't open a portal within the mountain itself, but rather just outside. Once satisfied he was on the correct spot, David pushed his location toward it and felt time and space bend. With great care, he funneled the energy he was receiving into a singular point from his end and condensed the atoms within it further and further until the area in front of him appeared to bend outward into nothing. At its center was a small dark mass that grew as David transferred the energy to condense the matter to many times more.

"Magnificent," Leonard said.

The mass grew until David could no longer rely on outward energy alone and pushed his own power into it. Flames erupted from him, and his face strained as the singularity grew, but both he and it remained stable as the two realities grew closer, until finally Chelsea could see through to the fields in front of Valhalla. The portal widened, and she saw the mountain, the clouds, and finally three figures growing larger. She realized they grew larger because they were approaching.

Rose, flanked by two women with armor and glorious wings, emerged from the portal, and Chelsea felt tears fall from her cheeks to the rich soil beneath her feet.

"Something's wrong," Leonard said.

"What could possibly be wrong? He's done it," Chelsea said.

Rose fell to the ground and looked at her hands, her form becoming translucent before her very eyes.

Ω

Rose saw David straining and cloaked in fire from the green fields she'd become so comfortable with. "Let's go," she said.

Mist and Sigrun followed her without word. She passed through the portal and felt a slight pull as though the very rules of creation were resisting what she was doing, but it lapsed, and she was released back into the world of the living.

Rose made to rush for David, but her strength left her legs the instant her knees flexed to propel her. She felt thin, and she fell.

"What is happening?" she asked.

"We didn't know what would occur when you reentered your world without a body. This is the unfortunate answer," Sigrun said. "I'm so sorry, Rose."

"Rose!" David cried.

"The poor boy has to watch her leave him twice," Mist said and looked away.

Rose heard the words from the Valkyrie and couldn't help but feel like a science experiment. The callousness of the beings from the veiled world was well storied in myth and legend, she supposed.

"Rose, get up, sweety," Chelsea ran to her but was called off by David.

"No, Mom. It's too dangerous. Stay back," David said.

The proximity to the singularity didn't seem to bother the Valkyrie, but he didn't think its effect would be so kind on a mortal's body.

Rose scrounged the world for purchase. *How do I stay? How do I stay? How do I stay?*

She thought of Freja and Samael and couldn't conceive that they would put her through this just to fail. Rejoining her in the belly of Ammit, housing her in Fólkvangr, taking her to Baba Yaga, confronting the stag— Rose thought of the stag and the saplings, and her salvation surfaced to her. She reached down and picked up a handful of soil, pulling it close to her chest as it sifted through her steadily fading spiritual form. She concentrated on the earth, from which she and all humans came, and placed her will into it.

David saw Rose grasping at the dirt and strained to keep the portal open. It snapping shut could have rended her in half.

He didn't despair—not yet. Knowing her nature carried with it a belief in her. He saw that she was putting her mind into a solution, and he concentrated on his part.

Ω

"He's done it," Freja said.

"They've done it," Samael said. "But that's only half of the hard part. Now comes Rose's last test."

Freja smiled.

Ω

Rose knew she couldn't will herself to remain here in this form for any longer than natural law would allow. She channeled her power as a seed of Rhea and caused the earth to sprout her form as she had the sapling plants and flowers before it.

The process wasn't strictly physical, nor was it magical, at least not to Rose, but a combination of many things all at once. The building blocks of an organism live within the seed, and that conduit made Rose's power easy to use. She simply accelerated and cultivated the process of growth and left a lasting piece within the plant to keep it strong. An animal was much more intense to foster. Each being utterly unique, even within the same species, and the elegance of how they are constructed, made for a much more difficult process. Still, by forced circumstance and quick thinking, she had handed life to a cursed stag while it tried to murder her. Rose was confident there was a way to conjure flesh from the earth.

The soil resonated in her hands, and the girl who was not just a girl felt it speak to her. No words registered, but a common intent, and both the earth and Rose conjoined in purpose. The ground lifted in granules around her to gently fill her vacating form. Leaves swirled to the portal and decomposed to create a slurry of matter. More and more life answered the call and found its way to Rose to provide the building blocks she needed to reconstruct her body, until the weight of her torso was familiar to her as she pushed it off of the ground.

Rose stood and sent her appreciation to the outer world for its aid in giving her form once more. She could feel its delight in her return. Something that before might just have come as a feeling of belonging or contentment now felt of communion, and she knew it was from finding her true nature in the veiled world.

Chelsea ran to Rose after shucking Leonard off of her. David raised a hand to ward both off. The power continued to flow through him and would take a small time to slow down safely, but he smiled at Rose.

"It'll only be a minute or two more," he said and mouthed *I love you* to her.

Chelsea, caught up with hugging Rose, didn't see Dodd running through the trees until she heard him casting timber to the side as he came.

"They're coming, David!" he shouted. "All Century is coming, and they have masses of troops. I think they're going to try and kill you."

David had assumed it would be Lilith's children he'd be contending with. All Century posed more of a mystery to him, but he felt the result would be the same. He'd annihilate them before they came within a mile of Rose and his family. "I'm shutting this thing down first, Dodd. I'll deal with them in a second."

David had been worried the power he'd receive from the nuclear power plants would not come near what he needed to create the singularity necessary to bend time to his will, and he was right. He had relied almost entirely on his own power, but the surge of electricity did afford him the ability to reliably generate it slowly and safely. His own power still spiked and surged at times as he grappled with the sheer magnitude of it, and having the birthing singularity to pour that energy into made this successful. Now he needed to shut the process down just as safely.

"They're still far out," David said. "This shouldn't take too long."

Dodd looked at Rose and broke stride. "It... it worked." The simple statement was all he could muster as he joined Chelsea in hugging her.

"Don't crush her, galoot," Chelsea said and squeezed harder.

Rose reached up and brought Dodd's cheek down to receive her kiss. "I am so happy you're okay. But you're different somehow. There's a fight going on inside of you."

Dodd simply nodded and looked away from Chelsea's probing stare. "It'll be fine. Let's deal with this first and me later."

Rose broke the awkward moment by nodding toward Leonard, who was shaking hands with Sigrun and Mist. "He's gotten bolder," she said.

"A little," Chelsea said. "It's nice to watch."

"Never underestimate what a dollop of recognition and esteem can do for a person," Dodd said.

The trio, reunited under the stars of a coming spring, held fast to one another and watched as the portal began to lose its definition and shrink in a moment too perfect to be lasting.

David registered Sigrun's actions first as she grasped Leonard and flung him through the air in the direction of the group. Dodd let the women go and leaped to catch his friend, who appeared dumbed by what had just occurred. Their attention being on Leonard, Chelsea and Rose looked back in surprise to see a man grasping Mist by the throat and forcing her to the ground, his eyes smoldering to illuminate a manic smile. Dread fell upon Chelsea in a way she hadn't felt since the night Asmodeus entered her home.

"Little toys. Pretty ones, but just trinkets. That's all you are," Flueric said and used his free hand to stop Sigrun's mace from its downward arc toward his skull.

"Leave them alone," David said. "You're here for me."

"Why do humans always make things about them? Me, me, me, me. It never changes, and it's so fucking boring. Why yours was ever put on a pedestal on equal footing as mine is still beyond me," Flueric said, squeezing Mist's neck tighter. Her grasp on his forearm loosened. Sigrun, frenzied from trying to free the mace from Flueric's grasp, refused to accept the futility.

Flueric pulled the mace, toying with Sigrun before eying David. "What makes you think I'm here for you?"

David concentrated on finishing powering the reactors down to normal output and was nearly done. The process was infuriatingly slow for him, given the circumstances. "If not me, then why?"

"Well, you were needed to conjure up this little ditty here," Flueric said. He cast Mist aside before turning to Sigrun, smashing her arm to the ground with ease. "I needed you to do something I knew I couldn't on my own."

Dodd resisted the urge to help the Valkyrie in lieu of ushering Rose and Chelsea behind him to where Leonard stood. He was thankful Flueric's attention hadn't fallen on them.

"Hard to believe you would admit that with your head so firmly embedded up your own ass," David said.

Flueric laughed. "I admire your own cockiness, Dolan. With everything you care about within my reach, you still mock me."

"Consider it a symptom of my youthful arrogance," David said. "I've taken your measure, and the way I see it, you fled from Azazel in that desert."

"I don't flee, little boy. I execute," Flueric said.

He reached his hand into the portal and grasped the slimming edges. His smile, already threatening to rip his face in half, broadened. The portal exploded in size and at a speed that made reality feel as though it whipped their consciousnesses like a rubber band snapping back to flesh.

David's eyes widened as he realized he'd lost control of the portal. But the last remaining dregs of power from the reactors ebbed, and he was free of his responsibility to it. As his knees bent to surge him toward Flueric and begin a contest of astronomical proportions, he heard the same desirous howl that had marked the end of his journey in the veiled world.

Leviathan had awakened.

CHAPTER THIRTEEN
THE WORLD SERPENT

Bulwyf left his chambers and walked through the corridor in a direction he had not taken in many calls of the horn that commanded those within the hall to their endless battles. Sarena, too, emerged but ventured opposite toward chambers filled with revelers and training. She had come to him to deliver the news. A rip in their reality had formed near the mountain, as they'd been told it would, and the time to act had come to pass.

Climbing innumerable stairs to the highest chamber of the hall, Bulwyf entered Odin's chamber.

"It has happened," Bulwyf said.

A single eye opened in the darkness and blazed azure at the large warrior.

"Ready the warriors."

Ω

Barbara saw the anomaly ahead just before Blakely registered it. "Is that the signal?" he asked.

Barbara kept her eyes on the blue skies and clouds seen through the portal as they contrasted with the deep night above it. "It has to be. Flueric said we couldn't miss it, after all."

"Couldn't miss that," Blakely said as he turned to the private army behind him. "Loose the HOVAS."

A man serving as what might have been considered a lieutenant in this outfit held a tablet in his hands. "Which units, sir?"

"All of them save the UHOVAS," Blakely said. "Flueric is the only one who has full command over those."

The trucks had maneuvered as close to the site as the terrain had allowed before Flueric left them. He had cautioned Blakely to follow his directions to the letter. "When you see the sign above the trees, let them loose. Set the program to Maraud."

That will make them kill every living thing they chance upon, Blakely remembered Barbara commenting. *All those without a chip, like our people have, yes. Every living thing without that chip is the enemy. Don't forget that.*

Blakely felt a surge of dread, considering the weight of his actions. How would he be judged if the HOVAS were never called back to their barrack units and left to continue their rampage unchecked? How would he judge himself?

Ω

Flueric stepped back and kicked Mist to the side. "Oh yeah, that's not closing anytime soon."

David watched the mountain through the portal as it began to crumble, the glow from Leviathan's green scales overpowering the natural light from above.

"What the hell are you doing?" David asked. "It'll destroy everything. Is that what you want?"

"No it won't," Flueric said. "It'll destroy *a lot*, sure, but not everything. What's left is what I'm seeking. Scores of scared and easily manipulated puppets. They'll fall over themselves to stand with me, and won't that just be the icing on the cake? The creator's experiment failing so spectacularly while he's out to lunch."

Dodd grasped Chelsea and Leonard by their waists. "Hold onto my shoulders so the speed doesn't give you whiplash," he said. Neither protested.

A moment of hesitation was pushed aside by David as he considered attacking Flueric, but the warmth of Rose drew him. He leaped to her and lifted her into his arms. Rose watched Sigrun rise from the ground to collect her mace and Mist, fly through the portal and back toward the field opposite the mountain, and disappear out of sight. She settled into David's grasp and reached around his neck, knowing he was about to move.

David and Dodd sprang clear of the area as Leviathan's head demolished the gates to her lair, and it breached the portal, entering the world of the living. Flueric stood beneath her, bathed in green, and smiled upon the world serpent—their eyes meeting for an instant before Leviathan's curiosity of his presence was outweighed by the freedom it had desired for so long. The monster snake smashed through the same hill that had marked the approach of David's electrical current and continued eastward with its impossibly long body continuing to follow through the portal.

Flueric laughed and danced beneath the waves of the serpent, only to step aside if its body would by chance come down to crush him.

"I know you have to go," Rose said as David set her down on the ground. "But give me this first." Rose pulled David into a kiss that he delivered all of himself to. No errant thought occupied his mind as his lips met hers, and he felt time slow to a crawl in their moment.

Dodd arrived soon after and dropped Chelsea and Leonard. He looked back at the spectacle behind them. "You aren't going anywhere," Chelsea said and hit Dodd's shoulder.

"You know I have to help David," Dodd said.

"No you won't," Chelsea said. "You're just dumb enough—and good enough—to go on over there and die. I'm not letting that happen. You stay here with me and Leonard and help me stop my stupid son from doing the same stupid thing you want to do."

"Well, he certainly has to do *something*, Chelsea," Leonard said.

"A mythical world-ending snake is cascading toward the Atlantic Ocean. If not David, then who?"

"He's still a kid, Leonard," Chelsea said.

"They all were. Draupadi, Perseus, Kundalakesi, Ivan Tsarevich—you know as well as I do that the young are always called to be tested," Leonard said.

"This isn't a fairytale!" Chelsea cried.

Leonard gestured to Leviathan. "Then why are we being inundated by them?"

"He's right, Chelsea," Dodd said. "If not David, then who?"

"One of these stupid angels. One of these stupid creatures from back there." Chelsea pointed to the portal, tears falling from her cheeks.

David and Rose approached them. "Don't cry, Ms. Dolan," Rose said, wiping the tears from her face. "It has to be us."

"How do you know?" Chelsea asked.

"Something happened to her over there," David said. "I can feel it."

Dodd patted Rose's hair, and she gave him a sideways smile that said she both loved and hated the gesture. "Rose is a super doodle now, too?"

"Not in the same way," Rose said. "I can't explain now, but I can help, I know that."

"I feel like that missing part of me is back," David said to his mother. "Rose and I are better together."

"Well, I already knew that," Chelsea said.

"Yup," Leonard chimed.

"It's different," Rose said. "I wouldn't have been able to pull my body together if David wasn't nearby. I can feel a difference here by him. It's like someone turned up my amplitude. I *sense* things more clearly."

"Exactly," David said as he watched Leviathan's body begin to thin as it continued to surge into their world. He looked to Flueric. "Now I'm going to head over there and sense that asshole right into the ground where he belongs."

"He's the devil, isn't he?" Chelsea asked. "I've never felt anything like being near him. It's pure malice."

"I think so, Mom," David said. "Rose, you should still hang back. I don't want you near when things heat up down there."

"I will," Rose said. "Dodd will look out for us up here. Lilith's children are stirring. I don't think they're close yet. Probably worried about being caught up in that thing's wave of destruction."

David kissed his mother's cheek, patted Dodd's shoulder hard enough to remind him how strong he'd become, and kissed Rose shamelessly before turning and walking toward Flueric—who continued to watch Leviathan. He surmised the snake's body, already countless miles long in its emergence from Valhalla, was somewhere in its latter half of emerging. If he could deal with Flueric quickly, he may have an opportunity to cleave the thing in half and mortally wound it by closing the portal, if such a thing was possible.

Flueric turned around at David's approach. "You took your time. I'm surprised. The boy I met just a little while ago would have surged over here to confront me."

"Look who's talking," David said. "You waited ages for me to come along and open this for you. It honestly wasn't even that difficult."

"Oh, don't mistake my not doing it for not knowing *how* to do it. Just remember, little scamp, there are some rules even I won't break." Flueric winked at David. "I don't blame you for not getting that yet. Not so old and not so wise, eh?"

"Sometimes wisdom gets delivered in large dollops, asshole," David said.

He leaped into the air and propelled himself into Flueric, remembering Azazel's skillful use of distance to keep him at bay. Flueric managed the contact with some strain and countered David with his own strike, which fell heavy on David's blocking arm.

"Hand to hand combat? How boring," Flueric said. "We're entities of near infinite power. Let's dial things up some, yeah?"

The sky did not cloud over or promise apocalyptic electric current, nor did Flueric emit a scaled down pulsar to fend David off.

Instead, the atmosphere around David became concentrated until he felt sluggish within it. Somehow, Flueric was adding density to the air, and David's speed fell as he blocked the blows Flueric rained on him. He tried to ignore the anger rising within him at Flueric's smile—which never faltered—and received Flueric's blows, crushing him into the earth. Somehow, he continued to throw attacks in response, but he knew they wouldn't meet Flueric by sheer will alone.

Rose steadied herself on the hill and tried to ignore Chelsea's anguished cries as her son was pummeled. Dodd saw to her, and Rose concentrated on finding her calm and reaching her will toward David, who seemed to find it and reverse his course of action.

Remembering Azazel's lessons, David thought of how Flueric might be concentrating the space around him by conjuring mass from his energy, since the two were counterparts. David focused on his own energy and moved to counter Flueric's. He found himself moving more freely, and it took only a matter of seconds to neutralize the trick.

"You're such a fucking nerd," Flueric said and opened his mouth to engulf David in flame so white hot that the boy didn't hesitate to dodge away.

"A fast nerd, though," David said, producing his own flames to bathe the devil himself. When they subsided, David smirked at Flueric, who had lost his own grin.

"You've got the nuts and bolts down, sure. But do have the toys?" Flueric said. He placed his hand at his chest and pulled forth a trident that appeared to devour the light itself.

David knew he hadn't gotten any closer to being able to wield the sword he'd used both to escape the veiled world and to free his father.

Flueric smiled appeared once again, and he flicked the trident with his finger. It hummed and resonated like a tuning fork. Rose, Chelsea, Dodd, and Leonard grasped their ears as the sound pulsed through them. The noise didn't bother Rose, though, so much as the disharmony it caused. The very beings that sang to her subconscious now cried out as they became malformed by the pulsing waves from the trident.

David's vision scattered, and when it refocused, he saw before him innumerable Fluerics.

One dashed at him and struck, but David deftly blocked, and the form fragmented and fell to ruin—but as it did, a cloud of smoke enveloped David. From within it, David felt the onslaught of thousands of fists all at once, and he fell to the ground. Reality had betrayed him, and David struggled to retain his consciousness after the onslaught. His resolve to protect those he loved from Flueric may have been all that tipped the scales in his favor.

Flueric laughed from infinite directions and at varying volumes and placements, furthering David's confusion. "Just one shot and you're down? Imagine if I'd thrown a second."

David felt a similar sensation of being hit in infinite tandem as Flueric's boot connected with his chin. It sent him flying to land within the light cast by the portal as it slowly shrank. He looked up to see Leviathan's tail finally emerge and follow through the channel the serpent's body had carved into the earth before it disappeared beyond them. He'd missed his chance to deal with it, but he realized he'd better focus on his current dilemma.

Flueric landed upon David's back, no longer holding his pitchfork. "You're just the same as all of them. A malignant tumor on creation. Remember your station the next time you dare to even think of yourself as equal to me." Flueric smashed David's head with his elbow. "I'll let the HOVAS deal with you." Flueric stood, brushed off the dust from his suit, and adjusted his tie. "They'll be here shortly. Quite menacing and bloodthirsty, they are. I can't wait to see what they'll do to your little girlfriend up there." Flueric turned and walked off into the night, leaving David to try and find his feet.

Chelsea made to run for him and, to her surprise, it was Rose who stopped her. "You'll die if you go down there," she said. "David is going to be okay. He's just depleted from making the portal and fighting with Flueric, but he's not in mortal danger."

Chelsea looked at Rose, her motherly instincts at odds with her compulsion to believe what Rose had said. The girl stood and appeared unafraid, so much wiser than her years should allow. "Okay, Rose."

Dodd pulled Chelsea close to hug her before she could protest.

"I'm going. He'll need a hand," Dodd said and leaped down the hill in bounds.

"He's going to get himself killed," Chelsea said.

"Probably," Leonard said, and Chelsea hit him in the arm.

"What?" Leonard protested. "It's true."

Ω

Dodd reached David as he was rising to his knees and looking to the tree line.

"You okay?" he asked.

"No, definitely not okay," David said. "Whatever he did to me is having a lasting effect. Imagine having vertigo and then multiply that by a thousand."

"Better think twice if you plan to aim any fire," Dodd said.

David seemed to consider this and reached his hand toward the trees. A jet of flame emerged at an impossible angle and hit the ground next to Dodd.

"Jesus, kid!" Dodd said.

"I guess you were on to something," David said. "I'm pretty neutralized, Dodd. Can you get them out of here?"

Dodd looked to the car, destroyed by Leviathan's coils as they'd slammed the earth. "Maybe if I take two and circle back for Leonard. I don't think he'll min—"

He was cut off by the glow of thousands of men and women walking to the edge of the trees, their skin smoldering with the latent energy of the creator's first children.

"Okay, plan B," David said and regained his feet.

"What's plan B?" Dodd asked.

"You all run, and I nuke this place," David said.

"Kid, you'd likely end up incinerating everything from Harrisonburg to Culpeper and killing thousands. No chance that's the way we do this."

David racked his brain for some solution and found only one. "Okay, then plan C."

"And that is?" Dodd asked.

"We fight them hand to hand," David said. "I can manage that."

"I have my doubts, but I think you're right," Dodd said.

David stood as the HOVAS poured from the forest, everything they touched smoldering. He tried to step forward, and Dodd steadied him.

We are going to die, thought the retired detective who had aspired for little more than fishing trips and jaunts with Ramirez and some family just months before.

Rose looked to the portal and placed her hand on Chelsea's slumped shoulder. "They're coming," she said.

The sound of the horn atop the hall of Valhalla rang so familiar to David that he didn't bother looking behind him to the portal. A simple smile crossed his lips. He knew.

Dodd *did* look, and he saw a wave of warriors race toward the breach in the realm behind them. Though the portal shrank, it happened slowly, as if Flueric had placed enough power inhibiting its collapse to ensure Leviathan had enough time to emerge fully. The warriors of Valhalla cascaded through and raged toward the HOVAS, whose own lust for violence matched their own. Dodd looked to cradle David from them as they approached.

"Don't worry. They're on our side," David said. The warriors rushed by them, some reaching out to slap David's shoulder as they did, and speared the middle of the ranks of HOVAS before spreading out to confront the line as it formed with military symmetry from the trees.

Dodd marveled at the number of people afflicted with his condition, especially knowing in his heart that many had undergone this change voluntarily. At least at first. The dark presence within him raged at his proximity to the same cosmic energy that flowed through him. He knew many of them had been cultivated at the facility where he'd been taken prisoner weeks ago. The number of warriors from Valhalla was impressive, but so many were ill-equipped to battle the All Century's super soldiers. Many were thrown into the air as soon as they met their adversaries. Others appeared confused when their mortal strikes met the abominable soldiers and appeared fruitless.

David stood on his own and looked ahead. "Let's level the playing field a bit," he said.

Using the same knowledge he'd collected from drawing the current from the power plants, and what he'd learned fighting Azazel, David closed his eyes and concentrated. Moisture coalesced, forming clouds above the trees from where the endless HOVAS emerged. He felt the friction forming and channeled the current in bolts of lightning to the ground where Leonard's stakes still made their claim. The current traveled through the ground and ripped apart the lines of HOVAS before dispersing harmlessly through the ground. It hadn't been enough to do critical damage to their ranks, but it gave the warriors from Valhalla time to regroup.

"New tricks, I see."

David faltered, and Dodd moved to steady him, but a hand grasped the boy's arm first. "My master told me to ever adapt or die."

"Yes, I also left you on firm legs," Mukhulai said. "Gain your footing. It will give my blades a chance to taste the innards of these fools." The dual blades glinted in his hands as though they'd just been forged.

"Here," David said and placed his palms on the blades. They appeared unchanged but sang beneath the sword master's palms. "This will help them have a chance to bite."

Mukhulai smiled and turned to the HOVAS. "It is a good day to die," he said and raced to the line.

Dodd watch as his deft skill allowed for the Mongol sword master to easily outmaneuver the soldiers of All Century, his blades doing the work the other warriors' weapons could not.

"Can you..." Dodd began to ask.

"Working on it," David said. The scattering he felt was subsiding, but he was still incapable of moving with any surety, and he knew joining the fray would endanger their numbers and his own. He concentrated on the weapons and tried to remotely imbue them with the resonance that would give them use against their adversaries. "I just can't."

Dodd felt the resignation in David and knew he was spent. He looked up the hill to see Chelsea, Leonard, and Rose. Her expression remained calm. "Your girl seems pretty confident."

"I can tell. I think she knows something we don't," David said.

Dodd watched as a horde of the greatest warriors the world had ever seen endeavored in a battle without any hope of victory.

Ω

Anguished at the abuse Sigrun and Mist had received from Flueric, Rose felt an underlying current of strength from it, as well. The Valkyrie were charged with her safety and nothing more. The act of saving Leonard must have been simply from Sigrun's nature. She wasn't surprised to see the Valkyrie take flight once their task was complete and she was in the care of her own, in the same way she wasn't surprised to feel Freja's presence here about them. She knew the goddess would play her hand.

The horn cut through the night and pushed the branches of conifers back with its power. It was Rose's turn to smirk as she watched the Fólkvangr emerge from the portal in disciplined columns and organize behind the warriors of Valhalla.

David and Dodd, still perilously close to danger, observed them. Dodd never faltering at David's side, ready to whisk him away to Chelsea and Rose should the HOVAS continue their advance.

The situation appeared dire from the hill. Leonard noted the number of warriors being dismissed back to the hall of Valhalla by the HOVAS and wondered at the hesitation of the warriors of Fólkvangr.

The sound of the horn faded, and its source, in all of her radiance, floated down from the sky, Samael at her side. The angel who'd done little more than keep pieces on the board in check now showed himself. This signaled to Rose a different pitch in the song of their struggle. The emergence of Leviathan may have changed things.

Samael landed beside Freja and reached his hands toward the warriors confronting the HOVAS. Rose felt a similar resonant singing as she did when David had touched Mukhulai's weapons, and she knew Samael was repeating the trick, but on a larger scale. Not sapped of power nor befuddled as David had been, Samael's work was quick and precise.

Freja's horn emitted two more short blasts, and the captains who were organized at the front of each column signaled the advance.

The effect was noticeable, even before the Fólkvangr met the fray, as the warriors of Valhalla were beginning to dispatch HOVAS they struck, but many more flooded through the trees. A resurgence in bloodlust pulsed through the forward ranks of warriors, and the Fólkvangr greeted the HOVAS head on as reinforcement to those they so often met on the field of battle as adversaries. Their knowledge of one another only enhanced their battle prowess, and the HOVAS were put on their heels. As they died, some disintegrated into embers, while others exploded in a fiery display.

Dodd surmised that the HOVAS were an unfinished product, after all, and they struggled to channel their celestial power while also keeping it from consuming them. *Flueric overplayed his hand in deploying them to dispatch David*, he thought. As the battle raged and the scales tipped in favor of their allies, Dodd marveled at the spectacle. The warriors of the realm of Fólkvangr, who bore the same name, and those from Valhalla vented their rage at how they'd died to aid humanity one last time.

Feeling secure in their position, Dodd looked to Rose and saw her frantically pointing to the large hill beside the warriors. He turned to see the landscape shifting as though alive, and he realized the piece of the puzzle he'd forgotten was now in play.

David didn't look as he shook free of Dodd's grasp. "She's arrived."

CHAPTER FOURTEEN
FURLOUGHED

Lilith felt joy as she watched her children crash through the trees to descend upon David and his allies. It was the closest to warmth she'd experienced since fleeing Eden.

"We are in a good position," Tchakyen said.

"You've done well. The children are in motion and won't stop unless I call them," Lilith said. Tchakyen nodded, and she added, "It's time for you to surpass your brother and bring me the head of David Dolan."

He looked at his mother and to her swollen belly, which now glowed in the darkness. He could smell the sulfur leaking from her pores. "I should not leave you. You are vulnerable here."

"I'm not," Lilith said. "I haven't been this strong in my entire existence. This seed in my belly grows and shares what it has with me." She pulled her hands from her belly and laughed. If not for the commotion of the battle below and the crushed undergrowth, she would have filled the forest with the sound of her joy. "Go."

The tengu turned and spread his wings. David was looking away from them and toward the portal as Tchakyen took to the air to finish what Asmodeus had started.

Ω

Dodd watched David totter in the direction of the portal.

"It's good you can walk on your own now, but don't overdo it," he said.

David waved him off. "We don't have the luxury of time to rest. I'm going to head to the portal, and I need you to stay here and handle something for me."

"What can I do over here?" David pointed, and Dodd's eyes glanced skyward at a dark shadow descending toward them. "What the hell is that?"

"That's your shot at redemption. Give him a taste of what you can do now," David said. "I'll be back in a jiff."

Dodd wanted to argue, but the shadow was almost upon David already. *Friggin' kid,* he thought as he leaped into the air to crash into the winged assassin. Dodd felt the firmness and size of the creature as his shoulder connected with its midsection, knocking it off course. The two landed and rolled to a stop at the end of a blistered path.

Dodd flexed his hands as he stood. This marked the first time he'd attempted to take his new body on a test drive, and so far, he found it handled well.

"I am Tchakyen," it said as it rose in front of him. "If you mean to stop me, I must kill you."

"I'm, uh, Brendan," Dodd said. "I guess you'll have to kill me, then."

Tchakyen did not advance immediately, perhaps hoping for Dodd to reconsider, and the retired detective wished he could. The sight of the tengu was mesmerizing, and by appearances, it would not be easy to subdue.

"I would prefer if we could talk this out," Dodd said.

Tchakyen looked to David, who'd almost reached the portal.

Dodd leaped to action, knowing it wouldn't leave David alone. *Well, I guess that's that, then.*

The tengu wasn't taken by surprise as before and braced for Dodd's impact. Despite this, Tchakyen stumbled back when Dodd's shoulder crashed into its own. Dodd jumped into the air and brought his elbow down near the crown of Tchakyen's head, but he was shrugged off by the swipe of a wing. He rolled to a stop and gained his feet.

The air stirred and both gave pause to look to the battle raging beyond them before turning their attention toward one another again.

Ω

"That idiot is going to get himself killed," Chelsea said.

"Which one?" Rose asked.

Chelsea looked from Dodd to David. "That's a good point."

"I'm going down over there," Leonard said, pointing to the edge of the fray. "I think I might be able to see something that can help."

"Oh, you're going to round out the hat trick of men who have no sense of self-preservation?" Chelsea said. "Why not just go wrestle the Furby that Brendan is fighting instead? Seems like your idea is just as stupid."

"That's a tengu, and I want nothing to do with it," Leonard said. "I'm being serious about helping. I know Brendan's condition and can maybe spot a weakness those shoulders have. I'm not sure if you've noticed, but there are thousands pouring out of the trees, and they outmeasure the soldiers fighting on our side by a few orders of magnitude."

"Don't forget the new platoon of jag-toothed weirdos flowing in now, too," Rose said.

"Yes, and that," Leonard said. "We are going to lose."

"Rose, I really hate when you egg them on," Chelsea said.

"We have to leave too, Ms. Dolan," Rose said.

"To David?" Chelsea asked.

"Yeah," Rose said. "He's going to need us, I think."

"Fine." Chelsea Dolan unclenched her fists. "Leonard, don't you die over there, or I swear I'm going to make David bring you back somehow, and then I'll kick your ass."

221

"Yes, ma'am," Leonard said. "Good luck." And he was off and running to the trees to survey what he could.

Rose grabbed Chelsea's hand in her own and gave a squeeze before they set off toward the portal.

"Don't worry, the warriors will hold out longer than Leonard thinks," Rose said.

"Because they respect David?" Chelsea asked.

"No," Rose said. "Because they have been steeped in valor."

Ω

David shuddered at the familiar sensation of passing between the world of the living and Valhalla. A cursory glance at the shattered mountain took his mind from the task at hand. The Leviathan was loose in the world. By now, news organizations would be reporting the impossible occurrence of it passing to the east and on to, presumably, the Atlantic Ocean. From there, who knew what it would do.

He smelled the air and looked back at the portal. It was still fading slowly, but he didn't want to chance being trapped here once again.

Each step called on David to focus entirely on the act of walking. If he managed to fulfill his plan and somehow escape alive, he intended to devote all the time he could to unraveling the mysteries of Flueric's power, but now was the time for piecing together his perceptions. The turf, green with a life glow entirely different than what was emitted by Leviathan's scales, scrolled by maddeningly slowly.

"Why don't you take a seat for a spell?"

David lifted his eyes from the ground before him and looked to who spoke. A man stood beside what appeared to be a massive inkblot with fur. He wore armor, but not a full set, at least not that David could see with his patchwork of vision. One detail he could tell with some certainty was that the speaker had long pointed horns.

"I don't have time for a break right now," David said. He shuffled his feet onward in what must have appeared to be a feeble attempt to the wayward warrior from the hall.

"We will make time," the man said. He walked to David and took his arm to guide him to his seat without malice.

David knew he would not make it to the crags in the earth forming ahead that signified the emergence of what he had called the "ghoulies." He sat with a sigh and gripped the grass to find his center.

"That's good. You were never lacking in grit, but knowing when to stop is important." A snap issued through the air, and soon David heard the familiar sound of Heidrun's bell. "Let's have a drink and take the measure of things."

A hazy form of the massive goat came into view and stopped at the warrior, who knelt before it. David reached out and felt Heidrun's fur, running his fingers through the goat's beard, much to its satisfaction.

A cup was pushed into his hands.

"When we feel the world around us shattering, the reality moving in waves, it's best to grasp the framework and start from there," the warrior said. "Drink."

David smelled the mead and thought of Freja, whom he surmised helped to guide Rose back to him. He recalled what she'd said about Heidrun's owner not liking to share his mead.

"Do you own this goat, sir?" David asked.

The wind stirred.

"I don't adhere to the concept of owning another conscious being, such as Heidrun here, anymore, but I do keep her and the Læraðr tree she so enjoys."

"Then I might have an idea as to who you are. Sorry for not making your acquaintance while I stayed in your hall, Odin."

"How could you have? I wasn't here. Bulwyf did deliver up the incidentals of your short stay. You did well, but we knew you would. You are one who thrives in the desert, as is your counterpart."

"Rose?" David asked.

"Yes," Odin said. "A fitting name for a beautiful girl with thorns to bare for those who mean her ill. She is who I speak of."

"I get what you are talking about now. The counterpart thing. Her being nearby is all that's keeping me moving." David drained his cup and held it out. Odin took it and turned to Heidrun to fill its volume once more.

"Drink."

David took a smaller pull from the mug than the first and let the warmth pull his mind and body from tension. He'd thought relaxing his concentration would undo him, the patchwork of twigs holding him together set to tumble upon the forest floor, but the mead worked its magic once more and pulled him closer to the truth.

"There's a reason they call this stuff and its cousins *spirits*, I suppose," David mused.

Odin laid a heavy hand on the ground and lifted one toward the sky. "Mayhap there is a reason, though altering the mind without discipline is a holiday. You are not on holiday, David."

"No. No, I'm not."

I need you to dig into your mind and remember the ferryman. Do you remember him?"

"Bob Ross? Of course I remember him. He taught me how to paint those happy little trees," David said.

"Are you being glib, son?" Odin asked.

"Yes," David said.

"That's good. I'll need to know if you've been struck daft," Odin said. "Don't be glib. You are not on holiday."

David continued to drink his mead until the last drop flowed through the serpentine path from the cup to his throat. He placed the cup on the ground. Odin reached for it, turned to Heidrun, and then turned back to David. This time he placed the cup in front of the boy on the ground.

"What did the ferryman show you?" Odin asked.

"He showed me how to see through the murk," David said.

"What is the murk, boy?" Odin asked, his tone of voice sliding from gentle guidance to demanding.

"The murk is what hides the truth from us," David said.

"How does it do that, David?" Odin asked.

"It keeps the light from traveling between us and what we would like to know," David said.

"Did you lift the murk and see with the ferryman?" Odin asked.

"Yes," David said.

"Then do so again. Your light isn't traveling out of you anymore. You can't find what you seek. You merely need to remember the words of—"

"Bob fucking Ross," David said.

David scoured his memory for the feeling of lifting the murk on the boat with Kharon as he crossed the Styx. He recalled the rivers and the images of those in both the veiled world and the world of the living. He felt how his mind connected to his latent power and pushed the cloudy nothingness aside to let the light shine through, and he pulled his will to task to do so again.

"That's it. Don't press against the murk. Cast through it," Odin said.

David saw the cosmos once more in their infinite size and recognized that they were nothing more than a marble compared to the big picture. There were infinite cosmos astride their own, all flexing and grinding against one another. Flueric had blurred his perception of what was real by allowing him to feel those other realities as he felt his own. David knew he had been straining against this.

"Drink."

David reached forward, grasped his mead, and drank it until one sip remained.

"You see?" Odin asked.

"I see, yes," David said. "Or I guess it would be better to say that I understand. What I don't understand is why you are helping me."

"Because we all exist to push back the darkness," Odin said.

The master of Valhalla stood and strode toward what David could clearly see as a boar and mounted it. He rode toward the portal, and David watched him leave, wishing he had seen his face before taking the last sip of Heidrun's mead and standing on two firm legs.

Ω

Dodd had enough outer awareness to notice Rose and Chelsea scoot past them by the tree line on a trajectory toward the fading portal, but Tchakyen's fierce strength occupied most of his attention. The tengu was no monster. A monster is mindless and menacing, enigmatic and beyond understanding. Tchakyen was intelligent and calculated.

A wing flicked out and glanced Dodd's arm as he blocked, throwing him off balance before Tchakyen's clawed hand came careening down from a blind spot to gouge his eyes. He was lucky to dodge.

The voice in his mind, ever growing in fervent rage, was not what distracted him, not yet anyway. He was completely present and in command of his somewhat newfound abilities. He was losing because despite his training as a younger man in hand-to-hand combat, his understanding of how to dodge and counterstrike, and his much-increased speed and strength, because Tchakyen was simply more skilled than he was.

He thought of letting the power inside him grow, as the ifrit demanded he should, but he knew that the demonic consciousness would vie for control if he opened that Pandora's box. Dodd would rather fight and die in control of himself than allow some dark passenger to attempt to do the deed for him.

"Hrupp!" Tchakyen bellowed as he kicked Dodd through the air, the only saving grace for the man being that he hadn't anything behind him to crash into. He rolled on the ground to devour the energy of the strike he'd taken and stood to see his adversary was no longer in front of him.

A twig broke to his left, and Dodd swirled to confront a strike, but none came. He saw a stone had been cast upon the stick from above. Knowing he'd succumbed to Tchakyen's misdirection, Dodd curled himself into as tight of a ball as possible while maintaining his footing. No strike came.

Instead, he heard the ring of claws contacting a steel, a sound so pure it could only be generated by steel given name *tamahagane* by its creators.

"Tengu yo, tabemono de asobu no o yameru toki ga kimashita. Anata ga watashi to odoru toki ga kimashita."

Tchakyen snorted and pulled his claws back from the samurai's blade.

Dodd knew two things in that instant. He had just been saved from being mortally cleaved by his opponent, and the person who'd saved him was speaking Japanese.

"Do not worry, large friend of David. Jubei has asked for your blessing so he may challenge this…" Boris paused. "What do we call this thing, Lapochka?"

"It's a tengu," Mina said. "At least, that's what Jubei called it. He even knows its name. Must be a bigwig."

Boris turned to Dodd. "Jubei wishes for your blessing to fight the tengu. Do you give it?"

Dodd did not hesitate. "Yes. He may certainly challenge it."

"Junbi wa dekimashita ka?" Jubei asked.

"Watashi wa itsu demo junbi ga dekite imasu… Watashi ga shinu made," Tchakyen returned.

The two squared themselves to one another.

"What are they saying?" Dodd asked.

"Jubei told him to go and lay with his own mother," Boris said.

Mina slapped him. "They agreed to fight. They are going to begin. I am Mina, by the way, and this idiot is Boris. Boris, fire your rifle at the glowing red things, please. If you couldn't tell, we are struggling out there…"

"And your rifle is broken? Perchance you dropped it?" Boris said.

Mina laughed.

"You're David's friends from Valhalla," Dodd said. "It's kind of trippy to meet you in person."

"We saw you assisting David and angled to come help. I don't know how you know him, but we are definitely in his corner," Mina said.

Boris nodded but kept his attention on Jubei and Tchakyen, who'd begun circling one another.

"He's lucky to have made such good friends," Dodd said.

"You're one of them. He wouldn't have made it away from this monster without you," Mina said.

"Kare wa kokoro no nai kaibutsude wa arimasen. Kare wa watashi ni keiiwoarawashite au," Jubei said.

"Yes, we know. He is an honorable abomination," Boris said.

"You understand him?" Dodd asked.

"Yes, we all know one another's speech despite not knowing the language," Mina said.

"It is complicated, but it is simple," Boris said.

"Yeah," Dodd replied, scratching his head.

Jubei was content to allow Tchakyen make the first strike. Boris knew this was due to Jubei having watched the tengu's battle strategy against Dodd, but he thought the creature may use different tactics against his friend. For one, Jubei had an armament, and for another, Jubei reeked of skill. He dared not convey this to his friend, though. Jubei would not stand for it. Mina, Boris, and Dodd were to stand vigil over this conflict and ensure that no others interfered. That was Jubei's wish.

Tchakyen let loose a howl and raked the floor with his claw to cast a dust cloud before pumping his wings to send it at Jubei.

The samurai did not move—with the exception of closing his eyes.

He felt the air pulse with vibration as Tchakyen twirled through it to land on all fours to Jubei's left, and the samurai maintained his composure. He remained as motionless as a marble statue. It was only when the tengu believed his opponent had been disoriented that it came within striking distance to claw at Jubei's heart.

Two of Tchakyen's fingers were severed in an instant that felt to the creature as a breath of wind, and Jubei stood squared against him once more, but with his eyes open.

Mina whistled, and Boris cheered. Dodd simply stood with his mouth agape.

Jubei had timed his strike so perfectly that it was hard to discern exactly what had transpired in that fraction of a second. Once Tchakyen's arm reached toward the samurai's arm, within a foot of its goal, Jubei had slid his rear leg out in an arched semi-circle while bringing his blade down over the claws to deflect them and then changing direction once more to glance the biting edge of the sword skyward to sever Tchakyen's fingers.

"He's unbelievable," Dodd said.

"None can evenly match him, other than Mukhulai," Boris said.

"Don't forget David and Sarena," Mina said.

"Oh, no one else?" Bulwyf said.

Dodd was surprised that the giant had managed to approach them without his notice. He had become especially attuned to how difficult it was establishing stealth with a large frame, even before gaining celestial power within him.

"We rarely count you. You are our, how do you say..." Boris said. "Alpha?"

"Yeah, it goes without saying," Mina said.

"You two need to return to the fray," Bulwyf said.

Boris and Mina both looked to Dodd.

"I'll make sure nobody interferes," he said.

The two soldiers returned to their higher vantage and began to take long shots across the field of battle.

"So, you're the colossal Viking who tried to cut David in half before fostering him?" Dodd asked.

Bulwyf chortled. "The very same."

Dodd saw a figure standing in the shadow of the Viking leader.

"Couldn't hack it, eh?" he said.

Dodd felt a familiarity in the voice and turned his full attention from the battle for the first time to look closely behind Bulwyf. The figure stepped into the moonlight. He appeared pale with broad shoulders and peppery blond hair, but Dodd knew the man's eyes the instant he saw them.

"Ramirez," Dodd asked.

"Not quite," he said. "Not anymore, anyway. But yes."

Dodd remembered David's explanation of how the souls of the warriors fighting in the fields may merge due to mysterious circumstances. He reached out instinctively, and his friend, or the portion of the man standing before him that was, grasped it in the familiar way he'd come to know as they worked together over the years and missed terribly after they'd been separated.

"I looked for you. There hasn't been a day that's gone by that I didn't think about you," Dodd said.

"I know," he said.

Bulwyf leaned toward them. "It is time for us to return to the fray."

Dodd felt a pang of unease. He had so many questions, but most were answered by Ramirez's presence in Valhalla.

"I hope you found peace," Dodd said.

"I hope you find it, too," Ramirez said.

Dodd was left to watch as Bulwyf and the amalgamation of personas containing his best friend returned to fend off the creatures who threatened humanity.

Ω

David rose and cast his cup to the side. He tried to balance his will and his body and found that he was working to attain a goal he'd already reached. His senses had returned.

A cursory glance toward the portal showed that Odin had departed swiftly.

Permafrost glinted in the sunlight ahead of him, and he walked toward it before remembering himself. David leaped the distance to its edge.

The ghoulies of Helheim were climbing to the field in scores and finding no adversaries before them. They meandered about in a pitiful manner without anyone to assail.

"*Hey,*" David called to the pit and beyond. "This way."

He stepped backward and listened to the sound his heels made as they compressed the glazed grass.

The creatures all turned toward him with eyes wanting of purpose.

Yes, this way...

"He's on his feet!" Chelsea said.

"Shhh," Rose said.

David looked to his side and realized he hadn't fully regained himself. If he had, he'd have known the two people he cared for most were within spitting distance.

"You have to get back," David said.

"Not without you," his mother said.

Rose looked to her and then to David and braced for what she knew was coming.

David leaped to them and scooped both in his arms before leaping once again toward the portal that had reached a size that reminded him of what may happen should it close fully.

"Aghrehh," Chelsea said as she was wrenched into motion.

"We had to come," Rose said.

"I know," David said and paused to turn back and make sure the creatures were following. Scores of vacant eyes and moving claws affirmed things were going to plan.

"When we go through, I am going to toss you to Dodd," David said.

"Okay, but he's fighting something," Rose said. "He might not be able to catch us."

Chelsea continued to reach for purchase as she bounced on the shoulder of her son, who was moving beyond record marathon pace.

"Okay, then I'll take you with me," David said. "I need to guide these things to the center."

"Yes, to flank the monsters, who are flanking with—" Rose said.

"Monsters," David said.

CHAPTER FIFTEEN
HONOR

Leonard peeled branches from his path with as much delicacy as he could while he maneuvered to the rear of the line of HOVAS. He hadn't known exactly what he was searching for when he left Rose and Chelsea, but the quiet afforded by his travels allowed him to think.

These things are raging torrents of energy trying to take over their hosts. There has to be some means of controlling them.

He saw lights glowing in the distance and chose them as his goal.

A command center needs light.

Sidestepping heaps of leaves and errant branches, Leonard crept closer until he could see the clearing beyond the brambles.

"Our stock is declining much faster now."

"Do the drones give any indication why?"

"The drones were shot down the second they passed the tree line."

"Goddamnit, Barb. We need to consult the captains."

"I did. Their messages are that the HOVAS were suddenly falling, and then that an outside contingent had reinforced them."

"Outside contingent?"

"Their words."

"Fucking Flueric. Like letting us know what he'd planned would hurt us in some way rather than help us..." The man turned to look behind him at the container labeled UHOVAS.

Leonard observed how they consulted their tablets as they discussed their situation. He had no doubt now that the HOVAS were being controlled remotely. If David could somehow reestablish himself, he might put an end to this mess.

"What's the rate of loss?"

"Beyond sustainability now. The data from the drones showed a finite number of opposing forces, but the drones were lost before they could deliver anything on the reason for the shift. My guess is it's Azazel."

Leonard watched the man look at the woman and once again at the container.

"I don't want to do this."

"I know."

"He'll kill us if we don't."

"I know."

Leonard saw the door of the container opening. Oily smog drifted out just seconds before he smelled the sulfurous ichor. He'd learned what he needed to know, and it was time to begin his delicate dance through the foliage back toward safety.

Ω

Jubei leaped into the air and twisted his body so that Tchakyen's strike would be blocked—and the momentum afforded by it put to good use. He spun to the ground and let his blade move forward to strike the tengu's heel.

Dodd could hear the creature's angered response, but it continued to use Japanese, and he couldn't discern more from the words than their emotion.

The samurai remained stoic in his repose despite the tengu's increasingly frenzied approach to the battle. Dodd assumed that he, in his current state, was much stronger physically than Jubei, but he would last fractions of a second against the master swordsman in a duel. To think David had bested this man in armed conflict was baffling.

Tchakyen reeled and dug his clawed feet into the ground before pumping his wings, using the wind to bully the samurai off balance.

Jubei took the blast of air and switched his stance to the same wide-legged crouch he'd used against David in their duel and waited.

Dodd saw the writing on the wall. The tengu was primed to use all four of its powerful limbs to lunge at Jubei and attempt to overtake him with sheer speed. His wings would work to his advantage here as well. The samurai looked to have put himself in a position to take on this attack head on. Dodd felt a surge of adrenaline only known by those watching a contest teetering between life or death.

Tchakyen did not howl as his muscles tensed and he surged forward, but his expression showed he would be holding nothing back. As he hurtled toward Jubei, the sword master leaned his torso forward as though to spear the tengu. Tchakyen flared his wings and gained altitude, meaning to rake the man with his claws and end the contest, but Jubei turned his torso and arms with such agility that Dodd was left to wonder how any human could bend that far and still have the strength available to move with such speed.

Jubei's shoulders pulled his sword so the blade faced the sky and continued his push until it met with Tchakyen's chest. The tengu couldn't match the samurai's reach and flared his wings further to pull away from the biting sting of Jubei's katana, but not before the swordsman flipped his wrists and extended the strike through Tchakyen's midsection.

The tengu curled upon itself in the air and landed on the ground in a rolling heap before taking purchase on a single knee. Dodd thought it would surge at the samurai once more, but Tchakyen's expression faded from rage to realization.

He'd been bested, and his body held a mortal wound.

Jubei flicked his sword but did not bother cleaning or sheathing it. He exchanged words with the tengu, who knelt and labored to breathe while clutching his stomach.

Jubei bowed.

I'll be dipped in shit, Dodd thought. The warrior wasn't going to finish the job.

Jubei turned to Dodd and pointed to the portal, which had nearly escaped his attention as he watched the battle, before sprinting back to the fray of warriors beyond them.

Dodd looked and saw a hazy figure finding clarity as it drew closer to the portal from the other side. He gave a cursory glance to the tengu, who was trying to regain his feet, before watching as David surged through the gate.

Before Dodd could figure out what was happening, David screamed, "Dodd, think fast!"

David had thrown something high in the air toward him, and Dodd's eyes widened as he recognized Chelsea's screaming.

Damnit, David.

Dodd leaped into the air and grabbed Chelsea. "I gotcha, I gotcha," he said.

"I'm going to beat his ass when this is over," Chelsea said.

"I'll make the popcorn for when Rose and I watch," Dodd said.

The two landed, and Chelsea's eyes widened. "He still has Rose!" They looked to the sky to see her flying toward them.

"What the hell, kid," Dodd said, placing Chelsea on the ground before leaping for Rose. She found a niche within his arms as easily as Chelsea had, and Dodd concentrated on landing. "You were okay with this?"

"He knew you wouldn't drop us," Rose said. "Take it as a compliment."

Dodd smiled as the two landed near Chelsea.

"Where is that thing going?" Chelsea asked.

Dodd looked to see that Tchakyen had found his feet and was shuffling by in front of the portal back toward where Lilith's children had emerged before joining the fight.

"Back to Momma to lick his wounds," Dodd said.

The portal, now showing it had mere minutes left to remain opened, began to surge and morph as countless creatures emerged to follow after David as he ran to the battlefield.

Tchakyen had only a moment to see them marauding toward him before he was trampled. The tengu didn't make a sound, and Dodd felt a pang of sadness for the creature despite everything.

David reached the mass of Lilith's children, causing chaos at the rear lines of the Fólkvangr, and stopped in place. He waited for the ghoulies to be within paces of him before leaping through the air and out of harm's way. Their momentum carried them into the backs of monsters, caught completely unaware.

The creatures of Helheim had joined the fray.

Ω

Tchakyen's life ended with a miserable acceptance that Lilith felt in her marrow, and although she screamed into the forest, none heard or cared. The one who'd earned the title of "Mother of Demons" once again felt doubt creeping up inside of her. She collected herself and marched through the trees alone, save for the one growing within her.

The battlefield looked much as she'd expected, but her children were struggling between an odd assortment of monsters she'd never seen before and a rear facing line of well-trained soldiers. They were meeting slaughter, and many were breaking from the contest to flee into the trees and forests beyond where they'd often found succor in isolation.

Flueric's promises of glory and a stake in this world disintegrated before her eyes. A feeling of dejection so familiar to the one she'd felt when she had left paradise overtook her, and the one emotion that remained was a pettiness she intended to point toward revenge.

Lilith looked about the fray and saw the girl she'd ordered Asmodeus to abduct just months before. The quaint thing stood aside the carnage, and to Lilith's surprise, appeared to be looking directly at her.

She raked the claws that had once been fingers across her legs and let the pain draw her from the feeling of having been victimized. Lilith left the safety of the forest to inflict harm on David the only way she knew how.

Ω

Leonard continued his slow progress through the trees with growing anxiety. Unlike when he'd made his way out to spy on All Century behind their lines, now there were monsters crashing through the woods and away from the battle.

They weren't numerous, per se, but frequent enough to keep Leonard hiding behind trees and holding his breath to ensure he was alone before making progress a few paces at a time.

The sound of something falling through the canopy above and landing nearby caused him to crouch to the ground, shocked. The dust settled to reveal David had somehow found him.

"Leonard?" David said. "What are you doing out here?"

"I was coming back from seeing if I could learn something from the other side. You scared me to death," Leonard said.

David walked over and threw Leonard over his shoulder before making his way back toward Rose, Chelsea, and Dodd. Leonard hadn't been hefted like a child in some time, and the utter lack of control he held in the situation was a mixture of relief and defilement.

"I saw that from the look on your face," David said.

"The Lilith demons are running away," Leonard said. "I guess that means we are doing well out there now."

"Well," David said, "I made a decision to unleash a horde of creatures that'll kill anything they can reach. Not sure what I'll do when they run out of bad guys and are left with just our guys, but so far, so good."

Leonard remembered David recounting the creatures who'd been banished to Helheim for their involvement in battles on the side of what he'd consider to be evil.

"That is a bit of a pickle, yeah," Leonard said.

David's presence seemed to clear the forest before them of any creatures who might have considered Leonard fair game. They progressed through the trees quickly.

"Did you get any good information by risking your life for us?" David asked.

The recognition of some bravery made Leonard feel as though he'd been seen.

"Yeah, actually. All Century is controlling the HOVAS using chips to send commands," Leonard said. "Not that it matters anymore. You can probably burn them all out in a second now that you're back."

"Well, there are two problems with that," David said. "One, I'm not *back*. I don't know if I can channel that kind of power right now without killing all of us, too."

"You might just need more time to get settled. What's the second problem?" Leonard asked.

David sighed. "They are people. It feels like massacring them would be the same as me walking to the front lines of a conflict between two countries and wiping one out. I don't think I have the authority to just murder people. I don't *feel* like it's something I could ever do."

Leonard thought about how Dodd had been shackled down to the table for his experiment and then considered how many subjects were truly willing given that All Century could control them using a tablet. It was possible—likely, even—that they were not all willing participants.

"You're right," Leonard said. "I'm glad you have such good morals."

"Thank my momma," David said.

"I will," Leonard said.

"Plan B," David said. "I have enough going for me to take over All Century's computers. I'll just take away their control of the HOVAS."

Leonard felt relief when they broke through the tree line and sprinted directly toward his friends—all of whom were alive.

Ω

"There are catastrophic losses from each unit now, and we are out of HOVAS reinforcements."

Barbara scanned her handheld screen in a frenzied display Blakely knew only emerged when she was panicked.

"Let's wrap this up," he said before pulling a radio to his mouth. "Move out the containers and equipment immediately. We planned for a removal in thirty mikes, and I want to see it executed seamlessly."

"He will kill you for that," Barbara said, her face bathed in strobing light, signifying each time a HOVAS was going offline. "He is going to kill all of us."

"Probably," Blakely said. "But if he doesn't, I don't want All Century implicated in any of this damage out here. It will be noticed. It will also be noticed that this is where that massive fucking monster emerged from. The company won't survive that kind of heat."

Men had swung into action while the two discussed their situation, and the sound of containers being lifted by hydraulics onto truck beds filled the night behind them. Blakely and Barbara both looked to the ones labeled *UHOVAS*.

Barbara's cell rang, and she checked the screen before answering: *Unknown Caller.*

"It's time for you to let out the big boys, Barb," Flueric said.

"I... Do you know the current situation? We are being liquidated of inventory out here, and the enemy is likely to be upon us soon," Barbara said.

"I can hear your heart beating through the phone," Flueric said. "You're scared. That's understandable. I didn't convey the true goal of this exercise to you or anyone else. Things are going exactly as planned. You were never going to be reclaiming HOVAS at the end of this. We are liquidating outdated technology. Release the UHOVAS."

"But—" Barbara protested. Blakely looked to her with growing concern.

"Release them and then retreat to safety. You won't be reclaiming the UHOVAS either. This is the last directive," Flueric said, and the call ended.

"What does he want?" Blakely asked, the look on his friend's face enough of a clue to Flueric's command.

Barbara turned to the container. "He said to release the UHOVAS and to continue the retreat. No units are to be reclaimed."

"That's insane," Blakely said. "There's no way we can leave these things running through the wilds. They have our damned tech in their heads, Barb!"

"So do the HOVAS, and we can't possibly hope to reclaim them now," Barbara said. "If we let the UHOVAS out, we will buy time to make a clean exit."

Blakely considered their situation and landed on his conclusion. "Don't, Barbara. Please."

He was answered by the alarm that signified the imminent release of the UHOVAS.

CHAPTER SIXTEEN
LOUSING THE SYSTEM

David watched the battlefield and marveled at the skill and prestige of the warriors he'd once trained with. The abominations they fought, both man made and denizens of Lilith, were fierce. To continue to hold them at bay was nothing short of miraculous, and David felt pride at what humanity could accomplish—albeit with some extra time to practice in some supernatural form.

He reached out with his mind behind the broken lines of HOVAS to find the radiating signals from All Century's computer systems. He found it disconcerting how much more difficult it was to navigate through this system than it had been for the one governing the nuclear power plants. Private security coffers plumped up by the military budgets made for much more intricate programing. David explored the nuanced encryption methods and found pathways to the command network governing the HOVAS. It was a marvel what he could store in his brain after having used TinkerCliffs to gain a complete understanding of modern coding methods.

"All right, here goes," David said.

Leonard, Chelsea, and Dodd looked to the battlefield, while Rose kept her attention to the side.

David disengaged the control function on the HOVAS and then focused on dismantling the code that had been used to maintain control of them in the first place. He didn't want All Century to reclaim their ability to turn these things into soldiers again. At least, not tonight.

Dodd saw what looked like a glitch. One moment, the glowing monstrosities were destroying everything they could, and the next, all of them simply paused. Having regained free will, most made the decision to continue, but a contingent of the HOVAS raised their hands and attempted to remove themselves from the fray. The battle, having reached a fevered pitch long ago, didn't allow for many to escape, and they were overwhelmed by the raging warriors easily before being left on the ground to be consumed by the fires they'd been imbued with. Some did manage to find their way to the fringes unscathed, however, and appeared capable of controlling their energy in a similar manner as Dodd.

The advantage leaned away from All Century, but now the remaining HOVAS simply faced slaughter as they became more disorganized, and the sound of Freja's horn called through the night once more.

The entirety of the Fólkvangr turned their attention on the remnants of Lilith's children and the raging monsters from Helheim beyond them.

"That answers your question of how to handle them, David," Leonard said.

"Yeah, seems so. Mom gets a little fiery about the likes of Freja and Samael, and I get it. They meddle, but they don't leave us hanging out to dry," David said. "Speaking of meddling, did any of you see a big guy on an even bigger boar ride through the portal before?"

"Nope," Dodd said. "I was fighting a tengu, and then your samurai friend saved me. I also met Boris and Mina. Bulwyf, too. But didn't see a big horned dude." He paused for a moment. "Chelsea, I also saw Ramirez. Well, sort of."

Leonard and Chelsea both shrugged, and she turned to Dodd. "Really? As one of them?" Chelsea pointed to the warriors, and Dodd nodded.

Rose brought them back to David's question. "I saw him. He came through the portal just before Ms. Dolan and I made it through. He kept on going down the path that Leviathan made."

"That tracks, I guess. He talked to me over there. Got me back to square," David said. "I didn't get the chance to see him while I was messed up, though, and something about him is irking me."

"What?" Rose asked.

"He seemed familiar, that's all." David looked back to the battle as its tempo continued to decrease and appeared forlorn. "I wonder how many of them have flicked back to their halls. There's so few out here now compared to the start."

"It was a battle of attrition," Leonard said. "Truth be told, I wondered if they'd blink out of existence when the portal closed, or if they'd be trapped here."

"They would probably go back," David said. "There's a plan laid for them that's much more stringent and firm than anything anyone involved in this could challenge. Even Flueric. So that's my guess."

"Finally, be strong in the Lord and in the strength of his might," Chelsea intoned. "Put on the whole armor of God, that you may be able to stand against the schemes of the devil. For we do not wrestle against flesh and blood, but against the rulers, against the authorities, against the spiritual forces of evil in the heavenly places."

"I thought you were skeptical of the good book, Chelsea," Dodd said upon hearing her quote from the book of Ephesians.

Chelsea dug her toe in the dirt. "In order to be a cynic, a person has the onus to be educated on the topic. I don't have a problem with the book itself, but what it's been used for."

David hugged his mother. "Yeah, mom, he's the devil, and he's real. I also think his scheme has been in the works for a while. That's why Uriel set us in motion like he did."

"Well, why can't the angels fight him and leave us to deal with"— Chelsea hugged David closer—"human problems?"

"If you think back and remember the stories, he seems to be heavily involved in lots of humanity's biggest issues. I think it's always been our job to deal with him, honestly," David said.

"On that day, the Lord with his hard and great and strong sword will punish Leviathan the fleeing serpent, Leviathan the twisting serpent," Leonard said. "We have to deal with that, too, now."

"That is one issue we might have some more direct help with," David said. "Odin chasing it down seems to point that way."

"I can't figure what the endgame of letting Leviathan loose is, but I'm sure we can gain some insight from Samael," Rose said.

"Or Azazel," David said.

Chelsea looked to Leonard and said, "There's one thing we don't need them to explain to us, and there's no need to sugarcoat for you. Leonard and I have both read the book. Leviathan being released is part of the apocalypse."

Ω

Blakely was now the one desperately scouring his tablet for some form of control over the HOVAS. Their number, declining steadily before, was now plummeting. He didn't find this as concerning as the fact that he no longer had the ability to control their ranks on the field. Before, and despite having lost his eyes in the sky, he would bolster declining groups with reinforcements to buy them more time to clean up their camp and get out. Now he was incapable of doing anything.

"Blakely, I can't direct the UHOVAS," Barbara said. "They're released, and I can't send them out there."

Blakely looked at the containers and saw a gnarled hand emerge and grip the side. Acrid smoke poured from the flaring embers pock marking the thing's flesh.

"He didn't—" Blakely said.

"What?" Barbara asked.

"The UHOVAS," Blakely said. "That looks like what happens when the eggheads decrease the meds on HOVAS to the point where they melt down. Happened a lot during the experiments. I think Flueric let them reach the tipping point. Maybe he found some kind of equilibrium just before they explode, but I didn't think that was possible. Those things are the same as the monster that melted down the facility in Connecticut. But that was just one. How many are in there?"

"I think that container could possibly hold twenty. Not more than that, given the size of them," Barbara said.

"Let's get the hell out of here," Blakely whispered as he watched the emergence.

Barbara took Blakely's hand and drew him back, away from the sight line of the UHOVAS. The creatures had turned their containment unit into a smelter as they emerged in a fog of acrid smoke, and she hoped it would shield them from being spotted quickly.

Blakely looked back one last time to see the monsters first lumber and then run to the forest toward where the HOVAS had been engaged. A small feeling of sadness welled in the man as he thought of what he'd wrought on the world before he left the scene behind him.

Ω

"Where are they?" Chelsea asked.

Leonard looked at her, taking his eyes from the spectacle of warriors cleaning up the dregs of their enemies. "Who?"

"The bigwigs who always show up when the work's already done. The angels," Chelsea said.

"It doesn't work like that, Mom," David said. "They aren't allowed to directly interfere. We can never expect a legion of angels to come flying in to save us."

"A few of 'em sure danced with the line of interfering," Dodd chimed.

"And one was obliterated for his troubles," Leonard said.

Chelsea hoped the statement didn't cut into David too deeply, but she saw that he didn't seem as down at the mention of losing Uriel as he had in the past. She couldn't imagine the relationship he had forged with Azazel had healed the wound so quickly, but she thought better than broaching the topic at the moment.

"Those who directly interfere now are doing so because they believe this is what their creator wants," David said.

"*The* creator, by all accounts," Leonard said. "This journey with you has me thinking these supernatural beings at least believe there is a single unifying power or being they consider to be God. I've always noted the overlapping of myth and religions from across cultures, but to think they were true stories, at least in some form. It's baffling."

"You must be like a kid in a candy shop right now, huh?" Dodd said.

"I'd be giddier if the overlapping tales had something of a happy ending," Leonard said. "Chelsea touched on it before. The loosing of the World Serpent in Nordic tradition begins Ragnarök. The end of the world."

"Leviathan emerging from the sea is a sign of the apocalypse in Christian tradition, too," Chelsea added.

David looked away from them as he spoke. "All those stories are about a last stand between good and evil. If we can't count on the help of the archangels or their legions, then we will find a way to stand on our own. Don't forget that we were created just like they were. We weren't put here to be cannon fodder for their games. Rose can tell you better than I can, but there is power in humanity."

"The kid has a point," Dodd said, "but things are going to get real hairy when the world reacts to that thing. It'll be a while before we know just what humanity is still capable of bringing to the table after the chaos ensues."

"Nobody believes in anything anymore," Chelsea said.

"It's been a long time since anyone has seen a miracle, after all, so maybe it's time to give them one," Rose said, breaking her long silence, her statement casting a spell of contemplation on the others.

It was David who dispelled their thoughtful silence. "I need to rally them for what's coming. Rose, will you be able to face her alone?"

"Face who?" Chelsea asked.

"Lilith. She's almost here."

Rose turned to David and reached her hand out to his. "I can."

"I won't leave you again."

"Neither will I."

Ω

Mina and Boris had rejoined their compatriots on a field of battle so unlike the ones they'd been called to for what felt like an eternity. "So this is America, Boris. How do you like it?" she asked.

"It feels the same as my homeland. Could be that Boris just feels at home being back here on true soil," he said.

"We may find ourselves back again in some form or another, one day."

Jubei had come to stand with the two, and they watched as the warriors from their hall celebrated their victory while the Fólkvangr continued to round up the soldiers of Helheim.

"That may be. It's a nice thought," Mina said.

Jubei was the first to look to the sky and smile, just seconds before David leaped into their circle. He wasted no time embracing his friends.

"I can't thank you enough for helping us," David said when they finally separated.

Jubei, Mina, and Boris all gave their versions of a bow, with Mina's looking more like an aw-shucks.

Jubei surprised his friends by unsheathing his sword. "It was an honor to go to battle in this manner and to give you aid, David."

"You aren't planning to duel him again or something, are you?" Mina asked.

Boris pointed to the trees as they shone with a familiar glow that signified a coming wave of HOVAS. "The fight is not over for us, Lapochka," Boris said.

"It never is," Mina said, chambering a round in her rifle.

"This is different, guys," David said. "These things aren't some sci-fi berserkers like before. I can feel the angelic power within them going in and out of control. They're like walking bombs."

"I know bombs," Boris said. "They hit and blow everything to shit. Some live, some die. It's like every call of the horn for us."

"Yeah," David said, "but if you all get wasted out here, we can't stop them from wreaking havoc everywhere. I can't fight very well right now. It's a long story."

"Sounds like you laid with the wrong woman," Boris said.

Mina laughed despite herself. "Don't be crass in front of Jubei, Boris."

The Russian shrugged and pointed to a place for him and Mina to set up before jogging off.

"I hope we see you again, David," Mina said with a wink and ran to catch her partner.

David turned to Jubei. "I need you to take a message to the Fólkvangr. They know you and respect you without question. I think they'll listen."

"What is it?" Jubei asked.

David detailed the plan to his friend, and the ghost of a smile crossed Jubei's lips.

Ω

"They've overcome once again," Freja said.

Samael whistled. "It's not like you to put the cart before the horse. There's still quite a lot going on down there."

"True," Freja said. "Perhaps I just feel proud of what they've accomplished thus far."

"It's not every day a mortal is able to stand against the likes of Flueric," Samael said.

"And live to find a path to greater success, no less," Freja said. "I sense Odin's hand in that."

"That was a surprise, too. One I would not have bet on," Samael said. "Another player on the board." The angel shook his head and looked to the sky. "I hope we were right in trusting that they are ready, Freja, truly I do."

"I know you well enough to know you are not speaking for *our* sakes. I take it that means you don't think we should interject on their behalf," Freja said.

"No. Sending the Valkyrie now will not help them for the struggles to come," Samael said. "A child is born a weak and innocent thing. It is nurtured and nourished, but in the end, it is only by its own means that it will ever be able to rise and stand on its own two feet."

Freja looked at Samael as he turned his eyes from the sky to the earth and the forces regrouping.

"I am proud of them, but they are capable of much more. The hardest battles aren't fought with swords in hand, dear Freja. It's the ones fought to win over hearts and minds that change the world."

Ω

Mukhulai and Jubei returned with the Fólkvangr at their heels. A rear contingent of them remained to keep the creatures from Helheim at bay as they joined with the Valhallan warriors and formed ranks.

David was surprised to see the two sides cooperate so smoothly, but he understood that they were only separated in character by a hair's width. He'd often survey the Bacchanalia occurring within the hall at Valhalla and wonder how the warriors would behave should they be housed under a roof with differing expectations.

"When they come, the front lines engage them to give them pause," Mukhulai said. "From what David tells us, you will meet with a swift return to our halls where you may fill our cups and plates to make them ready for us!"

The warriors shouted their appreciation at his sentiment. "At the signal from Sarena over there"—he pointed to an area where tinder was being piled high off to the left of the approaching UHOVAS— "divide the lines down the center and let through the denizens of Helheim. The signal is white smoke. There will be flames and smolder aplenty beside it as we hold these huur gichii on our line, but our signal will be *white* smoke."

David moved to stand next to Mukhulai and received raucous cheers from the ranks of warriors.

"If our plan works, you'll see some fireworks," David said. "Wait for the battle cries of Jubei and Mukhulai before you rush in to finish them off."

"Are we together?" Jubei called.

The warriors smashed their weapons to signal their understanding and agreement.

"Will this work?" Mukhulai asked.

"I give it a fifty-fifty chance, at best," David said. "But it's all we've got."

"It will work, or we will cut them down in the manner our ancestors dealt with such abominations," Jubei said.

"I do love when his blood runs hot," Mukhulai said. He and Jubei hurriedly took their places as the UHOVAS threatened to emerge at any moment.

David ached to go to Rose. She would be confronting a terrible enemy as he made ready for their final stand here, but he knew that he was all that remained to stop the possessed soldiers, should their plan fail. Rose had grown strong in her time beneath the veil, this he felt from the very moment she arrived through the portal and their link had been reset. But her power stemmed from a source foreign to David, and he was unsure how she'd utilize it to deal with Lilith. Regardless, Rose didn't need him to protect her. In truth, she never had.

His attention shifted from his thoughts to the field as the UHOVAS finally broke the tree line in looping gallops that may have been comical if not for their behemoth size. These were not soldiers—even the HOVAS weren't truly soldiers. He'd learned what it took to earn and maintain that title by now. These were man-made demons. A perversion of the power of creation that had been imbued within him, and to the point where the soldiers held little to no humanity at all anymore.

Many held faces akin to those of Lilith's more recent children. Pointed ears, mangy manes of hair, and mouths overflowing with gnarled and pointed teeth, aching to sink into the living. All smoldered like a cauldron set atop kiln-hot flames stoked to melt lead.

The warriors on the front lines of their ranks showed patience in waiting for the UHOVAS to cross the field before breaking off to engage—the result David had expected. Strength, unimaginable heat, and blind rage were a fierce combination to contend with. Warriors utilized tactics he had not often seen when they answered the call of the horn to the fields. This time, they were the ones showing discipline and tactics as they worked to slow the progress of their supernatural foes. And slow them they did. UHOVAS paused to swat at the scores of men and women clamoring round them.

David watched Sarena signal her small contingent to pile live green leaves atop their pyre before dispatching them to aide in hampering the UHOVAS. Plumes of white smoke wafted to the sky, and the Fólkvangr parted their ranks. Without reinforcement from behind, the shield-bearing warriors who had been holding the creatures at bay were flattened, and the monsters funneled between the remaining warriors toward the easiest adversary. Those who broke to attack the soldiers were easily dealt with by well-practiced strikes.

The melancholic faces of the ghoulies cracked with a maniacal glee when they approached the UHOVAS, and they leaped in scores to sink their claws and teeth into the beasts. As it began, UHOVAS swept the creatures aside with broad strokes of their arms, but soon David saw signs of what he'd hoped to. The smoke emitting from the UHOVAS lessened, and with each slaughtered creature of Helheim, a release of the cold held within that realm was left upon the beasts. The creatures were cooling the infernal monsters.

When Leonard and Dodd explained to David what became of people who were overtaken by the power of the fallen angels, he'd wondered what, if anything, could cool the stable release of supernatural heat. It was only tonight when watching the spear of a Fólkvangr impale one of the ghoulies had he come to an answer—supernatural cold, of course.

As more and more of the creatures were slain, the UHOVAS fervor and pace slowed, and it wasn't until the final ones had been stomped into oblivion that Jubei and Mukhulai signaled to the remaining warriors to engage.

They flowed forward as a wave and attacked in unison. When the monsters before them retaliated in a frenzy, they fell back as one. The tactic worked well to preserve their number as they continued to chip away at their adversaries.

David watched the first of the UHOVAS fall to a knee and saw the expert marksmanship of warriors who fired arrows and bullets into the remaining leg to cast the monster down to its side. Mukhulai himself brought his twin blades together at the nape of its neck to behead the creature.

The warriors, operating with the knowledge that the HOVAS would fall into cinder or immolate upon death, backed away, but none were prepared for the size of the ensuing blast. A rising orb of heat and plasma engulfed all who were unlucky enough to be within its radius, and the shock wave that followed made many more lose their footing, stalling their advances.

Mukhulai is lost, David thought. The soldiers rallying to continue their onslaught had lost a step, and the UHOVAS began to gain traction.

"You can't let them regain their heat!" David cried.

He reached his mind to the chips within them and only confirmed what he'd suspected before: These monsters had been untethered from All Century's control from the very start.

It was Boris who sprang to action when the lines began to falter. He ran to the front and stopped short to sight his target. As a swipe of unguals the size of tree stumps glanced by just before him, the stalwart Russian soldier loosed his round into an eye of deep blackness, freeing its ink. The UHOVAS howled, and the soldiers redoubled their efforts to hack at its legs and bring it down.

Jubei furthered the pendulum of momentum in their direction by flinging himself on the back of another and burying his blade between its shoulders while hacking at its neck with his smaller weapon. His clothes smoldered and ignited, but the samurai remained steadfast until the beast was brought down.

Explosions occurred in succession throughout the field as the warriors traded their brief tenure back on earth for the glory of a mortal strike, and David let himself believe they'd get out of this alive.

CHAPTER SEVENTEEN
A GIFT

Where is the bitch?" Chelsea asked Rose, who continued to stand away from peering to the woods.

Rose's silence had unnerved Chelsea and Leonard alike. Dodd, too busy grappling with the spectacle of fiery explosions beyond them to have fully brought his attention, was also ignorant to Lilith's approach.

"She's here. You all should leave now," Rose said.

"Like hell we will," Chelsea said.

Dodd found himself at odds with his instincts when he said, "We should listen to her, Chelse."

Leonard headed off Chelsea's protests at the pass, "I know they're kids. They're *your* kids, but we can't help them right now. Our part was before—and hopefully after."

"*You* can, Brendan!" Chelsea tried to push him away before pulling him close again.

"Sure, I won't be broken into pieces as easily as last time," Dodd said, "but not all fights are about brawn. Took me a while to learn that, but it's true. If Rose wants to face her alone, we should honor that."

"This is insane," Chelsea said.

"David already trusted her," Leonard said.

"Oh, who gives a shit what he thinks. You said it before, he's just a kid," Chelsea said.

"Not anymore, Ms. Dolan. He hasn't been since he fell into that river and lost Tim," Rose said. "And my childhood ended when Asmodeus burned me alive."

Tears fell down Chelsea's cheeks, and Dodd leaned in to support her. She knew Rose was right, but the cruel reality she faced was that *she* could do nothing now but let them walk their paths. Her work, as Leonard said, had already been done by raising them.

"Rose. I don't know what you have planned, but you better show your teeth out here," Chelsea said.

"I don't have a plan," Rose replied. "I love you."

"I love you, too," Chelsea said.

"Let's go," Dodd said and guided Chelsea away to where he thought they'd be safe.

Leonard cast a last cursory glance to Rose's back and stopped. "Do you remember the amulet I gave you?" Leonard asked.

"Yes," Rose said.

"I know it didn't work," Leonard said. "I've thought a lot about that. I don't think it didn't work because it couldn't have, but maybe we went about it the wrong way. The amulet wasn't what held power, but the belief in what it could do did. I don't think it helped you because you didn't believe it could. To you, it was just a beautiful and unique trinket."

Rose stood silently with the night's breeze about her.

"Believe this time, Rose," Leonard said before he made off to catch Chelsea and Dodd.

Ω

Lilith emerged from the trees and saw Rose standing alone as she'd expected. David would be needed to finish cleaning up Flueric's mess, after all. She quickly stalked toward the girl being bathed in moonlight, but soon slowed, not ready for the stable eyes and lack of fear she sensed in the girl.

Rose looked to Lilith with what appeared to be an impossible mingling of wonder and inadvertence.

"Are you proud of yourself?" Lilith asked. "It's not often a mortal finds her way back here with her vitality intact."

"Not half as proud as you are of yourself, which strikes me as strange since you weren't able to accomplish the same thing," Rose said.

Again, the even tone and steady look of the wispy girl put Lilith to her heels. "You'll regret that, girl."

"Rage," Rose said.

"What?" Lilith asked.

"It consumes you. It's all you are now besides ashamed. There was a time when you were too proud to bow to the whims of an unfair edict, but now you slink so low using some kind of moral protest as an excuse. It's sad," Rose said, speaking from the heart.

Rose, the girl who always had a habit of speaking her mind without worry, often leaving people stunned. Lilith now found herself to be counted amongst them.

"And you are any better?" Lilith asked. "Living rent free out here in this era of prosperity, and all your kind does is track mud through your own paradise. Yes, I steal the life of innocents to continue to exist, and I feel no remorse because they and their ancestors didn't *earn* that life. *I* earned it!"

"I know you feel remorse for sucking the vitality out of infants," Rose said. "I also know that feeling turns to anger in you, and you aim your rage at us. Why else would you have been so bold as to try to kill David? He's just another being born and placed above you. It's the only thing that makes sense."

"I'll kill you both, so you don't take what little I have left, that's why," Lilith said.

"No. That's just the excuse you tell yourself to rationalize it," Rose said. "My hair turned molten and melted to my scalp while I choked on the creosote-laden smoke that filled that cabin your son set on fire. I felt that. I suffered immeasurably in those moments that stretched on for a thousand lifetimes, and he lapped it up like a mutt at a filthy water bowl. Asmodeus wasn't an ounce human, and he relished in my agony. You, at your core, are human. Whether you like it or not, you need to rationalize your evil just like the rest of us, or it will devour you."

Lilith's hands had left their outward position and found their way to her belly—the slow pulsing glow matching what would have been the beating of her heart if the cold motionless muscle within her chest had the ability. She scoured her mind for purchase to retaliate after the awful truth she'd never been subjected to and was left wanting.

Rose was the first to move. She stepped forward as carefree as if she was crossing a field of lilies.

"Wait—" Lilith said. "Stop there."

Rose continued toward her, and Lilith reeled backward away from the girl. The internal meter within her signified the girl measured as a threat, though Lilith could not fathom why.

Somewhere, Dodd, Chelsea, and Leonard were watching.

Somewhere, Samael and Freja were watching.

Rose stepped forward, and Lilith stepped backward until her feet became tangled in the undergrowth, and the Mother of Demons fell. In a panic, she wailed to signal to her children to come to her aid, but she felt no answer from them. Those she'd raised to loyalty with the stolen futures of innocent children had been consumed by her errant campaign against David and Azazel. Those she relied on now were wild and devoid of piety.

"I have a gift for you," Rose said. "It's something you have always wanted."

"Stay back from me, you little witch," Lilith said, her howls having turned to whimpers as fire erupted far behind the girl and bathed her in red.

Rose stopped and knelt toward her would-be killer, whose backpedaling ceased as she realized the futility. Lilith's eyes widened as a slender hand reached out. She guarded her unprotected belly, but Rose placed her palm on her tormentor's cold bosom.

Tepid warmth spread from Rose as Lilith's reflection danced in her eyes. The feeling, so alien to a being who'd known only cold, overwhelmed her senses and paralyzed her. Rose took her fingers away, but the feeling persisted, and Lilith gasped for air. Vitality surged through her veins for the first time to carry oxygen and extend the feeling to her extremities as the night air betrayed her for the first time by applying its chill.

"What have you put in me?" Lilith asked.

"Life," Rose said.

Ω

In the end, the portal between realities closed with a feeling of slight static for those in its proximity. The last of the residents of the veiled world, having been dispatched by the final blasts from UHOVAS as they were exterminated, were again nestled beneath its cover as was in line with the order of things.

David lamented the loss of his friends once more, but he took some solace in the fact that they were continuing on their path as he was his. His focus had turned to Rose the instant his instincts had allowed, and he found her standing in the moonlight, looking after Lilith as she crawled back into the trees from where she'd emerged.

"Should we follow her?" David asked.

"No. She's not a threat to us any longer," Rose said.

"Mom would have killed her," David said.

"She still might, if the sad thing doesn't scurry off fast enough." Rose pulled David into her arms. "What now?"

"We regroup, I think," David said. "There's no telling what's going on beyond here with Leviathan on the loose."

Rose looked up to him. "But first, we rest," she said and kissed him.

"If there's nothing dire," David said, but Rose's expression didn't yield, so he quickly added, "Yeah, first we rest."

David looked up the hill opposite, where Dodd, Chelsea, and Leonard approached from.

"They're up there?" Rose asked.

"Our chaperones? Yeah, they're up there."

"Let's go to them."

"We don't have to. They're coming to us."

Samael and Freja appeared and reached the couple opposite the side of the approach of their human company. David and Rose stood tall between them.

"You've done well, little Rose," Freja said.

"I was hoping to see you again before you left," Rose said. "I needed to say thank you for helping me to find myself again."

David left Rose's arms to walk to Samael. The feeling of being pulled and pushed reverberated through the onlookers as the two neared one another.

"It's nice to finally meet, Sam," David said.

"As I told your friend there…" Samael pointed to Dodd. "It would have inevitably happened sooner or later."

"Thank you," David said. "I know you're putting yourself at risk by doing this."

Samael waved his hand. "Think nothing of it. When the doors are closed and the windows are locked and there aren't any others to point the finger toward, we own our choices in solitude. I am fine with mine."

Freja sniffed the air about David's neck. "You've been back into Heidrun's mead, you scamp. Tsk, tsk."

"Yeah, about that," David said. "This time, I was handed some by the owner himself. Your buddy is back in town." Freja didn't appear surprised.

"In truth, I wonder if he ever really left," Freja said.

David extended his hand, and Freja took it. He turned to Samael and put forth the same gesture of good faith, and the angel considered it for a moment before taking David's grip. The odd sensation of riding a tide ceased for Leonard, Chelsea, and Dodd until they released.

"You've come far, Rose, and you, David," Samael said. "But you've much farther to go. Let's hope you can bear the burden of the tasks ahead."

Chelsea broke from her ranks and marched toward him. "You leave them out of your sordid business now, you hear me, or it'll be me *you* will be having nightmares of."

"It's a wonder she hasn't wrung you out yet," Freja said to Samael, whose hands came up in a palm-out gesture.

"I wouldn't dream of it, ma'am. Well, not right away," Samael said, and Freja gasped at him in an exaggerated manner. "It would be disingenuous to say otherwise—"

Dodd appeared to attempt to calm Chelsea, while Leonard stood in the background.

Samael looked at Freja. "Leave off being wrung out—you've hung me out to dry!"

"We'll take our leave," Freja said. "Be wary. Your world is likely to fall into turmoil soon. The serpent will aim to devour what's yours."

David remembered how Leviathan hungered for knowledge about David, and he shuddered to think what it would do now that it had access to the countless spoils it had dreamt of for thousands of years.

Rose and David nodded and watched on as the two turned to leave.

"Goodbye," Rose said.

"Farewell," Freja said as her chain glowed and cloak danced upon her shoulders. She lifted from the ground and rode the wind away.

"See you soon," Samael said, and Leonard felt a chill. The angel lifted upon his black wings to follow the goddess.

Rose and David held each other once more, having their moment before the realities of the outside worlds called upon them.

EPILOGUE

Deep within the Atlantic Ocean, somewhere east of Puerto Rico, Leviathan coursed. Down and down, she dived to evade the pursuer she felt gaining on her by inches at a time. First to the sea floor and on through a chasm she surged, displacing water by volumes incomprehensible to the creatures pulled within her wake.

She dived between a rift in the North American and Caribbean tectonic plate boundaries to the deepest depths, shedding green light where the sun had not shed its own for millions of years. It was here, cornered by her size and out of places to flee, that she was confronted.

"You won't take me back," Leviathan hissed through the abyss.

A lancing light split the dark as Gungnir was hurled to impale her to the seafloor by her tail. Leviathan coiled and uncoiled to escape, threatening to tear the very crust of the earth apart, but she could not break the bonds Odin had laid upon her so quickly.

Unsuspecting people on the islands to the west and as far north as the US Capitol were thrown as the ground betrayed them.

ACKNOWLEDGMENTS

Continuing this journey with Rose, David, and company has been a remarkable escape for me over this past year. While finding the time to sit down and discover their journey has been difficult, in many ways it's also been a necessary distraction from the rigors of reality. We share something in common in this regard, you and I. We both enjoy a good escape.

Once again, a debt is owed to the horror community for helping me to find the proper tone for this novel. Far less horror has found its way into the second installment of The Valor of Valhalla series, but the stakes and undertone of this story are terrifying, if you've been paying attention. On this note, I will be taking the time to release an anthology of short stories detailing some of the *happenings* which occurred during the time when Lilith's children were unleashed on my unsuspecting neighbors. It will be entirely horror, and it is both an answer to the call for more work of its kind within the same VoV universe, and something I've been aching to do for some time. A few of the stories have been penned already and are available through my very reliably unreliable newsletter, if you'd like to take a look.

This book wouldn't have its polish without the exceptional work of Angela Traficante at Lambda Editing. She is second to none in the field and damned accommodating too. That's a nice combination to find for a shlub like me.

Todd Keisling at Dullington Design once again took on the formatting job for this novel, and he once again did an exceptional job with both the cover and the interior. If you're a horror fan, grab his work. *Scanlines* will knock your socks off.

Maurice Mosqua crafted the beautiful cover art that caught your eye and has a large catalogue of fantasy work for you to check out on his artstation page. We've become friends over the short time I've known him, and Maurice's work never fails to tend to the needs of my imagination.

I'd like to acknowledge the patience, understanding, and interest my wife Kim has shown throughout this process. I thank my lucky stars daily that I managed to find a partner who isn't afraid to be silly or weird with me, and who always encourages my lunacy. There's something to be said for that when it's laid atop all of her other virtues.

Last, and certainly not least, I'd like to acknowledge you for taking this journey with me through the perilous landscape of a world not so far off from our own. Let's hope the trip leads us somewhere special.

Martin Kearns
Putnam County, New York
September 16th, 2022

Martin Kearns is the author of *The Valor of Valhalla* series and select short fiction. He is a special education and English teacher and lives with his wife and children in the Hudson Valley.

"Stories were my first love and during rare moments of quiet my mind turns toward those I've watched, read, and lived. They bring to mind possibilities, which are really where the seeds of a story begin. I truly hope to bring creative tales to readers who, like me, enjoy finding themselves lost somewhere in a world of endless possibilities."

DON'T FORGET TO
LEAVE A REVIEW!

Independently published authors are at the mercy of online reviews. With that in mind, I have a favor to ask of you.

If you've the time, it will greatly help my cause for you to leave an honest review on your preferred vendor platform.

Thank you very much for your help and don't hesitate to reach out to me on social media or through my website.

www.readkearns.com